Praise for *The Beauty That Remains*

"A **beautiful, touching, and heartbr**... portrayal of love and loss from the lives of ...
—*BuzzFeed*

"**An emotional must-read story** of the way music connects us, the way tragedy threatens to break us apart, and the way life can change, for better or worse, in an instant." —*Bustle*

"If you're looking for **a book that truly hits the heart strings,** *The Beauty That Remains* is it." —*Seventeen*

"A **breathtaking YA** read about life, death, grieving, and healing." —*HelloGiggles*

"In her debut novel, Ashley Woodfolk delivers **a moving tale for young readers that will touch mature audiences as well.**"
—*Essence*

"**A stunning, heart-wrenching** look at grief that will stay with you long after you put it down. **Be prepared to be broken, be prepared to feel whole again.**"
—Angie Thomas, #1 *New York Times* bestselling author of *The Hate U Give*

"Woodfolk's debut cuts deeply and then wipes your tears away. **Wrenching, heartfelt, and vividly human.**" —Becky Albertalli, bestselling author of *Simon vs. the Homo Sapiens Agenda*

"**Haunting, heart-wrenching, and powerful. . . .** This book will remind you to hold fast to those you love, share your heart while you have time, and find the music that makes this wild ride of life better. **A tearjerker must-read for teens!**"
—Dhonielle Clayton, author of the Belles series and coauthor of the Tiny Pretty Things series

the Beauty that Remains

ASHLEY WOODFOLK

EMBER

Text copyright © 2018 by Ashley Woodfolk
Cover art copyright © 2019 by Zeke Peña

All rights reserved. Published in the United States by Ember, an imprint of Random House Children's Books, a division of Penguin Random House LLC, New York. Originally published in hardcover in the United States by Delacorte Press, an imprint of Random House Children's Books, New York, in 2018.

Ember and the E colophon are registered trademarks of Penguin Random House LLC.

Visit us on the Web! GetUnderlined.com

Educators and librarians, for a variety of teaching tools, visit us at RHTeachersLibrarians.com

The Library of Congress has cataloged the hardcover edition of this work as follows:
Names: Woodfolk, Ashley, author.
Title: The beauty that remains / Ashley Woodfolk.
Description: First edition. | New York : Delacorte Press, [2018] | Summary: Autumn, Shay, and Logan, whose lives intersect in complicated ways, each lose someone close to them and must work through their grief.
Identifiers: LCCN 2017000495 | ISBN 978-1-5247-1587-8 (hc) |
ISBN 978-1-5247-1589-2 (glb) | ISBN 978-1-5247-1588-5 (ebook)
Subjects: | CYAC: Death—Fiction. | Grief—Fiction. | Friendship—Fiction. |
Music—Fiction.
Classification: LCC PZ7.1.W657 Be 2018 | DDC [Fic]—dc23

ISBN 978-1-5247-1590-8 (trade pbk.)

Printed in the United States of America
10 9 8 7 6 5 4 3 2 1
First Ember Edition 2019

To my beautiful grandmothers,
whom I loved and loved and lost.
My heart still breaks.

What is bravery
if not the marching forward
though all may be lost?
　　　　—Tyler Knott Gregson

TAVIA'S LAST PHOTO

 Tavia_Violet

♡ 183 likes

Tavia_Violet How, exactly, does one become a professional shoe shopper? #brightfuture #alltheshine

18 HOURS AGO

1

AUTUMN

I just saw you yesterday.

There's no way this is real. It can't be.

I keep waiting for you to call.

Tavia may not be on Hangouts right now. She'll see your messages later.

From: HeCalledItAutumn@gmail.com

To: TaviaViolet@gmail.com

Sent: Jan. 16, 5:17 p.m.

Subject: <none>

I stared at my phone through most of your funeral.

I could have said goodbye to you in my room with

some vanilla-scented candles, a few of your favorite
songs, violets, and a can of orange soda. But instead
we had to do this public ritual where we all stood
around, watching each other cry. When I woke up, I
already knew today would be the worst day of my life.

When we get to the church, your brother walks straight to the
front and kisses the top of the casket, but I can't go up there. So
I just head to the second row of pews and sit down at the very
end. I look at my phone, at the infinite stream of pictures of you,
and I try not to look anywhere else. For the first time ever, I feel
grateful for how many selfies you took, and I feel bad that I always teased you about being conceited. If I didn't have hundreds
of digital squares with you in them, I'm not sure how I'd remember to breathe. After a while, when I do look up, I use different
squares—ones of tinted sunshine spilling through the stained-
glass windows—to mark time as they move across the room.

I'm sitting with your family. Your mom is squeezing rosary
beads in her hand, weeping in a way that doesn't make any noise.
Your dad's staring straight ahead, but not really looking at anything. Dante sits down beside me after he kisses your casket, and
I can feel that he's crying by the way his shoulder moves against
mine.

Part of me wants to shift away from him, but I'm frozen.

My family's sitting a few rows behind me. My mother's dress
is impeccable, but her blue eyes are sad, and my dad has had
his head bent the whole time, like a world without you is one
he doesn't want to see. Between their blond heads is Willow's

angled black bob, and you'd love this haircut on her if you were here. Sometime between winter break ending and yesterday, she bleached the bluntly cut ends and dyed them hot pink. She looks like a K-Pop star despite her puffy, red eyes. When she flew in from college yesterday, she crawled into bed with me the minute she got home and rubbed small circles on my back.

Willow sees me looking at her, so she squeezes out of their pew and comes up to mine. You know I don't really look like my sister, even on a good day. But with her hair the way it is now—so full and sharp and pink (and mine the way that it always is: too long and fine and flat)—we could be strangers. I look like the "before" scene in the Korean dramas we watched together, where the girls miraculously turn pretty.

But when Willow reaches me, she touches my flat black hair, like it's silk. She holds my hand, as if it's made of glass, and looks at me a little too closely. I squeeze her fingers before letting them go to look back down at my phone, and she steps back and stays quiet. She doesn't try to make me talk, which is a miracle, because I thought she was going to be pushy—you know how my sister can get. But she was perfect. People forget how much silence can help at times like these.

No one in my family has said anything, but I can tell how they feel by the way my sister reaches for my hand. The way my mother stares at me. How differently my dad says my name. They're so happy I wasn't with you that night that they can't keep their hands, eyes, and voices away from me. But every time I think about the fact that I wasn't, I feel like I'm drowning.

When you went to Alexa's party without me, I was upset that you didn't beg me to come out with you; that you went, even though I didn't want to go. It's stupid, but it *hurt,* and Margo and Faye were there too, so there wasn't even anyone for me to text and complain. I was just going to eat ice cream, read a book, and go to bed early.

Then Dante called.

I went to your house to hang out with him—to have some fun without you because you were doing things without me.

And now I have to live with this: I was *flirting with him* when I could have been *stopping you.*

For some reason, the priest asks everyone to stand. I wasn't paying attention, so when Dante pulls me up and into his side, I don't realize right away that it's time to pray. His touch takes me away from the world inside my phone, where you're still grinning and singing and alive. And for a second, I just collapse against your brother.

I can't stand on my own in a world where you don't exist.

Dante reads the weight of my body as an invitation. He tucks my head under his chin, and I feel a few of his tears hit my scalp where my hair's parted.

It's so complicated—the way I feel about him, but I can't think about that now, when I can barely stay on my feet. So I hook my hand around his hip and hold on tight. And when the sounds around me return and I hear the priest praying, I look at the photo of you that sits at the front of the church in a wreath of violets instead of closing my eyes.

After a few minutes of standing here anchored to Dante, I start to feel a little less like I'm sinking. Or at least like if I'm going down, he won't let me hit the bottom alone.

At the cemetery, Willow holds my hand again like a good

big sister, and I lean into her like I did with Dante at the church. She cries and cries while the priest sprinkles holy water over the grave, and I just stare at the dirty hem of the priest's robe. He says your full name the way your grandmother says it, at the same time as I read it in the obituary I'm somehow still holding.

"Oak-TAH-bia Bi-oh-LEH-tah SO-toe."

Octavia Violeta Soto.

And my whole body goes cold.

I'm supposed to drop a handful of dirt into your grave like everyone else a few minutes later, but after your dad starts crying, I just can't. By the time it's my turn it's raining, and most of the soil has turned to mud anyway. So instead, I shove the damp obituary into my pocket. I pull petals from a yellow rose, one at a time, and let them fall—bright against the dark earth all around them—right before the casket sinks into the ground.

I don't try to figure out if anyone loves me as I yank away each velvety petal, the way you used to (*He loves me? He loves me not? Autumn, he loves me!*). I just tell the rose how much I'm going to miss you. How much I already do.

I miss you.

I miss you.

I miss you.

There's never an *I miss you not.*

And there aren't enough petals on the flower. There aren't enough petals in the world.

In the limo, Dante has to pull the thorny stem out of my trembling hand because I'm still gripping it, even though the naked and ugly bud is the only thing left.

Hours after our friends and your extended family and my

family leave your house, I stay. I help Dante inventory all the frozen casseroles and stews and empanadas that people leave behind on your kitchen counters.

When we finish, I pull out my phone again and get lost in it. But Dante starts pacing around your living room, very much in the here and now.

He kicks the leg of your dining room table. He punches a wall and says it's all bullshit. I don't want to be here to witness Dante explode, but it's been almost impossible for me to leave your house since you died. I still can't make myself go.

Dante opens and closes his hand after he hits the wall. It settles into a tight fist, like he's holding one of his drumsticks. He aims his angular dark eyes at me, and says, "You think it's bullshit too, don't you?"

He's talking about the comments on your photos. They've been rolling in nonstop all week.

I stay quiet. I look down at my phone and read a few of the newest ones.

I don't have a right to say anything. I've been looking through your photos since the accident, just like everyone else. I've been clicking on every single picture you ever posted, reading over your captions and hashtags, like they're prayers. I've been ignoring the "Rest in peace," "We'll miss you," and "Only the good die young" messages people who barely even spoke to you have been leaving beneath your selfies. There are more broken heart emojis in the comments than there are kids at our school.

But Dante's right. They are all bullshit. So I look back up at him and nod.

With my approval, Dante turns to look at the other side

8

of the room. I don't know what he's going to say next until he says it.

"We need to get it deleted."

I'd forgotten your father was in the room, but that's who Dante's talking to now, probably because your dad has always been the kind of dad who gets things done. Like that time he argued with our teacher for giving us detention for passing notes, when really I was giving you a Tylenol in an origami box because you had cramps. Or the time he volunteered to coach our girls' soccer team when we were in middle school after the paid coach got let go. But ever since your accident, he just kind of sits there, like nothing matters. Or maybe like everything does, but he doesn't know where to start.

Dante can't delete your accounts. Your mom already cut off your cell phone. I only know that because I was calling your number over and over again on speakerphone while I sat in the school parking lot yesterday, just so your voice could fill the air like it used to.

I wanted to memorize the way you sounded. Where your tone changed and how I could hear a song playing softly in the background. Now I can't get your voice out of my head.

Hey! You've reached Tavia's phone. It's probably in my pocket or in my purse or on my bed, and I'm sure I really want to talk to you. So leave me something lovely because I love you.

The last time I called, I got an automated message instead. And it was so shocking, to go from hearing you to hearing *We're sorry. You have reached a number that has been disconnected or is no longer in service. If you feel you've received this message in error, please check the number and try again.*

9

I didn't need to check the number, but I did try again.

I don't look at your dad or Dante as I find your name, press down to call you, and put my phone on speaker. And when that recorded robot voice tells us your number's been disconnected, your dad looks at me from across the room. He shakes his head, like he can't deal; mutters something in Spanish; and stands up to leave. A minute later, I hear the front door slam.

I look at Dante, and everything about him softens. The hard angles of his face become curves. The onyx of his eyes melts into molasses.

"Did you know," I ask, "that her number was already dead?" I flush a little after I hear myself say that word. He shakes his head.

I wish I'd taken screenshots of every photo you ever sent me, every selfie with filters that made your eyes sparkle or gave you the ears and nose of some adorable animal, because those were private, meant only for me, and the ones Dante wants to delete are public, for everyone to see. But the private stuff only lasted a few seconds, and now those are gone forever, just like you. With your phone turned off too, I need to preserve every piece of you that hasn't disappeared.

So while he seems gentler, I ask Dante not to get rid of your accounts.

"With her phone gone, these pictures are some of the last things we have left that are purely her."

He still looks like he wants to punch something, but he just keeps watching me, quietly.

Even though I know there isn't, I say, "I'll see if there's a way to disable the comments."

He frowns, but then he nods.

10

"And I'll post something asking people to stop," I add.

I don't say that I know all your passwords and that I could erase every trace of you in a few seconds.

I don't say that I still send you instant messages and emails or that during every free moment I have I watch the long-ago-posted videos of you singing and playing the piano. I don't tell Dante that as soon as I walk out of his house, I'll put my earbuds in and dial my own voice mail because you left me a funny message six months ago that I'm so grateful I never got around to deleting.

I haven't cried, but I don't say that, either. My hands shake every time I think about your name, and Dante can't know that.

He has enough on his mind.

From the look on his face I can tell he's thinking about how we found out about the crash. Some idiot from our high school took a picture of your upside-down car and posted it to his story with a black-and-white filter and the caption *SHIIIIIT. Just saw the worst accident.* Perry, of all people, texted a screenshot of the picture to me with a message:

Holy shit. This isn't Tavia's car, is it?

It was. The Unraveling Lovely bumper sticker, the one we designed for the band's tour last summer, was a dead giveaway.

I knew you were on your way to see Perry, but he had no idea. I didn't even message him back.

I can feel Dante looking at me. He probably knows I'm remembering that night too.

"You okay?" he asks.

We say this to each other all the time now, whenever one of us catches the other zoning out; whenever it's clear we're thinking about you. I nod, even though I'll never be okay again, but I don't know what else to say.

I ask him the same question. "Are you?"

And he nods too, completing the circular lie we've been telling each other for days, since we first saw the photo of your car.

Lying is the new language we speak. It's the only way we can talk at all.

Dante's been looking at me a little too much all day, and it's starting to get to me, so I stand up. I haven't seen your mom in a while anyway. Your brother's heavy gaze follows me like a shadow as I make my way out of the room. But I don't look back.

When I find your mom, she's sitting on your bed. Her rosary beads are in a pile on her lap.

I sit on the floor by her feet. She smiles and pets my head, like I'm a puppy, and the whole room smells like you. Vanilla has always come from your open bottles of shampoo, your hand lotions, your candles. Today's no different, except you're not here, and the smell seems all wrong without you, like an echo heard miles from its maker. It's almost too much to take.

From across the hall loud music starts to play. Your mom sighs and I turn my head, but neither of us gets up to check on Dante.

She says "Hey, Autumn" a bit late, but she's smiling a real smile. Your mom has always been so steady, but her hands are shaking, just like they had before she fainted at the hospital.

"Hi," I say back. I pull my sleeves over my own trembling fingers.

Then we just sit there, silent and lonely for you together, because hellos are nice and neat and so much easier than goodbyes.

BRAM'S LAST 2 POSTS

 @Bramisbored
New video coming soon . . . Here's a hint:
this milk smells funny.
44 ↰ 31 ⊏ 320 ♡

 @Bramisbored
It tastes funny, too.
51 ↰ 35 ⊏ 334 ♡

2

LOGAN

BRAM IS BORED so he drinks expired milk.

160,791 views | 1 month ago

Shit.

Bram's face is on the news again, and I feel like I'm gonna puke.

You would think they would do the right thing and ask his mom for a picture. But apparently, reporters are lazy douchebags. So they just threw up the first photo they found. They probably just image searched his name. Awesome journalism, assholes.

It's been weeks, but they won't stop showing the last picture he ever posted. So he's always in his uniform. Forever on the field. Immortalized with his helmet in one hand, the ball in the other. He's grinning his cocky grin because he was a cocky bastard, but it seems like there should be a protocol in place for things like this. It should be his graduation picture or something more dignified. He looks too much like himself in this photo, and some part of me doesn't want the world to see the real version of him.

Plus, I didn't think it would still hurt to see him like that.

Lively.

Fucking *alive.*

His name is scrolling along the bottom of the screen, like he's a thunderstorm warning and not a dead kid.

New evidence in Bram Lassiter case . . .

Bram Lassiter . . . Bram Lassiter . . . Bram Lassiter . . .

I used to tell him his name sounded like a serial killer's. Or a horror movie director's. Or like the bad guy's name in a really shitty book. He used to say he liked my red hair best when it was short and we were sitting in the sun. "I have a thing for gingers," he'd say, with that beautiful grin of his splitting his face wide open.

But that was before. And we hadn't spoken in months. That, like most things, is all my fault.

> *"We go again tonight to Bayside High School, where varsity quarterback and popular video blogger Bram Lassiter was found dead in the boys' locker room on Christmas Eve.*
>
> *"Local law enforcement originally believed Lassiter's death was the result of a hate crime because his body was found beaten. A video of the student engaged in a homosexual act circulated online three*

weeks before his death, and though most of Lassiter's
close friends and relatives knew of his sexual orienta-
tion, many of his online followers did not.

"Lassiter received numerous threats of violence
following the video's release, but an autopsy revealed
that the visible injuries were not the cause of death. A
tox screen recently confirmed a drug overdose. NYPD
are now completely eliminating the possibility of foul
play and are ruling the death a suicide."

"Maybe this will help," Aden says, and I snap out of my Bram haze for a second. Aden crosses his small dorm room, going from his bed to his desk in two big steps, thanks to his long legs. He turns the TV off and pulls something up on his laptop. Then music—my music—fills the air. It's a song by my old band, and while he's a huge fan of our stuff, he only plays Unraveling Lovely when we're working on a song if he knows I'm stuck.

He walks back to his bed and quietly strums his guitar along with the music, and I give him a small smile. This song, a new one I'm trying to write, has had me stumped for a solid three weeks. When Bram died, so did my ability to write. Aden's patient with me, though, because when we met at a show a few months ago, I was turning out some okay stuff.

I could tell right away that Aden was everything I needed after the Unraveling Lovely fiasco—everything that everyone in my old band wasn't. Aden's quiet. Uncomplicated. Nice. Predictable. Plus, he isn't some lame high school dude who's not sure if he's serious about music. He knew like I did. Like I *do*. He's in the freaking *music performance program* at Queens College. And if I can get my shit together, I know we can make beautiful music.

But when Bram's face is *fucking everywhere,* the way he kissed me, the way I felt when he touched me, is all I can think about. It makes writing music with Aden nearly impossible. And lately, my mind is always somewhere else. On some*one* else.

Bram.

"Logan," Aden says. My small smile hasn't lasted. I'm staring at the floor biting my thumbnail—the dark blue polish I'm wearing is flaking off and onto my teeth—and not because I'm thinking about the song I'm supposed to be writing.

Aden's voice doesn't sound impatient, but I can tell he's called my name more than once, by the way his eyes look.

"Do you want one?" He's wiggling a can of beer in his hand.

I blink and lick my lips. I smile again. I nod. I need to stop thinking about Bram when I'm supposed to be working on this song. *Jesus.*

"I know you're trying to write," he says. He tosses me the beer. "But we need to find a drummer. That's a little more pressing than you finishing a song."

I nod again as I drain the beer like it's a glass of water. He doesn't get it. Not being able to finish this song is stressing me out.

"We need a band name, too," he adds. "Want to brainstorm that?"

Aden looks over at where I'm sitting on the floor after opening a beer for himself. I shrug and reach for another can.

"Or . . . we could make some audition flyers," he suggests next, completely undeterred by my silence. "We can take some to The 715—UL used to play there, right? And put them up online. We can say something like 'Former lead singer of Unraveling Lovely seeks badass drummer,' maybe," he says, and I roll my eyes so hard, they hurt a little. "What do you think?"

"I don't want to use my old band's name anywhere. You're new here, but last summer, we were kind of a big deal," I tell him, because he doesn't know any of our history. Last summer we also bombed at Battle of the Bands big-time. He doesn't know that, either, but it's a detail I decide to keep to myself.

Aden nods and sips his beer. "That's my point. We can use that. We can attract a drummer with the name Unraveling Lovely alone."

"We're not using UL's name," I say again.

He sits down across from me on the floor, and his dark eyes sparkle. I can see his expression softening, that he's morphing into flirty-Aden, but I did not come over for this. You're not supposed to date your only other band member, so on a good day, I try to pretend I don't notice when he flirts with me. On bad days, I flirt back.

He touches my knee. "Sorry, L," he says. He only calls me L when he's hitting on me. "I can respect that. And I know the music is important to you. It matters to me too. But there will be time later to write the perfect song." He reaches for my phone because I always write in my notes app. But the song is still shit, and I don't want him to see.

I put my phone facedown on the floor before he touches it, and I sigh. "It's fine. You're right."

The thing is, I know exactly what's broken about this song: it's the first one I've tried to write that isn't about Bram.

Aden nods, bats his dark eyelashes, and smiles. But when I lean forward for beer number three, he says, "Whoa. Trying for a record?" He reaches for the can sitting on the floor in front of me and shakes it to confirm it's empty. It is.

I shrug and say, "I guess not," but my head is screaming *Hell yes* as he turns the music off and the TV back on.

Aden pulls his laptop onto the floor, and we design some calls for drummers that he says he'll hang up around campus and I say that I'll post online. Then we make out a little, because we do that sometimes, and I can almost forget about everything for the first few minutes when Aden's lips are pressed against mine; when hands are impossibly everywhere at once. But when he laughs and breaks contact and then says, "Jeez, L, let me catch my breath," I can't help but remember how Bram and I wouldn't stop kissing until we were both gasping for air.

I'm a little buzzed—the promise of oblivion almost close enough to touch—so when Aden goes down the hall to use the bathroom, I root around under his bed for the whiskey I know he has stashed.

I tip the bottle into the Cherry Coke I brought with me, and when Aden comes back, I'm sipping it. I'm the most innocent, not-trying-to-get-drunk kid in the world, and I'm staring at my song again.

Some dumb reality show comes on, so Aden changes the channel, and there Bram is again—his name, his face, and one of his videos frozen behind the newscaster's head—just when I thought I was rid of him.

"You knew that kid, right? He went to your school?" Aden asks, as if proximity is all it takes. As if closeness is what makes people close.

This isn't the first time he's asked me about Bram, so it's not the first time I've lied about him.

"You're from a tiny town, where everyone knows everyone else," I say, because he is, and high school in Queens is different. "There are thousands of kids in my high school, hundreds in my graduating class. I didn't *know* him," I lie. Again. "But yeah, I knew *of* him because of football and his dumbass videos. Everyone knew Bram Lassiter."

I kinda want to say his name again, but I know I shouldn't, so I try to act like I don't notice Bram's face on TV anymore. I ignore the news the way I've been trying my hardest to ignore the conspiracy theories that have been all over school and the Internet. There are a million rumors about what really happened to Bram, and suicide has always been one of them.

But when we were together, Bram was a fucking ray of sunshine most of the time. I don't get how he could go from the happy-go-lucky goofball who loved sports and doing dumb things on camera for laughs to a guy who'd off himself the way they say he did: in a locker room, with pills, all alone.

Aden asks me to sleep over. "Just sleep," he insists, and I agree because I don't want to go home, so I text my mom to tell her. We order pizza and watch more TV with the lights out, and I forget about Bram for a while until Aden passes out. Thanks to my spiked Coke, I'm left lying there, wide-awake, tipsy and alone in the dark.

I slide my phone out of the pocket of my discarded jeans. I

go to Bram's profile without really deciding to. I start looking for the photos of us together that I untagged months ago.

My phone is like a time machine. My thumb is the key. I travel back through the last six months with a flick of my finger, and I'm not there, not there, not there.

Until I am.

Thumbnails of Bram and me fill the screen, more than three hundred altogether. I can't believe they're all still here. I look over at Aden to make sure he's still asleep, then back at the pictures on my phone, wondering why (how?) Bram never had the heart (or the balls) to erase them.

In the photos, we're at my apartment scarfing down take-out. We're high off our asses on my stoop, red-eyed and laughing. We're on the subway and then the Long Island Rail Road. We're on his fire escape and at the beach tanning on matching bright green towels. In one blurry selfie, we're in his bed, sheets of paper covered in math equations scattered all around us.

Bram sucked at algebra. It's the only reason we met. Freshman year, he went out for football and made second-string varsity while I was writing sad songs and experimenting with liquid eyeliner. By sophomore year, he'd become the starting quarterback, and I'd joined a pretty crappy band. So the odds were against us. We were on opposite ends of the popularity spectrum. But he was shit at math, and even though I kind of hate school, math's the one thing I'm good at. Last year, I was already in calc, but he was struggling through algebra 2. I was assigned to be his tutor.

I didn't know that I was into him right away. I knew that I liked the way he kissed his mom on the forehead every afternoon, as soon as he stepped into their apartment. I knew that I liked the way he twirled one of his curls around his finger like a five-year-old girl when he was trying to work out a really hard problem. I liked the way he tried so hard to fix everything: leaky faucets, hurt feelings, his math grade. And I knew that I fucking loved watching the way the muscles in his forearms flexed every time he picked up a pencil. But I don't think I knew that I liked *him*, at least not for sure, until he kissed me the first time.

We were in his bedroom, studying for his midterm. I was solving for *x* when he made an *O* beside it in my notebook. I started gnawing on my thumbnail before I even looked up at him. He raised his eyebrows, grinned, and said, "You ever been kissed?"

I opened my mouth, but all of the smartass replies I usually have lined up were gone. I said "um," and that was all he needed to hear.

Bram grinned even wider. He picked up his phone and started typing, and a second later, that cheesy song about kissing, the one from every nineties rom-com *ever*, was filling up his tiny room.

"Oh my god," I said. "You're not serious."

He responded, "Dude, this song is awesome," and started singing along.

I couldn't stop myself. I laughed, loud. I stared at him, like he'd grown another head. And when the second chorus started, he narrowed his eyes and pushed his curls off his forehead. He looked serious all of a sudden.

"What?" I said. I was biting my nail again, because Bram was so damn cute and I'd never been kissed and he was licking his lips. He pushed my hand away from my mouth, and when I looked back up at him he smirked. Something about the light made his green eyes kind of sparkle. When he kissed me, I almost forgot who I was.

I didn't even smile when he pulled away. I just grabbed his neck, yanked him back, and made out with him until my lips went numb.

"I've never even kissed a girl before," I whispered to him. But what I didn't say was that now I knew I never would. We were standing at the door of his bedroom, and my lips were swollen, my face rubbed red from his stubble. He'd just handed me my bag.

When our fingers touched, he smirked and tucked a pencil behind my ear.

"I fucking *knew* it," he said. He kissed me again, his big, rough hand on my face like he needed me to hold still. A week later, we were official, and nine months after that, it was over.

I put my phone down and stare through Aden's window. I can't see the moon, just the top of a few buildings. And I wish I were on a rooftop. I wish I were anywhere I could say Bram's name out loud. Make him real again, even for a second.

When I lift my phone again, I go to his online video channel, BRAM IS BORED. He started vlogging right before we got together, and by the end, he had thousands of subscribers. It's funny because I was always the one who wanted to quit school and get famous, and Bram just wanted to play football and go to college. But my band broke up, and his channel took off. He became Internet famous, and I haven't written a new song in forever.

I pull up the last video he posted, where he chugs an entire gallon of spoiled milk. It's gross but also kind of funny. Plus,

Bram looks good, even when he's doing dumb shit. I've been a subscriber since he posted his first video, and sometimes I even commented, but he never knew it was me. Even when we dated, I never told him my username.

The views and comments on this video are blowing up. They always seem to surge whenever his face is on the news again, like everyone forgets that he's fucking dead, and when they remember, they can't shut up about it. But I'm watching too, as desperate to connect as everyone else. The difference is, I really knew him. We were *in love.*

I don't know if it's the booze or the stupid comments or the pictures of him smiling at me, but my eyes are suddenly pooling with tears. I feel angry and hot, sad and alone. I miss him, like we broke up last week and not six months ago.

I don't know the rules, because he's my only ex, but he kept our pictures. And the songs that I wrote and sang about him made me almost famous. So I click inside the comment box and stare at the blinking cursor. I feel like he deserves at least one honest message, even if it's too late for him to read it.

Bram's green- and gold-flecked eyes, his big hands, and his deep voice fill my head. I think about kissing him and about more than kissing him. I try to count how many times we said "I love you" to each other. And then I think about the thing I'm always trying so damn hard not to think about.

Our breakup. His face. The last words I ever said to him.

I swallow hard. I type out three tiny words, and I let them fly before I lose my nerve.

I'm so sorry.

Then I press my face hard into Aden's extra pillow, hating everything. Especially myself.

I don't know what I'd do if Aden woke up right now.

I shouldn't be crying about another boy.

A dead boy.

Even if he was the first boy and only boy I ever loved.

SASHA'S LAST BLOG POST

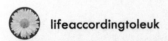

 **lifeaccordingtoleuk**

Dying flowers are the prettiest.

148 notes

SHAY

BAMF // SASHA'S SENSES REVIEW . . .
FASTEN YOUR SEAT BELTS

Looks like: a (New Age) boy band . . .

Sounds like: (with) damn good writing

Tastes like: Sour (Cabbage) Patch kids (this should be
the new name for this band. You don't even have to
give me credit if you use it)

3/5

Sasha died three months ago today. Ever since, I've felt a little
out of control.

But there's something about music that tethers me to the rest
of the world.

I'm screaming lyrics at the top of my lungs, so I barely even register the bodies pressing against me from all sides. The music is so loud that the bass is filling up my chest, so I can't feel my always-racing heart. I know the faces onstage, the set list, and that the people on either side of me are loving every second of sound as much as I am, so I don't have that clogged feeling in my throat that usually makes me want to sob or fight or run whenever I'm in a crowd.

Music is the only reason I can ever ignore the feelings that always have me on edge; that almost never leave me alone.

The set ends. I'm sweaty and smiling and tingly all over, and we're all still screaming—we're desperate for Fasten Your Seat Belts to come back and do one more song. But they can't tonight because the schedule is packed, and when I pull up the invite for this show on my phone, I see that Rohan's new band, Our Numbered Days, is up next.

Without music playing, the room fades into painfully sharp focus: Flashes of light from a dozen phones taking selfies in the dark. Scratches across the stage as stagehands dressed in as much black as I reorganize the setup. The clatter of glasses from people ordering at the bar, and voices shouting for friends or laughing. Hands, everywhere, reaching.

The space inside my head that the music filled up with warmth moments earlier overflows with something icy. It sends all the messed-up, mixed-up signals to the rest of me.

My stomach and chest flood with the hot, bad kind of butterflies. My palms get slick, and I instantly wish I had my sister's cool fingers to grab—she was always my safety net when the world got to be too much. Her hospital bracelet, the one I haven't taken off since the night she died, suddenly feels too tight on my wrist. I look at the glowing emergency exit sign, and I make my way toward it before the alarms sounding in my body get any louder.

When I come back inside, Rohan is onstage with Marc and Jo and Pooja. They're playing a song I don't recognize, but the melody is catchy as hell. I say hi to a few kids as I make my way through the crowd, trying to lie kinda low, so Ro doesn't notice me walking back in during his set, but kids keep shouting my name from almost every direction. It's hard not to know everyone in this scene if you go to enough shows, and I go to more than enough shows. I have to for the fan site I started with my sister: Badass Music Fanatics.

I holler a few more hellos, but I want to find the rest of the BAMF contingent (aka my real friends), like, *now*. I'm not sure how much of Rohan's set I've missed, so I pull out my phone to text Deedee. I'll never find her in a crowd like this, in spite of her hair, which is almost as big as mine, and that in a sea of white faces, she and I are the only two black girls here.

Deedee texts and says she's only a few feet from the stage and that she's found Callie, but before I can text back, Jerome is beside me with his lips against my ear.

"Shay," he says, and I can tell by his voice that he's been smoking.

I turn around and look at Jerome's lips, mostly to make sure I hear whatever he says next, but then I can't look away. They're heart-shaped and pretty, and he licks them, like he's going to start talking again, but I stop him by pressing my finger against

29

his mouth. I close my eyes, and I kiss Jerome's pretty lips because I've been kissing them (him?) all month. I don't want Jerome to say anything because I have a feeling I know what he wants to tell me: something about how he likes me; something about how we should be more than the occasional kiss. But I can barely stay in a room, so I don't even want to think about trying to stay in a relationship. I've never had a boyfriend, and I can't even imagine it.

I slip my hands into the pockets of his oversize cardigan and grab his lighter at the same time. Then my hands are in the back pockets of his saggy-bottomed corduroys, looking for what's left of his joint. "Aha!" I say, pulling my clenched fist from his pocket. He smiles, but he doesn't laugh.

"I saw you run outta here," he says. "You cool?"

I pull away and look up (because his lips aren't the only pretty parts of him), but his light brown eyes are searching mine for something I don't want to share. So I look back down at the things in my hands. He's one of the few people who understands that when I fly from a room, I need space to catch my breath. It's one of the many reasons I like kissing him. I nod.

"Cool," he says.

I give him a quick peck on the cheek before I flick open his lighter and hit his joint. The tiny flame illuminates the ripped band T-shirt I'm wearing, my arm full of bangles, how little space there is between the two of us. Jerome tucks one finger into the stretched out neck of my shirt and another through a loop in my jeans. I inhale smoke, and calm, and *him*.

This venue is teens only, which means no drinking and definitely no smoking, but I've never really let those rules stop me before. I feel my tense muscles relax the tiniest bit as I blow a thin ribbon of smoke into the barely-there space between us where no one will notice it.

He tips his head in my direction like I'm royalty, and the weathered metal of the vintage rings he's always wearing glint dully under the stage lights. He slips the joint from my fingers and puts it out between two of his own. As he moves away from me, I can see longing in his bloodshot eyes. I wonder if he can see the same thing in mine.

A minute later, I find Deedee. She's pressed against the wall on the far side of the stage with Callie and a few other people we know from school and shows like this one.

"Hey," I say. I wedge my shoulder between two guys I know from cross-country and nod at them. My heart revs up from their closeness, but I hook my arm through Deedee's, and I feel a little better.

" 'Hey'?" Callie says, looking annoyed. Her thin, dark T-shirt has holes in it, and her pale skin is almost glowing from beneath it, like pinholes of light.

"Yeah," Deedee agrees. "Where the heck have you been?" She slaps at my arm. She's pulled all her super-thick hair away from her eyes into a loose ponytail she probably can't get any tighter. Her glasses are fogged up, so I pull them off her face and wipe them with the hem of my shirt.

"You almost missed his whole set, and they're sooo damn good."

"Unraveling Lovely good?" I ask. (They're my gold standard for everything.) I place her glasses back on her nose.

"Close," she says. Then I look at Callie. Her hazel eyes and pursed, glossy lips seem to add, *But not quite.*

Deedee shows me a few pictures she took of Rohan when he got down on his knees during a guitar solo, and I post the best one to the BAMF account with just the name of his band: Our Numbered Days. I tag my location, and I add a rating: five shooting star emojis in a row. But I want to do a little extra since this is Rohan's new band. I add a trio of heart-eyed smileys, like I've fallen in love with music I've barely heard.

"Them likes, though," Callie says as she looks over my shoulder. She's a nerd for numbers, and my post has twenty-two likes and eight comments almost immediately.

"Pays to be a little bit Internet famous," I say, and Deedee adds, "At least on Long Island."

I silently wish Sasha could see how much our followers love that Ro is in a new band. BAMF was her idea.

The two of us have been obsessed with pop-punk and indie rock since our babysitter introduced us to some of her favorite bands when we were nine, the year before Sasha was diagnosed, so as I listen to Rohan's next song, I think about what Sasha might have said about it. She'd point out the lyrics of the bridge (something I never notice) or that the bass line is subtle but necessary. And I think that maybe that's why I love this music so much. Every piece of it—from the distortion on Rohan's guitar, to the way I can't help but nod my head to the beat—reminds me of her.

We were so into *our music* in a way not very many black kids are. So a few years ago, when we started going to shows and seeing how outnumbered we were, Sasha wanted kids like us to have a place where they could unabashedly love the music they love and not feel weird about it. BAMF was born, and the blog was how we met Rohan: he recruited Sasha and me to manage his old band, and managing Unraveling Lovely made us blow up.

Obviously, anyone who loves music is welcome in the BAMF community, but with our faces front and center on the "About" page as the creators—and Deedee as the photographer—we've always hoped to help other brown and black kids with our taste in music feel a little less alone.

Despite Unraveling Lovely's upset at Battle of the Bands, people still trust what we have to say about music. So I've always done show coverage. Deedee takes all the pictures. Callie does a pretty low-budget, biweekly podcast where she interviews aspiring musicians. Sasha used to do pretty much everything else, including writing demo and album reviews, so now we're going to have to find someone else to help us out.

I mostly try not to think about it.

"So, thanks so much for coming out tonight," Rohan says into the mike after the song ends and the audience quiets down. He pushes his dark hair away from his even darker eyes, and he's grinning, all dimples and whiskers. I'm pretty bummed I almost missed the whole set, and Ro won't be happy about it either. Still, I let out a long, loud *"Wooooo!"* before he says anything else, and he grins.

"This is the last song we're gonna play tonight. It's a cover of one of my favorites. Today is a pretty rough day . . . so I want to dedicate it to someone."

His voice sounds pinched, like it's too big for his throat, and my stomach clenches because I'm almost positive I know what's coming. Today marks three months since . . . And it looks like he might be scanning the crowd for me.

"This one's for you, Sasha," he finishes.

I just got back, and I want so desperately to hear the rest of his set, but her name rips me wide open again when I'd only just managed to put myself back together. I look at Deedee, and she's biting her bottom lip, already untangling her arm from mine because she knows what's coming.

Callie tries to stop me. She says, "Shay, just *wait*," but I can't. I shove my way through the crowd, back toward the exit, before he sings the first note.

In the parking lot, it takes me three tries to unlock my bike because everything about me is shaking. But when I push my headphones on over my hair and press play, the perfect song spills into my ears. I turn it up, focusing on the singer's desperate voice and pedaling to the bass line. I let the steady drums and the clearest notes from the guitar flow through me like a current.

The last time I heard the song Rohan was about to play, we were in Sasha's hospital room. His voice mixed with mine as we sang it to her. I was holding her hand, and when I looked around the room, Mom was shaking and the nurses were sniffling. There was Rohan, who I couldn't bear to watch, and a priest who I abruptly decided to hate.

Sasha looked at me when the song ended and said, "Fucking Luke," and we both smiled even as tears spilled onto our cheeks. When her eyes closed, and the nurses confirmed she was in a coma, Mom looked at me, and I knew her face mirrored my own expression. It was official: Sasha wouldn't wake up.

I couldn't watch. I didn't want to know which organ would

fail my sister first. I kissed her chilly fingers and wiped my tears away with my thumbs. I pushed my way out of the room because I knew Mom was too distraught to stop me, and I could feel the tension building in my limbs.

That hadn't been the first time my body betrayed me—my heart squeezing, sweat breaking out across my upper lip—but it was the first time I didn't have Sasha to bring me back from the edge, to tell me that I'd be okay. Ever since that night, whatever goes haywire inside me has been showing itself a lot more often.

"Fucking Luke" and sometimes "Motherfucking Luke" is what Sasha and I always said in unison whenever something new went wrong for her, as if the cancer were a crappy boyfriend she couldn't shake instead of leukemia.

The music is helping (it always does). I can breathe again, and I feel a little more in control. Even though I'm all alone, pedaling like mad down a darkened back road, when the song ends, I tilt my head up to the sky. I scream at the stars.

"MOTHERFUCKING LUKE!"

I'm only about a half mile away from home when Rohan catches up to me in the Band Wagon, aka his crappy black mini-van. The side of it is still spray-painted with a huge "Unraveling Lovely" from when the band went on their mini-tour, so there's no mistaking him for anyone else.

When I look over, I see my reflection in his window, and I wish it weren't an image of phantom me. I wish I were seeing Sasha, healthy Sasha, sitting in Rohan's truck. We were identical, so if I squint in this kind of dark, I can almost believe it's true.

We used to have the same wild, dark hair, precisely the same shade of honey-brown skin, round cheeks, and baby faces. But by the time she died, right before our sixteenth birthday, Sasha had wasted away so much that she only looked like an unfinished sketch of me—a half-drawn picture that hadn't yet been colored or filled in. I didn't even know it was possible for black people to *be* pale. Until there was no other word for what my sister's skin had become.

Rohan rolls down his window and then points to my headphones. I pull the cup off the ear closest to him, but I keep pedaling.

He says, "Shay, slow down" and then "Don't be like this." He drives slow to keep up with me, but I keep up my silence.

He tries "Stop" and then "Let me drive you the rest of the way." But I scrub at my face, in case there are still tears on my cheeks, and I stand up to pedal when we come to the base of a hill. I don't want his comfort. I want my twin sister. No one else, not even one of my best friends, will do.

"How much of my set did you even hear?" he asks, the hurt spilling into his voice.

I look over at him then. One of his arms is hanging out of his window, and he has to be cold because he's not wearing his jacket. He must have run out of the club to chase me as soon as he finished the last song.

I shake my head, and the tears bubble up and over again. I barely manage it, but I whisper, "I'm so sorry."

"It's okay," he replies, but we both know it isn't. I just hope he sees the BAMF post later and forgives me.

I'm huffing and puffing and still kind of crying, and it is so cold. I say the only thing I think I can without completely falling apart again.

"Just . . . Can you not play that song, again? At least for a while? I can't stand it."

I look back over at him, and the way he's looking at me makes me wish for a different face. I love my sister, but he loved her too, and I can't help but wonder how much of her he sees when he looks at me. I think the same thing about Mom.

He nods, and stops talking, but he follows close behind until I turn onto my street. As soon as I park my bike and pull out my keys, he drives away.

When I open the front door, Mom's not home (because she's never home), and I should be used to it. She's always worked a lot, but I miss her more at night now than I did before. Music will have to keep me company for now.

I unplug my portable speaker from the charger and sync it to my phone. I turn the volume all the way up. I just left a show headlined by Our Numbered Days, but I pull up my Unraveling Lovely playlist. My whole hand feels like its vibrating with bass as I carry the speaker from my dresser to my bed.

As I sing along to the soundtrack of last summer, I pick up my phone to check on the photo of Rohan I posted earlier instead of doing the homework I still haven't finished. It has 437 likes and dozens of comments, and I hope it will be enough to win Ro's forgiveness for missing the majority of his first show with his new band. Without really deciding to, I flick through my pictures, back to three months ago, when my sister was still here.

In the last photo I posted with Sasha, she and I are curled around each other on the roof of the hospital, wrapped in piles of blankets like newborns. It was October, two weeks before our sixteenth birthday, and when Rohan and I asked Sasha what she wanted, she said, "To see the stars." Rohan helped me sneak her into the elevator in a wheelchair; then he carried her up the last flight of stairs and out onto the roof. He took this photo of us.

Mischief managers, the caption reads. It has more than a thousand likes, and as in the comments of any picture of Sasha, all anyone ever says is that they miss her. It makes me feel less alone even knowing most of our followers don't really know her at all.

I'm feeling a little calmer after reading a few comments, and after the first UL song ends, but in that dreaded two-second gap between the first and second tracks, I hear the front door slam. A moment later, Mom's voice is fighting its way up the stairs, competing with Logan's as the next song starts.

"Shay, what have I told you about that noise? Turn it down before you and I both go deaf!"

I cut my music and examine my face in the mirror before I head downstairs. I look okay; not like I sobbed all the way home. I reapply some of my eye makeup, just to be safe. She's stepping out of her heels when I get to the bottom of the stairs.

"Hey, Mom," I say. "You're back pretty late."

"I know, sweetie. I'm sorry. Did you finish your homework? Have you eaten?" She starts walking toward the kitchen, and I wonder if I'll ever fill out like her—get the hips she's had for my whole life, or a butt that can actually make a pair of jeans or a skirt look good.

I dodge her first question. "I had something to eat at the show."

I stand behind her as she fills our electric kettle with water to make herself a cup of tea. She pulls down two mugs, and then I think it hits her; the mistake she's made. I'm not the twin who was an Anglophile—who drank tea and read British literature for fun and watched BBC documentaries with her every Friday night. I'm not Sasha, even though I look like her. Mom glances at me anyway, and I shake my head. I'm the twin who likes coffee, who likes music magazines, and who likes watching BMX videos. She puts one of the mugs back into the cabinet.

I pour myself a big glass of water and hop up to sit on the counter, like we're going to chat, because she and Sasha used to talk for hours. (I have no idea what about.) We both end up looking at our phones instead of saying anything else to each other, though.

When she says "Don't stay up too late" and heads for the stairs, I ease toward Sasha's room.

I open the door and just stand there for a moment, trying to decide how much I can handle today. With the song Rohan played still fresh in my mind, and my palms already turning a little sweaty, I decide I'm too on edge to attempt to lie in my sister's bed tonight and read the poetry and song lyrics she painted across her ceiling. I slide down by the door to sit on the floor because I don't want to walk in any farther, but I don't want to leave, either.

I turn on her TV and queue up our favorite show, *Intervention*. Rohan and I used to lie in bed with Sasha and watch hours of it on the weekends. I lean against the wall and watch as a girl only a little older than me tells the camera that she's been hooked on heroin since she was sixteen.

Sasha's favorite beanie, an all-black one with two cat ears stitched onto the top, is sitting in a basket by the door, the peak on a mountain of all the knit hats my sister collected once she'd lost her hair. I grab it, shove it over my own messy curls, and finish up the episode. Then I actually do my homework, trying to soak in the Sasha-ness of Sasha's room until I feel as calm as I would have if she were here beside me.

When I open the bedroom door to leave, I hear Mom in the kitchen again. I stand there for a second, hoping to wait her out because I don't want to have another awkward nonconversation.

"No, it's not that," I hear her say. She must be on the phone. "Sasha was so open, you know? She told me everything. But Shay doesn't talk to me, so I don't know how she's feeling or how to help her." She pauses, and I step into the hall, ready to assure her that I don't need any help, that I'm completely fine. I'm seconds away from turning the corner to the kitchen when she speaks up again, and her voice sounds almost weepy. "I just want her to be okay."

I stop. I take a few steps back toward Sasha's room, unsure of what to do. I knew Mom was sad about Sasha, but I had no idea she was sad about me too. I don't know what I could have done to make her worry.

When Mom goes back to her room, I head back to mine. But I can't get her words out of my head, which makes it impossible for me to fall asleep. Only twenty minutes pass before I creep back downstairs, lace up my running shoes, and grab my jacket.

Outside, in the cold, my feet pound the pavement, and my breath is a puff of white in front of my face. Besides music, running is the only thing that consistently helps to keep me calm. I run to the end of my street, then around my block.

I keep running. Past my old elementary school, its playground creating a shadowy silhouette in the moonlight. Past my high school, where Rohan, Deedee, and Callie cheered me on in a track meet earlier today. Up the hill that leads to the park where me and Sasha used to swap secrets on the swings, and farther still, to the parking lot of the hospital where my sister died.

I slow down and jog over to an empty spot in the lot. I lie down on the cold asphalt, and I feel unmoored, like I'm a ship, and the black concrete around me is the sea. While I wait for my pulse to slow, I stare up at the seagulls circling the lot—maybe they think it's a body of water. Sasha was my lighthouse, my north star, so I search for a sign of her in the dark.

Some people visit their loved ones' graves to talk to them, but for some reason, I like talking to my sister at the hospital. Maybe because this was the last place I saw her alive.

"Mom's worried about me," I say out loud. "But I don't really know why."

It's Momma, Sasha says inside my head. *She worries about everything.*

"Yeah, but I'm a pretty good kid," I say.

You are, but she must know something else is going on.

I shake my head. "She doesn't know about me staying out late."

Because she's never there.

"Right. She knows I go to shows all the time, but she has no idea about the smoking. And I guess my grades could be better," I say. Sasha doesn't answer, but I know she agrees.

I turn my head, almost expecting to see my sister beside me, because we would lie in bed all the time and have talks like this. She always stayed quiet when I talked about school because she hadn't been in one for almost a year. I close my eyes so I can picture her as clearly as I can summon her voice.

What about the running? Sasha asks.

"Track?"

No, the flipping out. The running away? I'm sure that worries her, too.

I open my eyes and look up again. "She's never seen it happen, though."

I'm sure she wouldn't be happy if she knew about it. And it's Momma. She probably knows about it.

"I hope not."

I think of Mom's words tonight: *I just want her to be okay.* And it's funny because I just want *her* to be okay. She shouldn't be worrying about me after she spent the last five years worrying about Sasha. She deserves a little peace.

I should go home right now. I never should have left. It's late, and I'm not stupid—I know I shouldn't be out by myself, running recklessly through the dark. But I think I've decided this is my last night doing things that would worry Mom if she knew about them, and I want to enjoy it.

I stand up, turn on the loudest song on my phone, and run in the direction of the beach. The wheels in my head are turning, and since I wouldn't mind being less like myself right about now, I hatch a plan to become the kind of kid Mom won't have to worry about.

4

AUTUMN

JAN. 17, 3:19 A.M.

My mom said I have to go back to school on Monday, so I'm not talking to her.

Tavia may not be on Hangouts right now. She'll see your messages later.

From: HeCalledItAutumn@gmail.com
To: TaviaViolet@gmail.com
Sent: Jan. 20, 1:41 a.m.
Subject: <none>

Alexa was crying when I saw her in the hall my first day back, and seeing her crumpled against her locker made me want to run to her. But when I got a little closer, she wiped her face really fast and pulled out her phone, and tried to seem surprised when I tapped her on the shoulder.

Because Alexa never wears makeup, she can look almost normal after crying. Her nose is all pink, and her brown eyelashes are pinched together because they're still a little wet, but no mascara is running.

It makes me remember how you'd attack her with liquid liner before we went to parties. How you'd send me links to your favorite Asian vloggers' makeup tutorials, hoping I'd follow the instructions to make my own eyes "pop." And I'm seconds away from bringing up your makeup obsession with Alexa. But then I realize she's pretending that she wasn't crying. She wants me to think everything is fine, and I don't really want to upset her again. So I try to stop thinking about makeup—about how much lip gloss and bronzer you owned—and I bump her shoulder. She smiles a little, and neither of us says a thing about you.

We walk to class together, and Margo and Faye join us on the second floor, but the balance of the way we take up space is off. Faye is supposed to be in front—walking backward telling a story, or facing forward, like we're a ship and she's at the helm. Margo and Alexa should be in the middle, and Alexa should be turning her head to tell me everything Faye is saying. Margo should be adding her own commentary to make us laugh. Your arm is supposed to be threaded through mine—the fifth point in our star.

Instead, Faye is next to me. She says, "How was your weekend?" But she doesn't sound normal. Her voice comes out a little higher pitched than it should be, and her eyes are too wide and wet-looking. Her head is tilted slightly, like I'm a small child or a puppy, and I know she means well, but I hate when people talk to me using their Sympathy Voice.

I don't say anything at first. But the truth is, I want to tell her everything: that my weekend was terrible, that I've been sleeping at your house, that being back here is harder than I thought it would be. That it took me twenty minutes to find something clean to wear and that everything with Dante is weird and complicated now. But telling her things that I can't tell you first feels strange.

Eventually, I say, "Weekend was fine, I guess." But still Faye stays beside me, looking concerned. Margo has her arm around Alexa's shoulders, and she hasn't said anything funny at all. Alexa hasn't looked at me since we were at her locker, and no one's really talking when usually, we don't shut up. I can tell Faye wants to say something else or wants me to, but when I stay quiet, so does she. She waves to some guy she knows and then touches my shoulder before she goes over to talk to him instead of me. I already want to go home.

I keep pretending everything is normal, even though nothing is normal, because I'm not sure what else to do. I roll my eyes when a teacher makes a dumb joke in homeroom, and I try to ignore the gaping hole your empty chair carves right through me. I compliment Margo's shoes before our next class, and she tells me where she got them, but her explanation is way shorter than it would ordinarily be. I even laugh when we watch an embarrassing video in health class, but when Faye looks at me as if I've done something wrong, I bite my lip. I feel like I have.

Between periods, a few people hug me or touch my shoulders as they tell me they're sorry that you're gone. They talk to me in their everyday voices, and it's a relief to hear them saying your name. I hug them back and say thank you. For some reason, it's easier for me to talk to random people than it is for me to say anything to our friends.

After a few more classes with the three of them barely speaking to one another or me, I decide to eat lunch alone. I'm tired of not knowing what to say or do around them, so I sit at the table near the bathroom, the one that smells kind of bad. I see Alexa look around for me when she first gets into the cafeteria, but Margo pulls her toward our usual table. Faye says hi to about a million people, the way she always does, but eventually, she goes to our table too.

I watch our friends until the scene makes my chest feel like it's caving in. I don't know where I fit inside the picture of us without you.

I've always felt a little . . . *optional* to them, and the lack of you in the lunchroom makes me feel more unnecessary than ever. Your absence is more shocking here than it's been almost anywhere else, like in one of those spot-the-difference games where something essential has been erased from one of the pictures. I'm an extra cloud in an already-cloudy sky, but you were the leg of a table. You were our sun.

Perry sees me sitting by myself, and before I can run away from his gaze, he comes over.

"Hey, Autumn," he says. He puts his tray down on the table. He's thinking about staying, but I hope he doesn't. He plucks at the front of his baggy T-shirt, like he's hot, and lifts his blond eyebrows higher than he needs to when he starts talking.

"That history test was intense, right? Tavia's like, a history genius, so I used a couple of her memorization tricks."

He smiles and taps at his temple, but that's when I notice that the whites of his small gray eyes are red, and I wonder if he's been crying, or having a hard time sleeping, or both. It's hard to look at him for too long knowing you were on your way to see him that night. *I* know you still loved him, but *he* doesn't.

I don't know how to process everything that seeing him makes me feel.

"Sorry, Perry. I gotta go," I tell him as I stand up. I'm too tired to come up with an actual excuse.

I've had my phone on all day. Between periods, I look at pictures of you with it hidden in my locker so it doesn't get confiscated, but right now, I don't really care. I call my sister and put the phone right up to my ear before I even get to the door of the girls' bathroom.

"Autumn," Willow says. There's a frantic edge to her voice, but she's working hard to sound like her normal self. "Everything all right?"

"Not really," I say. I tell her about Perry. Then about everyone else.

"Alexa has Margo, and Faye has never really *needed* anyone. It's like I suddenly don't have a place to stand. Like I don't fit anymore." I pause when a girl comes into the bathroom, and I wait for her to go into a stall before I say anything else.

"I guess I didn't think I would feel so out of place without her," I whisper, hoping the other person in the bathroom doesn't hear. Willow sighs, so I know she knows I'm talking about you. "And I thought I wouldn't want to talk about her, you know? But *not* talking about her is worse. It feels like we're ignoring the fact that she's missing. That she's gone."

"Sounds like they don't know how to process what's happening," Willow says after a pause. "They're probably not dealing with it, or whatever. Or maybe they feel weird because they don't know what to say since the two of you had been friends for so long before you even met them. She was yours first. But even if they don't know what to say, they should be trying harder to be there for you."

I can tell my sister's trying to analyze them, just because she declared her major recently: psych. But I can't deny that I find comfort in the fierceness of her love. I cling to her words about you: *She was yours.*

"I love you, Will," I say to her, even though we don't say that to each other very often. And that tiny truth is something I wish I told you every day. "It's just that . . . losing her was hard enough. I don't think I can handle it if I end up without them, too."

"I get it," Willow says. "But don't forget that you're not the only one hurting." I picture Alexa's face, and I try not to feel my own pain multiply. "You guys should be supporting one another right now, not, like . . . ignoring everything. Maybe try to do something small? Show them what you wish they'd do for you?"

It's not a terrible idea, but I'm not sure I can do it today. "Yeah. I'll try to figure it out."

"Call me later, okay?" Willow says. And I just tell her I love her again before I hang up.

I stay in the stall and text Dante. He isn't back at school yet, and he probably doesn't really care, so I don't bug him with the Alexa-Margo-Faye drama. But I do tell him about Perry.

I just don't get why he's talking to me, I send. He never talked to me like this before, even when they were dating.

Yeah, Dante sends back. But that's all he says.

Where are you? I ask. He never answers my question.

After school, I ask my dad if it's okay, and I drive to your house instead of mine.

I do my homework in your den, like you're right there beside me the way you used to be. I watch *Teen Mom* on your couch with your mom, but you liked that show more than either of us, so we switch to a weird indie movie. When it's time for dinner, I help her make a salad and pour your dad some wine. We listen to some contemporary classical, and they say it's a shame that I quit playing the violin. I talk about school when they ask me about it, but I don't tell them about how weird things are with our friends.

Dante isn't around all afternoon or evening, and part of me is relieved. But when my mom calls around ten and asks when I'm planning to come home, he comes through the front door, looking rosy-cheeked and pissed. When he sees me, his face doesn't exactly light up, but it's suddenly a little less shadowed.

"Is it okay if I stay the night?" I ask my mom while he's still watching me.

She covers the mouthpiece, but I still hear her muffled voice when she says to my dad, "I'm worried she's spending too much time over there, aren't you?"

That's when I remember that I wasn't talking to her for a reason.

"Maybe it's helping her, Abby," I hear my dad answer. "Maybe we just let her do whatever she thinks she needs for a while. Autumn's not Willow," he adds, as if I'm more fragile than my sister, as if I need to be handled with more care. And something about the way he says my name makes me angry. My face must have changed because when I turn toward him, Dante asks me our question with his eyes.

You okay?

I nod, deciding that maybe I shouldn't be speaking to either of my parents.

"Okay," my mom says, to me, finally. "Okay. Do you need a change of clothes?"

Dante finds me in your room after midnight.

I'm sitting on the floor beside your bed, and I'm holding that thin, hot pink scarf I bought for you because you said it looked like a wish. You were always saying stuff like that—making everyday things seem like magic.

Dante sits on the floor beside me, and he leaves a few inches of space between us.

He just showered. His too-black hair is wet, and he smells just like you. Without really deciding to, I lean toward the familiar scent. Or toward him. Maybe he's the one who moves. Either way, there was space between us, and then suddenly, there isn't.

He nods at the scarf and says, "You should take that. Tavia would have wanted you to have it."

Our shoulders are touching, and I can feel his warm skin through the thin fabric of my shirtsleeve. I can feel his breath on my cheek as he says it.

I lick my lips and try not to breath in the vanilla-y scent of him too deeply.

"Did you use her shampoo?"

His thick hair is dark as a shadow, and he runs his hand through it, then sniffs his fingers. I watch him out of the corner of my eye.

"Is that weird?" he asks me.

I shrug. "No, not really."

But when he sniffs his fingers again, something about his normally serious face being all scrunched up makes me laugh.

It feels wrong like it did in health class. But it's worse here, in your room, only a few days after we left you all alone, underground, in the rain. So I change the subject. I tie the scarf around my wrist, and I tell Dante about the day we bought it.

He watches me quietly as I talk, and his thick eyebrows lift as he grins. The story isn't really funny, but Dante laughs a little, too. And for a second, I feel better than I have in days.

When the moment passes, though, Dante picks up one of your frilly socks from the floor and starts to cry.

Usually, when someone cries, I don't know what to do. But right now, Dante smells exactly like you, so that makes things easier. I pull him toward me, and he buries his wide face in the narrow space between my cheek and shoulder. I hold his head and breathe in the vanilla scent of you that's spilling out of your closet and seeping from your sheets and that's threaded through your brother's hair.

But then I think about that night. About being with him while you were all alone. And I pull away.

He stares at me. His cheeks are pink, and his eyelashes are long and black and wet. His lips, for some reason, seem swollen, and he looks a little hurt, a little pissed, a little . . . something else. I look down at the scarf on my wrist.

"I'm not going home," I tell him. "But . . . I can't sleep in her bed."

I can't lie on your pillow or crawl under your sheets now that you won't ever touch them again. I still can't wrap my head around how *gone* you really are.

Dante nods, like he understands, and gets up, scrubbing at his eyes with his sleeve as he leaves your room. When he comes back, he has two pillows; an air mattress; and a thin, blue blanket.

He points over his shoulder, to his room across the hall.

"You can sleep in there," he says, and the thought of being in his bed makes everything about me run hot. I'm blushing all over the place, but he's leaning over with his back to me, plugging in the electric pump for the mattress. His dark hair is like a curtain between us, so he doesn't see.

As little as I want him to notice me right now, I still want to touch him. I want to say thank you to him for letting me talk about you, which is what I needed from our friends so badly at school. I want to thank him for offering me his room, but I don't have the words. It's so bad that I squeeze my fingers together, just to be sure that I won't reach for his shoulder.

I step back and take a deep breath to pull myself together, then shake my head when he turns back around. "I can't spend the night in your room, Dante." I say. He bites his lip in a way that makes me have to look at anything but him, so I stare at the air mattress. "I have to sleep in here."

The house is so quiet that the sound of the electric pump fills the air like applause. And when Dante starts drumming his fingers against his knee, I wish I could hear whatever rhythm was filling his head. I wish I could clap or sing along.

I watch him, hugging one of the pillows to my chest, thinking about last summer and how you and I went on the road with his band for those three days. I start humming, even though I don't mean to. Instead of leaving when the mattress is plump with air, Dante looks up at me through his lashes. His eyes are still a little wet.

I was humming the chorus from "Unmasked," but I stop when he looks at me, even though the lyrics are still floating through my head.

"That's our song," he says. I assume he means him and me, so I blush again. A second later, I realize the "our" he means is probably his band.

"I just meant—"

"I know what you meant."

Dante would always find me in the audience when the band played that song live, and grin because he knew it was my favorite. And he's still looking at me now, so I wonder if he's thinking about that. I know I am.

"Would it be weird if I sleep in here too?" he asks.

We both just want to be close to you, and this room is as close as either of us is going to get. I shake my head.

I lie down on the air mattress, and Dante lies on the floor right beside me. He falls asleep quickly, and his snore is soft and steady, and I almost feel better in your room with him here. But I can't sleep. I keep thinking about how awful school is without you. I keep thinking about Alexa's party. I reach for my phone and dial my voice mail. I push it to my ear.

"Summer," your voice says. "Spring. Winter. Autumn, my love. Where are you? There are cute boys here, and a few cute dogs, but there are no cute yous. Let's change that, and soon."

You pause, but I know you aren't done. I reach out to touch a strand of Dante's wavy hair and keep listening.

"I'm sorry, okay? What will it take for you to forgive me? Should I sing, horribly, in public? Should I sing, horribly, and embarrass myself on this park bench right now?"

There's a rustling sound, and I assume it's your collar rubbing against the phone's receiver. You sigh at this point in the message. I don't even have to close my eyes to imagine your puffed cheeks, your rolling eyes. But I do close my eyes. I'm that desperate to see you.

"Fine," you say, and then you start singing. It must be a song your mom taught you because it sounds like Spanish. And even though this is your version of bad singing, I still think it sounds pretty good.

"Happy?" you say a minute later, and then, in a much smaller voice, "Call me."

I don't even remember what I was mad at you about.

If I were normal, listening to the message would make me laugh, imagining you standing alone in a crowded park, singing at the top of your lungs as an apology. Or maybe it should make me cry, hearing the humanness of you: how your mood could shift from playful and confident to vulnerable and sad in only a few minutes. But I'm not normal, so I don't react at all.

And I also don't sleep. I stare at the back of your brother's head, his hair tousled and so, so black, and I play the message again.

5

LOGAN

BRAM IS BORED so he tries a makeup tutorial.

121,164 views | 2 months ago

"Absolutely not," I say to my mom.

We're sitting in the kitchen, and she's trying to make me take the phone. She just called Bram's mother for God knows what reason. And I don't know how the hell it came up, but now she knows that I haven't talked to Ms. Lassiter since Bram died. Not even at the funeral. That might make me an asshole, but I can barely deal with my own feelings right now. Between Aden blowing up my phone trying to find a drummer and having no idea where to start, and attempting to not fail my senior year of high school, I don't have the brain space left to deal with her, too.

"Mother. No way. I don't even know what to say."

I stand up and back away from the phone, but she follows me with it. I roll my eyes and cross my arms, but she won't let up.

"I wasn't even friends with him anymore," I plead, a whiny last-ditch effort. But my mother covers the mouthpiece with her hand.

She says, "Logan Gale Lovelace. If you don't take this phone right this second, you can say goodbye to practicing with Aden this weekend."

Even though Aden and I have been hooking up more than practicing, she doesn't know that.

My mother is tiny and freckled and fair. She's what a small vanilla latte with a dash of cinnamon sugar sprinkled on top would look like if the drink could become human. But she's scary as hell sometimes. She does that little mom-nod, with her eyebrows lifted and her lips pursed, like she's saying, *Did you hear me?*

I drop to my knees and breathe out an impressively throaty *"Ughhhhhhh."*

But then I take the phone from her hand. I put my thumb over the end button, like I'm gonna hang up without saying a word, and I toss her an evil smirk. My mom doesn't miss a beat. She mouths, slowly, deliberately, *Don't. You. Dare.*

"Hi, Ms. Lassiter," I say, my eyes rolling up to the ceiling. I lie across the floor dramatically, like it's my bed or a stage. But then Ms. Lassiter clears her throat in the same rhythm that Bram used to; three beats instead of two: *Ah, ah-hem.*

That alone removes the sarcasm from my voice. Knocks the attitude right out of my posture. I sit up and take a deep breath. That alone nearly rips me in half.

"Hello, Logan, honey," she says. Even though she cleared her throat, every word she speaks is still thick with sadness. "It's so great to hear your voice."

I nod. Then I realize she can't see me nodding. I cringe, thankful she can't see that either. Neither of us says anything for way too long, and I start to get goose bumps, something that always happens to me when I feel this fucking awkward—my skin starts to crawl. Then, because I don't know what else to say, I mutter, "I'm so sorry for your loss."

As soon as I say it, I regret it. And I want to throw the phone across the room because I feel like such a phony using that line. A loss is something that's missing or something you can't find. And Bram was a person—a vlogger, a football player, the boy I loved, her kid, for fuck's sake—and we both know exactly where he is: gone.

"Th-that's not what I meant," I stammer. "I meant to say . . ." And my lips start to quiver a bit. I look up, and my mom is staring at me, like she's done something wrong. Like she regrets making me take the phone. And I desperately want to toss out some smartass comment, but I can't. I'm too busy trying not to cry right here on the cold tiles of the kitchen floor. So I just stand up and walk away from her. I go down the hall and lean against the door to my dad's study. I clench my teeth so tightly that my jaw starts to hurt.

"I meant to say . . . this fucking sucks. Excuse my language, Ms. Lass, but it does," I say, slipping into what I used to call her when I went to her apartment every day. When Bram and I were crazy in love. "I mean, why did something so messed up have to happen to Bram? He was one of the good ones, you know? He was . . . better . . . more . . ."

But I don't know what he was better or more than. I just know that he was.

Then I'm crying, and it's so damn pathetic. Ms. Lassiter is quiet, but I can hear her soft breathing, so I know she's still there.

"I never said sorry after our fight." My voice is so soft it's almost a whisper. "And now I'll never get to tell him I'm sorry. It all seems so stupid now."

She sniffs, and I know that she's crying too, which makes me feel like the biggest asshole in the world. I push into my dad's study, and I slip open the drawer where I know he keeps his bourbon. I lean the phone against my shoulder, unscrew the bottle, and lift it to my lips, digging my nails into my palms against the violence of its burn.

"I'm so sorry," I say. "Is it weird that I miss him, even though I hadn't talked to him in so long?"

Ms. Lassiter swallows so loudly that I hear it through the phone. She says, "No, sweetheart, of course it isn't."

"It's just that . . . not talking to him by choice, and knowing that I can never talk to him again, is so much different than I expected it to be."

I press my head against the wall and squeeze my eyes shut, trying to will the tears to stop filling my eyes and falling. I take another fiery swig from the bottle: hot liquid courage. I say, "You don't have to answer this if you don't want to. And I know I'm probably an insensitive jerk for asking." I still myself. I wish I were talking to her in person. "But, Ms. Lass, I feel like I'm losing it. This just doesn't seem like something he would do, right?"

Ms. Lassiter takes a deep breath.

"Well, he's been different since this summer. We were put

in a tight spot, financially," she says. "I got laid off and couldn't find work for a while. And you know how he was."

"He wanted to fix it," we both say at the same time.

"Exactly. That's why he started making those videos," she continues. "And when they started making money, they helped for a while. But he changed. He . . . wasn't really acting like the Bram you knew, the Bram *I* knew, anymore."

We talk a little while longer, and by the time I hang up, the phone is almost dripping with my tears. I hide my dad's bourbon behind my back, leave his study, and edge up the stairs without drawing attention to myself. When I get to my room, I close my door slowly, even though a part of me wants to slam it shut.

I put the bourbon on my desk, open my laptop, and turn on some hardcore rap. The really nasty stuff that mothers everywhere hate. The angry, gravelly voices just speak directly to my angsty soul at times like these. People wouldn't guess that from the music I write, but sometimes I need this.

My mom starts knocking on my door before the first verse of the first song ends, and I just turn the music up louder.

I head to Bram's channel. I should be trying to figure out where the hell I'm going to find a drummer, and soon, but instead I take a swig of the bourbon and play a video of Bram where he's doing a makeup tutorial, which is about as far as I can get from my lack-of-a-drummer drama. It's on mute because the music is more important than Bram's voice right now, and I've watched it so many times lately that I can read his lips.

"I don't know how some guys do this." I know that's what he's saying, even though I can't hear him, as he tries to steady his hand to apply mascara. I glance down at my chipped nail polish and then over to the mirror at my kohl-lined eyes. He says "guys," not "girls," and I know that's because of me.

After I tutored him in math, and he taught me how to kiss (*No, put your lips like* this), we moved on to a mutual education in other things. The first month of our relationship, he taught me how to catch and throw a football. I'd perfected a barrel roll by winter, so then it was my turn. I showed him my dad's record collection, and made a playlist for him with the best music from every decade for Christmas. By spring, he'd developed a healthy love for the good stuff, and that's when he decided to teach me how to cook.

When it was my turn to play teacher again, I decided makeup would be fun, mostly because I knew exactly how I could make his eyes pop like crazy.

I'd gone to his apartment the day our relationship went to hell to make him up for fun. It was a really hot day in mid-July, and I remember his window AC unit was on full blast. I had goose bumps. As I carefully applied liquid liner, we were staring at each other because I'd told him not to move. He was so beautiful that I didn't mind. When tears began to brim along the edge of his lashes, I thought it was because the tip of the brush was dangerously close to his eye and the vent from the AC was aimed straight at us. But then I realized what song was playing, and I grinned. I thought it might be the music (a song I wrote and recorded for him), and the sensitive side of Bram, the part that made him weep when he heard a beautiful song, was the side I liked best. He didn't know, but it was the song that had gotten Unraveling Lovely to the top of the leaderboard on the East Coast. My love for him had basically helped us qualify for Battle of the Bands, and I was planning to tell him about it that day.

"God, you're adorable," I said, picking up the mascara I was planning to use next. "Are you seriously crying because of this song?"

But when he looked away from my face and started wringing his hands, I knew something else was going on. I put down the makeup.

"At camp," he started, "we made some prank calls." He said it so low, I almost couldn't hear him. He was talking about football camp. He'd been gone for all of June and most of July. He'd just gotten back a few days earlier, which is why he'd missed Unraveling Lovely's mini-tour.

"Okay . . . ," I said. "So what? You called a strip club and asked to speak to fucking Rose Thorne or something?" I grinned. "Oh wait, or Candy . . . Crush?"

He didn't smile. He swallowed and cleared his throat a little, with three beats instead of two, like every other human on Earth.

"No," he said. "We called the cheer camp. And I talked to this girl Yara. She's new, but she's starting at Bayside next year."

My first thought was, *What kind of fuck-up transfers for their last year of high school?* But I bit my lip and stayed quiet because I didn't know where this was going and he looked like he had more to say.

"Since the call," he continued, "we've kinda been texting. A lot. And she's amazing." His eyes were shining, like he was gazing up at the fucking stars instead of slowly destroying the best part of my life. He kept talking, sounding like he was her boyfriend instead of mine.

"You'd love her," he kind of whispered. "And I guess what I'm trying to say is . . . I think I already do."

He said it like it was nothing. Like with those words he didn't care that he was stomping on my heart.

It was so sudden, and I was so shocked, that I didn't do anything for a few minutes. I sat there and stared at the one eye of his that was surround by a decorative, thick black line.

"Logan," he said. And that brought me back from wherever it was I'd gone. I blinked. I registered that the song he'd put on before our first kiss was playing—a song he'd added to my playlist to be cute. Then I lost it.

"Seriously?" I started. And I don't even know what else I said. I know I screamed a lot. I know I threw a few of his things across his room. I remember being grateful that his mother wasn't home.

He kept quiet and let me freak out, just waiting for Hurricane Logan, as he used to call my temper tantrums, to pass.

When I finally stood still, I was out of breath and shaking. He looked at me with his sad, green eyes and asked me to sit beside him on the bed.

His hands were sweaty when he pulled me toward him, so it was easy for me to twist my wrists out of his grip. I sat down across the room, where he couldn't touch me.

"I know this changes things," he said, like it was raining and we had plans to have a goddamned picnic.

He said, "You're a huge part of my life," like I was just a sport he liked to play. "I don't want you to disappear on me."

I flared my nostrils and kept staring at him because I couldn't believe he'd think I'd be okay with him loving someone else. If I couldn't be with him, I knew I'd have to disappear. He must have known it, too.

I could never be just his friend. On top of the agonizing heartbreak, the asshole had left me all alone with this undeniable knowledge about myself: *I liked boys.* Bram was the first boy I'd ever kissed. The first person I'd ever loved. But loving Bram was one thing; it was easy. It felt right. Being gay was something else entirely—and it was scary as hell.

People had already given me shit my whole life about being weird. The first time I wore nail polish to school, a kid punched me in the stomach. So to be honest, I was kinda pissed that I was gay. I was definitely pissed that Bram wasn't *exactly* gay. He didn't love me anymore—that hurt like hell. And the worst part of it all was Yara. That he was breaking up with me for a girl, when I didn't even know he *liked* girls. And on top of everything else, she's a *cheerleader*!

I stared at him for too long. At his golden-brown skin and dark hair. I thought about telling him I loved him one last time.

"It's possible to love two people at once," he said, and that was just way more than I could take.

His eyes were still shining when I stood up, walked over, and punched him in the face so hard, I broke his nose and one of my own fingers.

Most people would stop there, but not *this* guy.

We were both sobbing, covered in snot and blood and tears. But before I left his room I said it. The worst thing I've ever said to anyone, and I can never take it back:

I hope you die alone.

I guess I got my wish.

It hits me then, what Ms. Lassiter said: *He's been different since this summer.* And I wonder if he was different, sadder, because of me. Because of what *I* said in a moment of rage. A moment I didn't apologize for and that I'll never be able to take back.

My mom is still knocking. I slam my laptop closed before I finally go to the door, unintentionally killing the music because there's no way I want to risk her seeing his videos on my screen, seeing just how deep my obsession with Bram goes. I scrub at my face, like there's a hope in hell I can make myself look human again before she sees me. But when I open the door I can tell by her face that mine is still red and blotchy, swollen and ugly.

"Oh, Lo," she says.

She only calls me that if I'm sick. Or when she's scared.

I've been bigger than her since before I started dating Bram, but sometimes it seems like she forgets. When she hugs me, her face just kind of smashes into my chest.

"I had no idea you were this upset."

I want to say *No shit.* But I don't.

My chin trembles against the top of her head, and I squeeze the soft fabric of her sweater so I don't hold her too tightly. Her wavy red hair sticks to my damp cheeks.

They say that dead people who have unfinished business with the living become ghosts. That their spirits linger here, or in limbo somewhere, and that they can't rest in peace until they've done whatever it is that they needed to do. But no one ever talks about the living who have unfinished business with the dead. Where is the plane they're banished to, and how do they ever find peace again?

What's to become of fuck-ups like me?

"Logan?" my mom says, bringing me back to my room and her warm, soft arms. She backs up a little so she can look up at my face, but then she looks around me, and I follow her line of sight. She puts her hand on her hip, and that means trouble.

"Is that your father's bourbon on your desk?"

Shit.

6

SHAY

BAMF // SASHA'S SENSES REVIEW . . .
REVENGE OF THE TERDS

Looks like: poop
Smells like: poop
Sounds like: poop
(If it looks, smells, and sounds like something, it's
probably that thing. Also: See band name. I wonder
if their pun was intended.)
0/5

I'm exhausted at breakfast the next morning because I ran until
dawn, thinking things through. Mom was sleeping when I got
back, so she has no idea I was out that late. Her eyes are puffy

this morning. She's playing her go-to sad music almost as loudly as I was playing Unraveling Lovely last night, so I know she probably spent most of her time in the shower crying. She's never let me see her lose it, but I heard it in her voice last night on the phone. I know the signs of her sadness. I kind of want to lean toward her now and say something annoying like *I thought we'd go deaf from music this loud?* to make her smile and say something like *You can blast your music when you own a house.* But I don't.

Her dark eyes linger on me for a beat too long when I first step into the kitchen (probably because I actually ironed my shirt today), but she's the one who taught me to dress the way I want to feel. This lesson is why Sasha had so many floral dresses and brightly colored sweaters—she always wanted to look better than she felt. And since I want to try to *be* better, for Mom, I thought a wardrobe change was in order. I'm still wearing jeans (Rome wasn't built in a day). But I thought a nice shirt wouldn't hurt. So Mom looks at me but doesn't say anything. She's dressed to the corporate nines as usual, so maybe she just gets it.

We fall into our normal routine. In the mornings, Mom and I move around each other like planets in orbit. We're used to living without Sasha, because she was in the hospital so often, but somehow, she still left this gaping hole right through the middle of everything. Sometimes the morning is the only time Mom and I will see each other all day, but we still don't say much.

When I go to the cabinet and pull down the cereal, Mom is at the sink, filling the kettle for her tea. I open the fridge for the milk and I grab Mom a yogurt while I'm in there. I don't toss it to her, the way I normally would. I set it on the table beside her, and she seems surprised by the change. She had already put down her mug, prepared to catch it, but she just says "Thanks." She hands me a banana as I fill my bowl, and then we both look at the empty toaster.

If Sasha were home, I'd drop the bread and Mom would lay out the butter and jam. Even if she were at the hospital, I'd text Sasha and ask what she wanted and then show Mom my phone with her answer. But Sasha isn't here. Sasha isn't anywhere. So I say "See ya," and Mom kisses my forehead before I push open the door.

It starts then. The hungry kind of missing-Sasha that makes me feel like she's just out of reach, not gone forever, and I'm just not trying hard enough to get to her. The thing inside me that's always on edge drops off its cliff. And I don't know if it's because I'm tired or if I'll never get used to something as simple as not making toast for my sister, but as I climb onto my bike, I feel overwhelmed and alone again. I manage to make it to the end of the block before I'm crying, my chest tightening, like someone has me pinned and is sitting on top of my body. I pull up behind an empty bus stop shelter and lay my bike in the grass before sinking down beside it.

I take out my phone and pull up photo after photo of Sasha, and when I can swallow without it making my entire throat ache, I open my browser. The cursor blinks defiantly inside the search bar, and my thumbs hover over the keyboard for only a second.

I type: *Are you still a twin if your twin dies?*

I slowly scan the results, but before I can even find an answer, I see the word "twinless" so many times that my throat tightens up like it did at the club, and starts to hurt again.

I didn't even know that was a word. It *shouldn't* be a word.

I stare down at Sasha's plastic hospital bracelet. I can hardly make out her name anymore because the ink is so badly faded. But it's there, just barely: MALONE, SASHA. I kiss it the way I've kissed it a few times a day since the night I slipped it off her skinny wrist and onto mine. I look back at the screen (at the unbearable "twinless" search results) and throw my phone into my backpack.

At school, I wait for Rohan in the parking lot. I wave to Callie and Deedee as I'm locking up my bike. Deedee comes over and hugs me, and Callie asks if I listened to the edit of her latest BAMF podcast. "Not yet," I tell her. "This weekend for sure."

She points at me and says, "You'd better." She looks me up and down, her eyes settling on my shirt. "Why are you dressed like you have an interview?"

"Just, you know, trying something new. 'Dress to impress' and all that?"

Callie frowns. Then she shrugs. "If you say so."

Deedee loops her arm through mine the way she always does, like she doesn't want me to float away.

"Come in with us," she says.

"I'm waiting for Ro," I tell her. "I need him to help me with something. Save me a seat in first period?" She pouts a little, but she nods before heading inside. Callie waves and follows her.

I joke around with a few kids from cross-country, and borrow some chemistry notes from a guy in my class, and still no Rohan.

My fingers are getting cold, and I'm just about done waiting when Jerome spots me and heads in my direction.

"Hey, Shay," he says, and somehow my name sounds different when it's coming through his lips. He's wearing a fedora today, and a big overcoat, so he looks a bit like an old-school mobster. His fingers stay tucked in his pockets, but the way he gently taps my arm with his elbow makes me wish he'd touch me with his hands.

"You ready for today?" he says. He's not referring to a test or anything. It's just something he always asks me, like every morning is something to prepare for, something harder than the day before it. And I guess, sometimes, days do feel that way. I smile.

"Yeah, I guess."

"Cool," he says. He bends his knees and cups his hands over his mouth. His rings shine as he blows against his fingers and watches me. He has bristly black hair that I always want to touch, and his skin and eyes are almost the same shade of coppery brown. There's something so familiar about his face, even though I'd never seen a face like it before I met him. If I look at him for long enough, I start to feel a little less lost.

And how do you tell someone that their face is your compass, your North Star, without sounding like a weirdo?

My eyes flicker from his eyes to his lips. I'm trying to be a new and improved version of myself, but I think it's okay if I still kiss him. So I kiss him, because it's easy and he lets me, and I feel in control of my body and my life during every precious second our mouths are touching. I wonder how these kisses make him feel, but I don't ask.

"It's cold," he says. "Walk in with me?"

I scan the lot one more time, but I still don't see Rohan.

"'Kay," I say.

When I find Ro at lunch he's bouncing the way he always does right before band practice, like the music is under his skin or inside his bones and it can't wait to get out. But when he sees me leaning against his locker, his walking immediately loses a bit of its rhythm.

He breaks away from his other friends. I wave to them as they move farther down the hall.

"Hey," he says, stopping a few feet away from me. He dips his thumbs into his pockets and looks at me through a mop of dark, messy hair. His eyes are a murky blackish-brown, like tea leaves or rain-soaked branches. They make me want to tell him everything.

"Hey," I say. "Look, I'm sorry about last night. I totally freaked, but can we talk?"

I try not to look as pathetic as I feel when I reach out my hand, which is full of my weak attempt at an apology—watermelon taffy. This flavor is his favorite, and his breath is always grossly sweet with it. He doesn't reach for it right away, which makes something inside me flicker, like a dying lightbulb, or a star. I bite my lip and lift my hand a little higher.

He keeps watching me, like he's trying to see if my apology is real. Or because I look exactly like his ex-girlfriend.

I'm wearing another one of Sasha's beanies today, so I pull it off, hoping to look less like her and more like me. This one says

BAD HAIR DAY, and I got it for Sasha a few days after she shaved the last of her hair. She thought it was hilarious.

"Of course we can talk," he says, hitching his bag higher onto his shoulders with both thumbs. "But I'm still pissed you missed so much of my set."

I grin and push away from the lockers. I stick my arm between his backpack and his body, and I hug him from the side as he puts in his combination. "Please, please, *please* forgive me?" I beg.

"Fiiiiiine," he says.

Rohan is tall and narrow, with wiry guitarist arms and lengthy runner legs, and I'm built pretty much just like him: long-limbed, boyish, and flat (just about everywhere). I can see our reflection in the mirror he has on the interior of his locker door. He musses his hair. I muss it too.

He ducks and says, "*This* doesn't happen by accident, you know," gesturing at his sloppy hair, his crooked, dimpled grin. I roll my eyes.

"Whatever. So," I say. I turn around and glance at the thick swirl of bodies all around me, and it makes me feel a little dizzy, so I turn back to Rohan.

"There's something I need your help with."

"Okaaay," he says, turning to look at me.

"I need you to cover the Revenge of the Terds show tonight. For BAMF."

It isn't like Rohan to be quiet for long, but he doesn't say anything for almost a whole minute (which seems like forever).

"Why?" he finally asks. He glances down at me. "And what are you wearing?"

I roll my eyes. "Oh my god. It's just a shirt."

He flicks the collar and points to the center of it. "It has buttons," he says, smirking. "It's not all wrinkly. Wait, did you iron it?"

"Can you focus?" I ask. "The show, tonight. Can you do it?"

"*Why?*" he says again. "You've never asked me to do anything for BAMF before. If I remember correctly, you said it would be a 'conflict of interest.'"

He's right, I did say that. And it would be since he has a new band on the scene, and BAMF prides itself on its objectivity. But there are more important things than BAMF (though Callie would be pissed if I ever said that out loud). Plus, if I'm being honest, Sasha's terrible review of Revenge is already posted. I don't care too much about missing them, and anyway, I don't want to be out late another night this week.

"I have to study," I say.

Rohan blinks at me. "You have to study," he repeats, and it doesn't sound like he's asking me a question, but I nod.

He closes his locker slowly and presses the back of his hand against my forehead and then my cheek. I slap his hand away, and he laughs.

"Since when do you study?" he asks.

"Since now!" I say.

Rohan's face changes then. He squints at me.

"Sorry," he says. He stuffs his hands into his pockets. "Is this about what happened last night? I'm sorry I played Sasha's song, okay? I'm not going to play it again. I promise. You don't have to skip tonight because of me."

Rohan lets his messy hair fall across his forehead. He hides his face if there is even the smallest chance he might blush or look sad. So now he hides his face every single time he talks about my sister.

"It's not that," I say, touching his shoulder. "I swear. I just have a chemistry test. Look," I say. I unzip my backpack. "I borrowed notes from a kid in my class."

Rohan looks at me, as if the notes aren't proof enough. "I believe that you have a test," he says. "But you don't miss shows." He doesn't ask out loud, but I hear the question anyway: *What else is going on?*

I stick the notes back into my bag. "It's Mom," I tell him. "I don't want to stress her out. She's been worried about Sasha for practically my whole life. I don't want her to start worrying about me now. So I'm just trying to pull some of my grades out of the gutter. For her."

"I get that, I guess." He nods and starts tapping his fingers on his thigh. "Speaking of BAMF, I saw the photo you posted last night," he says. I look over, and his eyes are playful. "Trying to get hired to manage another band?" he asks.

I smile, knowing that he's changing the subject to make me feel better.

"I already told you," I say, rolling my eyes and playing along. "I'm done working for amateurs."

Rohan smiles. "That was really cool of you. We got, like, two hundred fifty new followers from that one post."

"No way," I say. I take out my phone and go to his band's account. They only had seventy-three followers yesterday. Now they have more than three hundred.

"You didn't even hear our songs," Rohan continues.

"Well, I guess I have faith in your musical abilities. Besides, Callie and Deedee said you didn't suck," I say.

But Rohan shakes his head. He's done joking around.

"No," he says. "Thank you. Really."

I shrug.

"So, will you cover for me?" I ask again. "I'm not telling Dee and Cal because they'll be pissed, but if I totally flake without even sending a replacement, Callie might actually murder me."

"Deedee will probably cry if she has to be by herself at any point, and you know Callie is a lone wolf," Rohan says. I know he's right, but I need to pass this test.

"So maybe stick with Deedee as much as you can, too?" I smile really big, like "please" is written across my front teeth.

He clears his throat, like he's about to make a speech, and I'm kind of expecting him to say no and then give me a long list of all the reasons why he can't do it: his band is performing; he needs to practice; Revenge of the Terds sucks; he doesn't want to.

But all he ends up saying is "Sure."

7

AUTUMN

I went to the library, but I couldn't decide what to check out. I just stared at the shelves.

Then I took my sketchbook with me to the beach, but my fingers were trembling too much to hold the pencil.

It was pretty pathetic.

Tavia may not be on Hangouts right now. She'll see your messages later.

From: HeCalledItAutumn@gmail.com
To: TaviaViolet@gmail.com
Sent: Jan. 22, 6:57 p.m.
Subject: <none>

Your brother texted and said he's coming over. He
wants to talk, so I'm out in the cold waiting for him.
I like him, Tavi. I don't know what to do about it.

My swing set will always remind me of you. I can't even count
how many secrets we whispered to each other out here; how
many times you braided long blades of grass into my hair. How
often we fought and then apologized to each other while pump-
ing our legs, hurtling ourselves through space, like wind itself
could solve all of our problems.

My mom finds me out there with my earbuds in and my
sketchbook open. I'm sitting on the ground by the swing set,
and it's freezing, but she sits down in the grass with me anyway.

I pull my earbuds out, but I can still hear Unraveling Lovely's
song blaring through them from where they land in my lap. My
mom eyeballs my phone, like she's about to lecture me on ruining
my hearing, but I guess she decides not to. Instead, she threads
her fingers through mine and presses on each of my knuckles,
like she's playing the piano—something she's done since I was
small.

She brings the back of my cold hand to her warm cheek and
looks away when she starts crying, but I still notice her using her
shoulder to awkwardly wipe her face.

"What are you drawing?" she asks. I aim the blank page I've
been staring at toward her.

"Am I still getting the silent treatment?"

I shake my head. "I was going to do the swings, but I just
started thinking . . ." I don't finish. I can't *stop* thinking, mostly

about you. I poke holes in the blank page with the hand that isn't holding hers, the one that still holds the pencil.

"You know it's okay to be mad, right?" my mom asks. "To scream into a pillow or scribble all over a page in your sketchbook. To even break something if you need to?"

I roll my eyes a little because she is so dramatic. I shrug.

"Well, I'll just have to be pissed enough for the both of us," she says, and her voice sounds like someone has just hit her in the stomach.

I look at the rest of her face. Her tears *are* angry ones. I can tell because when my mom sad-cries, her mouth is turned down and her light eyebrows crowd together in the center of her forehead. When she angry-cries, her nostrils flare, and she turns a little red, and she presses her lips into a tight, thin line.

She stands up and kicks at the base of the swing set, where it meets the frozen ground. She kicks it again and again.

"Jesus, Mom," I say, crab-walking backward a little. But she keeps kicking.

"It shouldn't have happened," she says between the solid sounds of her sneaker hitting the wood. "Not. Like. That."

She's breathing hard when she sits back down a minute or so later. Tears are all over her face, and her thin, blond hair is falling out of its ponytail.

"And it should never have happened to our Tavia."

She says it as if you dying broke a law of physics. Like it should have been impossible.

I nod and pull my sleeves over my hands, wishing I could be more like her. Wishing I could get what I'm feeling inside, *out*. For some reason, I pick that moment to tell her the story of the day I explained to you what adopted meant, right here by the swings. We were both seven when my family moved in, and you asked me why Willow and I didn't look like our parents a week later.

"By then we'd already decided to be best friends," I tell her, and she laughs. "And Tavia cried when she found out someone gave us up. She couldn't understand how someone wouldn't want to keep me," I say. "She didn't know someone could decide not to keep a kid."

I still remember how you looked, like it didn't make sense. That made me feel . . . I don't know. Special. Like I was extraordinary. I'd never felt like that before. But being friends with you always made me feel that way.

"She cried?" my mom asks, and I smile a little and nod.

"That's just like our girl, isn't it?" she says, looking up at the cloudy sky. "What I really came out here to tell you is that we're having kimchi jjigae for dinner."

My mom's been watching cooking shows and videos online and making more Korean food lately. I think she feels like the big flavors, harsh spices, and strong scents will fortify me with the kind of resilience I need to get through this—losing you. Maybe she fears I'm missing some kind of strength I would have had if I'd grown up in Korea instead of in a big house on Long Island.

"Also," she continues, "Dante's here. I told him to let me check on you first. Do you want to see him?"

I always want to see him, but something about that feels like the wrong thing to say.

So I just nod. She stares, like she's trying to see inside me.

You know the look: Raised eyebrows. A jutted-out chin. I smile so she'll believe me, wondering how I got so lucky. I was born into a family that couldn't keep me. But then I got her.

"I promise. It's okay."

"Ask him if he wants to eat with us because I'll make the soup a little less spicy if he's staying."

She squeezes my shoulder, then walks back to the house. A minute later, Dante steps through my back doorway.

His cheeks are pink, and his breath puffs in front of his face like smoke, but I try not to look at him for too long once he gets up close. He looks more like you now that he's the only person walking around with that hair and those eyes and a strange, thicker version of your lips.

There's more to it than that, though. Since I don't look much like Willow, and I obviously don't look at all like my parents, I'm jealous. There's no reason for me to feel this way, but I kind of hate that you belong to him in a way you'll never belong to me. In a way my own family even doesn't. You and Dante were a matching set, with barely a year between your birthdays.

But we were a pair too.

He sits on one of the swings and hangs his hands between his knees. His text said he wanted to talk, but it's ages before either of us says anything. I'm the one who breaks the silence.

"I'm worried about your parents," I tell him, because your mom won't stop moving. She's reorganized the garage and raked the yard and cleaned the house from top to bottom at least half a dozen times. Except your room. She still goes to her book club meetings and volunteers at the art gallery on the weekends. I don't know for sure, but I think she still wants to go on the senior trip as a chaperone, even though Dante said "Hell, no" when I asked if he was still going. I'm skipping it too.

Your dad, on the other hand, is motionless. He goes to work during the week, but if he's anything like how he is at your house when he's at his office, I don't see how anything gets done. Whenever I'm over, I might see him get up to use the bathroom or to make coffee (never to eat), but then he just sits down again. I've only heard him say two complete sentences since the morning you died.

Dante shrugs, like he doesn't care that his parents are falling apart, but a pained expression crosses his face. His fingers go all twitchy, and he starts chewing on his bottom lip before he says, "I didn't come here to talk about them."

He takes a deep breath, and I don't know why, but I pick up my pencil again. I start sketching the oval outline of his face. I feel something inside me open as I look for differences between his face and yours, and I draw them. First I sharpen the shape of the oval to echo his square jawline.

"I'm listening," I say.

"I know what you're thinking," he starts. And I wait. I add his stubble to my drawing—another difference I can cling to. A million tiny dots and super-short black lines all over his chin and cheeks.

I glance up at him and then back down at my sketchbook.

"What am I thinking, Dante?" I ask.

He stands up and starts pacing, and I want him to sit back down so I can keep adding to his face on the page. I need to see his long, dark eyelashes (they're straighter than yours). I can't get his nose right (broader than yours was, and a little crooked from when he broke it) without having him in front of me.

"You're thinking that you were with me when it was happening, right? You're thinking you should have been at that dumb party with her."

He jams his hands into his hair, and I look back down at paper-Dante, because that version of him doesn't have eyes filled with tears. Paper-Dante doesn't have eyebrows yet, so he can't frown.

"I know you, Autumn. I know you're freaking out, even though you're just *sitting* there." He throws his arms in my direction, like sitting is a crime. "You're thinking this is on you."

I feel myself pressing my lips together like my mom did when she was angry-crying, and I wonder if expressions can make you look like someone you love, even if your features are from strangers on the other side of the world.

He shakes his head, but he doesn't tell me it wasn't my fault.

His voice goes all shaky as he says, "You're not the only one who feels like that."

He comes over to me then, and sits down in the grass right in front of me. And God, I feel like I might burst into flames when he reaches for my hand. But he just slips the pencil from my fingers. He sticks the pencil between his teeth as he pulls off his gloves and shoves them into his back pocket. Then he reaches for my sketchbook, turns the page, and draws a quick, sloppy portrait of me. The only part he gets right is my messy, elbow-length hair.

I take the sketchbook back and trace over a few of his most carelessly drawn lines. I darken my narrow eyes, and I make my cheeks a little rounder. And just when I'm almost done, lost in a self-portrait he started, he touches my arm, and I shift away from the weight of his warm hand, like it's a reflex.

"So, what?" he asks loudly. Meanly. "I can't even touch you now?"

I open my mouth, but no sound comes out. I close the sketchbook and watch real-Dante's eyes turn stormy.

"That's it, then? This, whatever this is—was—is done?"

I shake my head, because the thought of losing him terrifies me. But a second later, I shrug, because I don't know how I can keep him.

"You're not the only one hurting, Autumn," he says through his teeth. I think about Willow telling me the same thing, and I feel a little ashamed.

"I *know*."

He looks at me, and his black eyes are shining like they're made of glass. He clenches his teeth, and his jaw moves, as if a tiny wild animal is stuck inside his cheek.

"I missed you at school today," I say.

I don't add "and yesterday" or "and all week." I want to tread lightly because ever since your accident, Dante is a stick of dynamite with a lit fuse. But my change of subject has the desired effect. The sentence calms him down, puts out his always-burning fire. He squeezes his eyes shut and stands up. Paces for a second.

"Yeah?" is all he says back.

"I know it's only been two weeks since . . . But are you going to come back soon?"

He shrugs and runs his fingers through his dark hair again,

looking out across my yard. I stand up too and tug at his jacket so he'll look back down at me.

I want to tell him that I feel better when he's around. That as complicated as things are between us, at least I feel a little less alone. But I can't figure out the right words. I swallow, hard, before I say anything, but I don't look away from him.

"It would be easier, for me, if you were there."

It's a selfish thing to say, to put on him. I feel like I'm tricking him into coming back, even though it's true. I can barely be with him, but I'm so sorry, Tavia, I don't think I can be without him, either. And I know there's something not fair about that. It's not fair to him or me. Or you.

I squeeze my fingers together and yank at my sleeves because my hands are shaking, and Dante thinks I'm doing it because I'm cold. He pulls his gloves out of his pocket and hands them to me. I hesitate, but then I take them just for something to do.

"No one else knows what it's like," I say as I pull on the too-big gloves. I look down at my hands, at the flat flaps of fabric at the end of each of my fingers, so he can't see my eyes. There aren't any tears, but there doesn't need to be for Dante to know what I'm feeling.

"Not even Alexa or Margo. Definitely not Faye."

I don't know if he gets it, because things are different with boys. They don't claim one another the way girls do. They don't learn who they are because of their friends.

"I hate taking the bus without her. Being at school without her. I text Willow constantly or look through Tavia's pictures, just to be less miserable."

I even tell him that I listen to that one Unraveling Lovely song, "Unmasked," over and over again, to drown it all out, and how it doesn't really work. It's the most I've said at once in days.

Then I bring up Perry again. "He keeps talking to me," I say. "Not just small talk. He's talking about *her*."

"He's still bugging you every day?" Dante asks.

"Pretty much."

I know Perry's sad. He's been in love with you since we were eleven. But God. I can't talk to him. Especially since he's the whole reason you were even in your car that night. I hate talking to anyone lately who isn't Dante. Or you.

I reach for his hand. I squeeze it once and let it go.

"I don't know what I want yet, with us," I say. Dante crosses his arms. His eyes are hurt. He knows what he feels, what he wants, but he stays silent.

"I don't know what you want me to say," I whisper.

And because your brother's heart beats for everyone but himself, he rubs his eyes and nods.

"I'll pick you up on Monday," he says. I'm about to ask if he wants to stay for dinner, but before I can, he walks away and slams my back door.

I don't know if his words mean he'll drive me to school and drop me off, or if he'll actually come inside and go to classes, but it's a place to start.

When I pick up my pencil to start drawing again, I stop short. I'm still wearing his gloves.

8

LOGAN

BRAM IS BORED so he sees how many times he can scare his mom in an hour.

10,231 views | 3 months ago

I guess when you lock your mother out of your room for a solid half hour while you blast angry music and drink your dad's expensive stolen booze, you're not exactly a picture of mental health. So it's no surprise that I'm sitting in a shrink's office right now.

I take out my phone to check Bram's channel for new comments, and to look at the Battle of the Bands leaderboard, something I do every now and then. Obviously, my unnamed, drummerless band isn't on it, but before I even type a word I slip the phone right back into my pocket because I'd forgotten that none of my apps work. My parents canceled my data, so the only thing my phone is good for now is texting. Or talking. Or trying to fix that same damn song because I don't have any new ideas.

I have a text from Aden that I don't want to answer. So I look at the shrink. I don't want to talk to her, but I know if I refuse to say anything here, I won't get my data back.

The psychiatrist has tiny, pale green eyes and a nose that's a little too big for her face. But she's young, and healthy-looking—one of those people who could model because her features are so originally arranged. I don't know how to describe it exactly. She's not beautiful, not even close. But something about her face is . . . striking. Anyway, her name is Gertrude Stein, like the writer, and she has a similarly bad haircut. Her hideous shoes and brown sweater make me sad. Wasted potential, if you ask me.

"So, Logan," Gertrude says.

"Trudy," I say back.

She cringes a little, and says, "Gross."

I kind of grin because I was not expecting Gertrude to say "gross."

"Only my grandmother calls me that. You can call me Dr. Stein, or Gertrude, obviously."

I smile again. "Okay. *Trudy*," I say.

She looks down at her notebook and doesn't acknowledge me repeating the name. It bugs *me* a little that it doesn't seem to bug *her*.

"Your mother tells me that you're here to talk about someone you lost pretty suddenly around Christmas. And I wanted to start by saying I'm incredibly sorry for your loss. Would you like to tell me about him?"

I hate every second of this, but her casual mention of my mom isn't lost on me. I wonder if she meant it as the thinly veiled threat it came across as. I look right at her.

"What else did my mom tell you?" I ask, frowning.

"Just that you seem to be having some trouble dealing with what's happened." She smiles. "I'm only here to help, Logan."

I let my eyes roam around her office. Then I stand up, walk to the window, and squint at the tiny people eighteen floors and a fancy-ass lobby away from me. I watch a plane disappear into the clouds while I fiddle with the thin strings of my hoodie. I flip up the hood and then yank the strings tight. When I turn back around, the fabric is over my eyes, but I can feel that the shrink is still watching me.

She probably thinks she's hot shit with her swanky Manhattan office. I loosen and lower my hood. I run my finger along the windowsill, and I make a big fuss about the city grime and dust that's there, but you'd never notice it if you were sitting on the leather sofa.

She writes something down. I stick my hand into my pocket and tap the surface of my useless phone. I sigh, feeling stuck.

"Well," I start. "He was my ex. The guy who died."

"I see. How long had you two dated?"

"Nine months," I say, walking back over to the couch. I pluck a tissue from the tissue box. I rip it up into tiny pieces in my lap. "We got together first semester junior year, and we broke up this past summer."

"And why did you break up?" she asks.

I gnaw on my thumbnail while I try to decide how much to tell her. I've never said any of this stuff out loud, and I hate that

I have to say it for the first time to a stranger. But I can feel the weight of my phone. It slides around in my pocket as I shift in my seat. I don't have much of a choice, so I keep talking.

"He was interested in someone else. A girl. We hadn't spoken since the day he told me about her." I hear the poison in my voice when I say the word "girl." I don't try to hide the disgust on my face, either.

"Were you upset that he was interested in someone else or that the someone else was a girl?"

"I mean, it would have sucked regardless, obviously. I fucking loved him."

Gertrude nods. "Of course."

"But yeah, I guess it added insult to injury that it was some basic bitch cheerleader and not another guy. How could I even compete with a girl?"

"You can't," she says, shrugging.

"Exactly," I say. "If it had been another guy, I could have convinced him I was the better choice. But if he wanted a *girl*, he couldn't also want me."

Gertrude doesn't ask "How do you know what he wanted?" But something about her face makes me feel like that's what she's thinking. She makes a few notes in her notebook, and I notice that her short hair has a curl to it. I wonder if it would look like Bram's if she grew it out.

"Do you want to talk about how he died?"

I told him I hoped he'd die alone, and then he did, I think.

But "Suicide" is what I say out loud. "Which makes zero sense. He loved his life. I don't get how he could just off himself like that. The Bram I knew never would have."

I didn't mean to say his name, but now that it was out, that urge I always feel to say it again and again tricks my brain into talking about him more.

"Bram was so happy," I say. "His favorite quote was that cheesy one from *Slaughterhouse-Five*, you know the one I mean?"

"'Everything was beautiful, and nothing hurt'?" Gertrude asks.

I point at her. "Yes. He said that all the time. He was a hopeless romantic if I ever saw one. He was one of the happiest people I knew."

My eyes get a little blurry.

Gertrude straightens her glasses but doesn't say anything for a while, like she knows (or hopes) I'm working something out in my head. But I can tell she's dying to know what I'm thinking. I look up at the wall, and I can't stop staring at my own pale reflection in the gilded mirror she has hanging up right behind her head. There are shadows under my eyes, and even my freckles look a little faded. I pull the hood back on, but it doesn't really help.

Sometimes when I look into a mirror for too long, I start to look like someone else.

She keeps watching me, so I stare back and say, "Isn't it weird that eventually, someone will say your name for the very last time, and then it will never be said again?"

This occurred to me when I was high last week, and it's only made my obsession with Bram's name worse.

Gertrude kind of frowns, but she looks interested. "What do you mean?" she asks.

"Think about it," I say, leaning forward. "It might not be for twenty or thirty or fifty years, but eventually, your mom will say it for the last time, or your friends, or me." I look at her, and she's still watching me, wondering what I'll say next.

When I had this weird epiphany, it freaked me out pretty badly; that someone's name could just disappear like that. So every day since, I've whispered or shouted or said "Bram" out loud whenever I'm alone, thinking about him. I'm sure Trudy would have a field day with that if she knew about it.

"Yes," she says. "I guess that's true. Are you worried about that happening to Bram?" she asks.

Duh, I think.

I sit back and shrug. I know he's gone, but I won't let his name disappear. I don't say that to Gertrude, though.

"Have you found anything that helps?"

Before the chain of thoughts that fills my head—*drinkingsmokinghookingup*—even split into individual ideas, she puts up a hand and says, "And I don't mean any of the self-destructive behaviors that landed you in this office."

I think about it. I let my mind drift back over the last month. I've felt like shit so often since he died that the few moments I've felt okay that aren't *drinkingsmokinghookingup* bubble to the surface almost immediately.

Aden helps a little, even when we're not kissing, because he's so annoying about the band stuff. He keeps me focused, I guess. And then, for some weird reason, the phone call with Ms. Lassiter pops into my head. Even though it was hard, it was kind of a relief talking to someone who knew and loved Bram—someone I didn't have to hide my real feelings from.

"I talked to Bram's mom," I tell Gertrude. "She's the only

person who I've told how I really feel about everything. She told me some stuff about him, too. How he'd changed."

Gertrude says, "Did that help?"

When I nod, Gertrude takes her glasses off and chews on the earpiece.

"Maybe talking to other people who were close to Bram near the end of his life will help give you perspective on where he was emotionally when he died. Maybe if you understand how *he* was feeling, *you* can feel better. Talking to Ms. Lassiter seems to have given you the beginning of what might lead to closure, a place where you feel safe enough to share. Grief is tricky, and it's something that will never go away. But I think getting what you're feeling out in the open is part of the first step toward finding peace."

I nod again, like I agree, but she doesn't know that I practically wished this on him. She doesn't know how much I hate myself because of what I said, and that no degree of talking can fix me when I don't trust my own voice. She didn't hear Ms. Lassiter say *He's been different since this summer.* I don't know if I deserve closure; I definitely don't deserve to forget or move on. But I like the idea of talking to people who were close to him. Maybe they can help me figure out what happened—how he went from the Bram I knew to a stranger who wanted to die. And if I can figure that out, maybe for the first time in months, I can write a song that isn't about him.

As soon as I get home, I log on to my mom's computer. She locked mine in a drawer but left hers out in the open, like I don't

93

know her super-obvious password (it's my birthday) and like incognito windows don't exist.

Like I do every day, I lie to myself. I sit down and swear that I won't look at Bram's profile, pictures, or videos. I read some news. I try working on the song, but everything I come up with is crap. I check out a word generator to try to think of a name for the new band. I even do some homework. But I know I'm fighting a losing battle.

I haven't watched Bram's sex tape since people started giving him so much crap about it online, but now that I've been given a directive to talk to people close to Bram, I feel a little more justified being as obsessed with him as I am. I decide to skip his profile, pictures, and the videos on his channel. I go looking for the sex tape instead.

The day it first showed up I watched it over and over, trying to figure out who the other dude in the video was. I didn't watch it right after Bram died because the cops were still investigating everything, and after they questioned me, I was paranoid as fuck. Now that they know what really happened, and *I* know I'm not on some kind of watch list or anything, I can watch it again. If I can figure out who the guy in the video is, maybe I can talk to him about Bram.

The sex tape was originally on Bram's channel, and he deleted it as soon as he realized it was there. But by then, thanks to his mild Internet celebrity, dozens of people had already downloaded it, taken screenshots, uploaded it elsewhere, and shared it all over the place. I heard more than one person say that *I'd* released it because I was bitter and wanted to ruin Bram and Yara's relationship. That rumor died pretty fast because, even though it's dark in the video, it's obvious that the other guy isn't a ginger. Lots of people said it could have been recorded before Yara even came to our school. I just hope it was recorded after he'd already dumped me. But who knows.

It's been yanked from every respectable site, but nothing ever really dies on the Internet. I know a few shady sites that have probably reposted it.

It only takes about fifteen minutes to find it. And then, there he is. The first frame of the video is Bram's face really close to the screen, like he was just using the laptop normally and the webcam came online without him knowing that it had turned on. His eyes are so green that they seem electric, and his lash line is so dark that it almost looks as if he's wearing makeup. His hair is short, so you can't tell that it has that crazy curl, and it's sticking up a bit in the front. When he smiles, my eyes blur with tears. He just looks so much like himself: young and beautiful and *alive.*

I can hear another guy's voice in the background, but it's muffled. Bram laughs at something the guy says before standing up. He's already naked and so hot that I close my eyes for a second, slowing the thoughts his body brings to my mind. I'd forgotten how tall he was—he's towering over the other guy, whose back is to the camera. At nearly six foot four, Bram was even taller than me.

They don't really waste much time, and though I can never make out the face of the second guy, I can see all of Bram. His broad shoulders, the trail of hair below his belly button, the two dimples in the small of his back, just above the tight curve of his ass. I watch the video again and again, until I'm remembering what it was like to be with him.

The jealousy hits me like a shot of whiskey—I'm burning from the inside out. The feeling that he's mine has never fully gone away. There's no angle where the other guy's face is showing, and I already *knew* that, but I got myself all riled up anyway. I kill the browser and close the laptop. I walk away, trying to calm myself back down.

I leave my room and go into my dad's study. I don't admit to myself that I'm looking for booze, but I'm looking for booze. I put on one of his records and stare longingly at his liquor cabinet, but there's nothing I can do about the locked glass door. I contemplate putting my fist through it, but it seems like a bad plan.

I get drunk on music instead. I sit in my dad's big leather chair and put my feet up while the first track plays. I pace while humming to the next few, hoping inspiration for my own music hits. When it doesn't, I stare through his window and outright sing the last song. I leave his office, but I let the record restart—music playing to an empty room.

Luckily for me, my parents are out for the evening, but that means they're calling the house phone every goddamn half hour to make sure I don't go anywhere. It could be worse. They could be here hovering, like I'm a four-year-old with scissors, the way they did all weekend after my mom found the bourbon in my room.

Back at my mom's computer, I go to Bram's channel and watch a video where he sneaks up on his mom a bunch of times in a row and shouts "Boo!" She spills soda all over herself the first time and nearly smashes a vase the second. By the third time, I thought she would have wised up, but she almost rips a page out of the book she's reading.

It goes on and on (he gets her eight times), and as I smile at his antics, I scroll down through the comments. There are a few of the clickbaity memorial posts, like *RIP, I was here the day he died* and *Live fast. Die young.* And Yara posted an entire goddamn poem. But since this video went up a while back, it's mostly still populated by normal comments.

I see one comment from Nico, this kid who was sort of my friend until a few months ago. We'd go to shows together and swap music recommendations whenever we bumped into each other in the halls at school. But when I heard he hooked up with Bram at a party over Thanksgiving weekend, it really pissed me off. It's so dumb because Bram and I had been broken up for months. But my heart is a fucking drama queen, so I haven't really talked to Nico since.

His comment was posted two months before Bram died, so you know it's one of the real ones. It says *You can scare me any-time,* and it makes me want to punch something. Instead, I click over to Nico's channel, planning to leave a few nasty comments.

But I'm stopped in my tracks because all of Nico's uploads are videos of him sitting behind *a drum set.* He's doing a bunch of drum solos, and in most of the videos he's performing on corners and in subway stations, the full drum set right on the pavement or platforms. The craziest part? He's damn good. *"Shit,"* I mutter, impressed, wondering why he never mentioned to me that he was a musician too.

The house phone rings, and I literally jump and slam the

computer shut, as if I hear my parents coming through the front door. When I pick up the phone, it is my dad, so I wasn't completely wrong.

"I'm home. I went to therapy. I have no booze. Anything else?" I say before he even says hello. I obviously don't mention the computer.

"Well . . . good," my dad says, sounding kind of flustered. He's not the disciplinarian in the family. I hear my mom asking him questions about me, and I roll my eyes.

"Hello, Logan, sweetie." She must have taken the phone from him. "How'd it go?"

"Not bad," I say, thinking of Gertrude. "Can we talk about it later? I'm kind of in the middle of some homework."

"Right, well. I'm glad. Go ahead and get that work done. We'll be home around ten."

When I hang up, I look through my phone to see if I still have Nico's number. I almost never delete anything, but he hooked up with Bram, so I can totally imagine myself deleting him at some point when I was pissed or drunk. Or both. But I find the number. And since the only thing I can do with my phone is text (or talk), I shoot him a message.

Seen any good shows lately?

Who is this?

Logan.

Long time, he texts back.

I feel like I should apologize for giving him the cold shoulder or something, but before I can, I guess he decides there are no hard feelings all on his own.

Rohan's new band is pretty badass.

Something swells inside my chest at the mention of Rohan's name. I fucked up big-time when we made it to Battle of the Bands, and I never really apologized—I just stayed away. I wonder if he hates me.

I'm actually going to a show of theirs this Friday, Nico sends. Wanna come?

I'm grounded, my phone barely works, and my parents are circling me like fucking vultures. So this seems to be a bad idea all around.

But Aden won't get off my back about the band. Plus, I'm supposed to be grieving or whatever. Nico is a drummer. And he knows Bram.

Sure, I send, thinking maybe I can kill two birds with one stone.

9

SHAY

BAMF // SASHA'S SENSES REVIEW . . .
SOUND/WAVE/LENGTH

Looks like: a beach party

Tastes like: bubble gum

Sounds like: earworms waiting to happen (aka the whole album is catchy af)

3/5

I ace my chemistry test. Mr. Tucker is surprised as he hands back our papers. "Nice work, Ms. Malone," he says, looking at me, as if I'm an impostor or something. He taps my paper with the remaining stack in his hand. "I hope this kind of work continues the rest of the semester."

I nod, and I'm so proud, I hold my breath so I don't start screaming right there. Studying was painful. I kept getting distracted by the pictures everyone was posting from the show, so actually reviewing the notes took freaking *forever*, but if this feeling is the payoff, and if it makes Mom less stressed, maybe pulling my grades up is worth the trouble.

I want to show this test to Mom right away, so I snap a photo of it to send to her. Aced my chemistry test, I include. When class gets out, I run down the hall looking for Rohan. I bump into Callie instead.

"Cal, look!" I say. I show her my test, but all she does is shrug. She's wearing a shirt that's falling off one of her shoulders, and that's the one she lifts, her bare skin sparkling because I guess she's wearing bronzer.

"Cool?" she says, like she's not sure it is, and she brushes by me. Deedee is right behind her.

"Oh, that's awesome, Shay," she says with a smile, but I see her eyes flick ahead to Callie, who keeps walking.

"What's up with her?" I ask as I start toward my locker. Deedee turns and follows me, even though hers is in the opposite direction.

"She's mad you missed the show."

I sigh. "I knew she'd make this into a big deal. That's why I sent Rohan. I had to study," I say.

Deedee nods. "Yeah, but you didn't tell us that."

She leans against the wall as I pop open my locker. Her glasses are dirty, so I take them off and clean them with my shirt before I do anything else. I actually need to put books into my bag, and Deedee looks surprised by how long it's taking me to swap things in and out.

"Callie begged her cousin for a couple of backstage passes to the show last night. You remember Ryan, right? He's a total—"

"Dick?" I fill in for her.

"Yeah," Deedee says, though she'd never call anyone that. "Cal had to, like, promise to work coat check at some shows all night for him for a few weekends in a row to get the passes. She wanted to surprise you."

"Oh," I say.

Deedee looks at her feet. "She thought it would be easier for you to watch from backstage, since crowds have been bugging you so much lately. I told her it was probably a good idea."

"Crap," I mutter, wondering if my friends are worrying about me too, which is a horrible feeling. I look over at Deedee. "That was really nice."

Deedee nods again. "She was really upset you didn't come, after all that, even though I told her you couldn't have known. She let Rohan have the passes, so the good thing is he got to talk to the band a bit, and I got some really awesome photos, too, even though Revenge kind of sucked."

She pulls out her phone and starts thumbing through her photos. "Which one should we post? I have some more on my DSLR if you don't like any of these."

I glance back at where Callie was a minute ago, but the hall is filling up fast as kids are dismissed from last period.

"I'm not sure, Dee. Can we talk about it later?"

She pockets her phone and hikes her backpack up higher on her shoulders. "Sure. Um, is it okay if I come to your track meet?"

I'd almost forgotten I had one today. I smile. "Duh. You know I love it when you guys come."

"Oh, I meant, is it okay if it's just me? Callie has a thing after school, and Rohan got detention. He said he'd drive us home after, but he wasn't sure what time he was getting out."

I look at Deedee, and I feel the nervous, scary feelings flickering inside me. I don't want Callie to miss my meet if it's because she's mad at me, and I want Rohan to be there, too, and my mom still hasn't texted me back. Maybe my missing the show made things worse instead of better. I wish Sasha were here to sit with Deedee, at least.

I just wish Sasha were here.

"You don't have to come and sit there all by yourself. It's an invitational, Dee, so it could go on for hours."

"No, it's okay. I really want to be there." She smiles, her glasses flashing in the hallway's bright lights.

I reach out and wrap her in the biggest hug, wrinkling my test, which was, a second ago, my crowning achievement, and not caring at all. Her bushy ponytail tickles my face and I wonder if my thick hair is doing the same to her.

"Thank you," I say.

For a few minutes today, I was happy. I was proud that I'd studied and it had paid off. I've been home before curfew every night this week, and I haven't been late to track practice once. Mom hasn't cried in the morning in days, and I'd like to think that has something to do with me. But when I step into the gym to start warming up, I see a set of twins from one of the visiting teams, and now that they're both standing right in front of me, I'm not happy anymore.

I know Deedee is here, and I should be grateful. But Callie isn't, and Rohan isn't, and Mom hasn't come to a meet in forever. And seeing those girls, feeling twinless all over again, makes it impossible to ignore how *not here* Sasha is too.

I start scanning the bleachers, looking for Deedee, but I can't find her. I'm supposed to be stretching, hyping myself up, talking smack with my teammates about all the other teams. But after I can't find Deedee, I just keep staring at the twins, and their matching faces and long, dark ponytails are making it hard for me to stay calm.

I shake out my hands because they're getting tingly, like they're about to go numb. And I know if that happens, I might lose feeling in my feet too. I can't run—not like this, because track is all about control, discipline, and focus. I stare at my sister's hospital bracelet, but I can't even focus on that. I jog over to Coach.

"I can't run," I tell him, feeling like a failure, a flake.

"What do you mean 'can't'?" Coach asks.

I feel tears fill my eyes because I don't know how to describe it. I need to run, but not in here.

Away.

"I just . . . It's hard to explain," I say, but it's not just hard. It's impossible.

"Okay, Malone," Coach says, softening because he can't take it when anyone on the team cries, and he can probably tell I'm right on the edge. "Go sit on the bench. Drink some water. See if it gets any better. There are three other events before yours, so you have some time."

I go to the bench, but it doesn't get better. Those twins are still there, and they fist bump before one of them lines up for the first event. I twist around, scanning the sea of faces more carefully, desperately, but I still don't see Deedee. The thought that she could have decided not to come too crosses my mind. I've never felt so alone in a room this full.

One of the girls on the team passes me a water bottle. She says, "You don't look so good," and I'm tempted to tell her to shut up, but I hold back. If I look anything like I feel, I probably look like I'm about to puke.

"Hey," I hear a familiar voice say, right behind me. I turn around, and it's Jerome, wearing a big ugly sweater and grinning. I've never been so happy to see him and his weird clothes.

"J," I say. "I have to get the hell out of here." I start crying for real then.

He nods. "Okay, it's okay. I think I see Deedee. Let me go get her, then we'll take you home, okay?"

I nod. I lean forward and put my head between my knees when he tells me to. It helps a little. And then Deedee is there grabbing my arm and explaining to Coach that I'm not feeling well, and then we're in the locker room getting my stuff. Deedee's voice is in my ear, and it helps too, and now it's a little easier for me to do what I'm supposed to be doing. After I change, we go out into the hall, and Jerome is talking to Rohan, who I guess got out of detention and has been waiting for us. We pile into the Band Wagon and pull out of the parking lot a few minutes later.

As we merge onto the freeway, I roll down my window, even though it's cold, because I'm trying hard to keep it together in Rohan's van. I'm hoping the wind in my face will remind me of running. I'm hoping I'll be able to zone out instead of freaking out. Deedee reaches forward and turns on some music, and Jerome puts his hand on my shoulder.

"You good?" he asks, and I nod again. "I think so," I say, but the truth is, I'm so grateful for these amazing people all around me that I'm fighting off happy tears as much as I am the other kind.

I'm still too hot, so I push up my sleeves, and just like that, Sasha's hospital bracelet pops off my arm and flies out the window.

I twist around to look behind us, but it's hopeless. It's already gone, and I get upset all over again. My friends are laughing, making fun of how bad the Revenge show was. But I can't breathe.

"Stop the car," I say.

Rohan doesn't hear me. "So SOUND/WAVE/LENGTH is playing down in Merrick."

"Oh, I love them!" Deedee cuts in. "Should we swing by and pick up Callie?"

"Where would she even sit?" says Jerome.

"You'd think in a van this big there would be more room." Deedee laughs.

"We can't. If we don't hurry—"

"Ro, I'm serious. Stop the car!"

They all look at me then, and notice that I am *not* okay. Rohan says, "Shay, I can't. There's no shoulder on this part of the highway. But I'll take the next exit, just give me a minute."

I look ahead, and there's a sign that says the next exit isn't for three miles. I'm not sure if I'll make it that long. Deedee takes my hand, and I close my eyes when Jerome tells me to try to breathe deeply.

"Talk to me," Rohan says as soon as we've pulled into the parking lot of a Dunkin' Donuts. I fling the passenger door open and start pacing. Jerome stretches out across the middle seat and lights a joint that he passes around. Everyone takes a hit but me, and when I refuse, no one says anything, even though I feel like they're all thinking it: I'm the main one who needs to chill out.

"The hospital bracelet," I say, feeling like I'm choking on the words. "It flew out the window."

"Oh shit," Rohan says. "Are you sure?" He walks over to the passenger side of the car and opens the door. He kicks around the trash on the floor but doesn't find anything. When he slides the back door wide, Deedee gets out of his way and sits on the curb with her arms wrapped around her shins. Ro keeps looking, a little frantically, and Jerome lifts his long legs so Rohan can run his fingers over the middle seat next. Rohan opens the back of the van, but it's not there, either. His eyes are glassy and fierce when he looks back at me.

"I'm sure," I say, because it looks like he's about to ask me if I am again. "I *saw* it." I feel tears spill over my cheeks. I start pacing and squeezing my hands. "Did you know that people who don't have twins anymore are called twinless? Have you ever heard something so horrible?" This is what I do when it gets bad. I make it worse. Sasha called it spiraling. And it's dizzying, the speed at which dark thoughts are filling up my head.

Jerome hits the joint and passes it through the open door to Deedee, who has come over and put her hands on my shoulders to stop me from moving. Deedee tries to hand it off to me, but I shake my head. Jerome says, "You could always get a tattoo."

For the first time since we pulled over I stand completely still.

I shove my hands into my pockets and frown. "What are you talking about?"

"You can't lose a tattoo," he reasons. "Plus, it would be bad-ass." He grins, and his coppery brown eyes sparkle in the dying evening light.

"Hell, yeah," Rohan says. "I could get one with you." He looks relieved—like it was his fault I lost the bracelet and now he can make it up to me or something.

"How about the fact that we can't *legally* get a tattoo? We're not old enough. Plus, we don't have that kind of money, and Mom would kill me."

Rohan lifts his eyebrows and grins, and he looks a little devilish whenever he makes that face. He pops open the glove compartment and pulls out something small and plastic.

"I still have Sasha's fake ID."

Deedee perks up at this. "No way! Sasha had a fake ID? For what?"

"Shows, mostly. Getting into the ones that were eighteen plus."

"Wait," I say. "When did Sasha ever go to eighteen-plus shows?" I'm thinking of Sasha, always reading books, watching documentaries, and drinking tea. I know she loved music as much as me, but I've never been to a show that wasn't teens only.

I guess I'm a little surprised that there's something I didn't know about her.

Rohan grins again. "Whenever she could," he says.

"There's no way in hell you're getting a 'Fucking Luke' tattoo."

This was my first idea, but everyone thinks it's a bad one.

Rohan had some cash from the last couple of shows he played still in his wallet. He and his band split whatever they make at the door and on merch. Jerome and Deedee donated to the cause, and now we have just enough to get two small tattoos if the place doesn't try to rip us off. The only problem with pooling funds is that my friends think they get to tell me what I can and can't get inked.

"You can't actually stop me," I say to them. We've just picked up Callie because I couldn't very well get a tattoo without all of my best friends there. She's still mad, and not really talking to me, but I'm still glad she's here. I point to the inside of my wrist, at the part that pulses; the part that, on a lighter-skinned person, the soft green of tiny veins would be visible right through it.

"I'm getting it right here," I tell Rohan.

"I don't know. Maybe you should get it done here," Deedee says, pointing around Callie, who is on her lap, in the backseat. Her pudgy finger pokes my shoulder. "That would be easier to hide from your mom."

"Truuue." I nod, considering.

"Actually, I can stop you," Rohan says. He holds the ID between his thumb and forefinger and bends it until it starts to look like it might snap in half.

"No!" I shout, and everyone, even Callie, laughs.

I reach for it, but he shakes his head and puts it behind his back. Like we're freaking five-year-olds.

"Seriously, Ro? Are you going to make me beg for it?"

"Nope," he says. He grins, and his dimples appear in his cheeks. "But I am going to make you pinkie promise you won't get a 'Fucking Luke' tattoo."

"Fine, fine, I'll figure something else out," I say, offering my hooked pinkie finger. "Promise."

When he hands it over, I see that the ID says I'm a woman named Lacy Pantese, from a town in Colorado that's probably more than a thousand miles away. The picture, which actually is a photo of Sasha in heavy makeup, is the most believable part of the whole thing.

"Seriously?" I say again. But he just shrugs.

Jerome takes the ID from me and uses the flashlight from his phone so the whole backseat can read it.

"This actually works?" he asks.

Rohan says "Yup" and tells us about the last show he and Sasha went to.

"When you guys moved her into the downstairs room, it just made it easier for her to sneak out," he says. "She told me she didn't want to worry your mom since she was working all the time. I think she thought it would stress you out too, if you knew. So it was something just the two of us did." He has a small smile on his face, but then he looks over at me, probably because I'm quiet. "Don't be mad."

"I'm not," I say. "Just surprised."

It's weird to find out that Sasha had secrets, even from Mom—even from *me*. But as I look in the rearview mirror at Callie, who's twisting her brown hair around her finger and looking through the window, I think maybe there are unknown parts of everyone. Callie's so intense, and a lot of people think she's mean. But then she'll do things like beg someone she hates for a favor, just to help out a friend. I look at Deedee next, with her honest eyes and big smile, and at Jerome, with his pretty lips and furrowed brow. I never know what he's thinking. And Ro, who looks at me like I'm an apparition half the time and teases me the rest.

We're all so much more than we seem.

When we get to the tattoo place, I hand the ID to a big bearded guy leaning on the glass case near the entrance; then I start fidgeting—sticking my fingers into my pockets and then pulling them out, wringing Sasha's beanie (I'm wearing a purple one today) in my hands. Rohan pokes me in the back with his keys and mouths *Relax,* so I stop moving so much and try not to look as guilty as I feel.

The guy looks at the ID, then up at me, then down at the ID again. Then he scans the room, looking at everyone else. Callie has her arms crossed, but I can see a brightness in her eyes that wasn't there in the car, so I know she's excited to be here. Deedee is walking around looking at the photos on the walls. Jerome has his legs kicked up in one of the waiting room chairs, and Ro is looking at the body jewelry. They are all playing it *so cool.* The guy smirks a little and tugs at his earlobe, which is pierced half a dozen times, but then he hands the ID back to me.

"So, Lacy, what can I do for you?"

Rohan looks at me with a warning in his eyes. But I'd decided in the car what to get instead of "Fucking Luke."

"My sister's name," I say, pointing to the inside of my wrist. Once I get the tattoo, every time I go running and need to check my heart rate, every time I'm waiting for my pulse to slow, I'll have to touch "Sasha." My heart will beat for the both of us now.

"I just want my sister's name right here." We all hold our breath as Rohan shows his fake ID, but it goes much more smoothly than it did with me.

While we wait for the guy to reappear from behind a velvety red curtain, I flip through a binder, trying to find a font to use for the tattoo.

"How often does that happen?" Rohan asks.

"How often does what happen?" I echo. I point to a fancy script on the third page of the book, but Deedee quickly shakes her head.

"That's too adult-looking, like it could be on a wedding invitation or something," she says.

Rohan clears his throat and tucks part of his too-long bangs behind his ear. "The panic attacks. How often do they happen?"

I look up at him. "Oh God, Ro. Don't be so dramatic. It's not a *panic attack*. I know I'm not, like, *dying*." But I look away when I say that, because pretty much the opposite is true. Sometimes, when it's really bad, it feels exactly like dying.

"Sorry," Rohan replies. "But what just happened back there was definitely a panic attack. I'm just wondering how much it happens, because I've seen it happen a few times this month alone."

Callie says, "They happen all the time," even though *nobody asked her* and I thought she was giving me the silent treatment.

I look back at the page of fonts in front of me. I'm about to turn the page when Rohan reaches for the book and closes it completely. He puts his phone on top, as if it's heavy enough to stop me from opening it again, and crosses his arms.

"Has it happened more than the ones I saw?"

I don't look at him when I nod.

"How many more times?"

I shrug.

Deedee steps closer and touches my arm. "I had no idea. Does your mom know?"

I look at her and roll my eyes. "If *you* didn't, what makes you think she does?"

Rohan bites his lip. "And they've been that bad since Sasha . . . ?"

I half shrug, half nod. "Have you thought about . . . I don't know. Talking to someone?" he asks.

I smile and nudge him, trying to keep the mood light. "I'm talking to you, right now."

Callie jumps in. "I think he means like a therapist or something."

I bristle, even though I don't mean to. "I'm not crazy," I say.

Rohan frowns. "Going to a therapist doesn't make you crazy."

"You can't just ignore it," Callie agrees.

"I'm *fine*. It's getting better. I aced that test. I'm not smoking anymore. I'm getting home by curfew. I'm good. I swear." But I see Deedee and Callie look at Rohan, instead of me, and I flare my nostrils because I'm so annoyed. Their eyes are having a conversation about me like I'm not even in the room.

The bearded guy pushes back the curtain a second later and waves us over.

"You pick the script you want?" he asks.

I shake my head and roll my eyes in my friends' direction. They distracted me.

I'm afraid that if I leave here without a tattoo, every time I look at my wrist without seeing my sister's hospital bracelet, I'll feel adrift and alone. Or I'll feel what's coming on again right now, the wave of worry that overtakes me before I . . . panic, if that's what they want to call it.

Jerome walks over to us and picks up Rohan's phone. He's been pretty quiet since we got here, and he doesn't say anything now, but he tilts the back of the phone in my direction.

At some point, Sasha must have doodled her name on Rohan's phone case. It's written in purple ink and sits in the center of a sloppily sketched heart, and it reminds me of her so much that I literally gasp.

"I'd forgotten all about that," Rohan half whispers.

I grab the phone and aim it at the tattoo artist.

"Can you do this?" I ask.

After some pretty searing pain, I stand up and twist my wrist toward the mirror. It looks like Sasha was here a minute ago with a marker and a grin; like she drew the name on my arm herself. While he was working, I remembered Sasha drawing all over me when we were little: hearts and stars drawn around my scratches and scars, promises written along the lines of my veins, like they were paper.

"I *love* it," I say too loudly in the small room I'm in with just the tattoo artist. I touch Jerome's hand when he holds my wrist to get a closer look once I rejoin my friends on the other side of the curtain. "Thanks for noticing her name on Ro's phone," I say to him.

He licks his lips, and his long-lashed eyes flick up to mine. "You like it, then?"

"Duh," I say.

Rohan won't tell me what he's getting. And he doesn't let me stay with him while he gets it done. When he comes out, and rolls up his sleeve, he has "LUKE" in a red circle with a red line diagonally across it like a no smoking sign. "You stole my idea!" I shout, but Ro just shrugs, and I can't stop laughing.

When Rohan drops me off, the house is still and quiet. No Mom, no Sasha, just me. I go to Sasha's room and grab another one of her beanies from the pile and pull it on. I've been wearing them until they start to smell like me instead of her. Then I lie down on her bed, and I stare up at her ceiling in the dark. I say, "I got a tattoo today." But the Sasha in my head who normally talks back is quiet. Maybe she's already asleep.

10

AUTUMN

JAN. 24, 3:16 P.M.

I watched High Fidelity today.

Then I watched School of Rock.

Then I watched Pitch Perfect.

A marathon of our favorites. I thought it would make me feel a little bit better.

It made me feel worse.

I think I should tell someone that I still haven't cried.

But the only person I want to talk to is you.

Tavia may not be on Hangouts right now. She'll see your messages later.

From: HeCalledItAutumn@gmail.com

To: TaviaViolet@gmail.com

Sent: Jan. 25, 6:11 p.m.

Subject: <none>

On Monday, Dante came over to drive me to school like he said he would. And when I ducked into his car, he threw a thumb over his shoulder, pointing at the backseat. I turned around to see what was there, and it was his beat-up backpack. The holey, pin-covered one you hated with iron-on letters spelling out "Unraveling Lovely." I think I'll buy him a new bag. It's the least I can do.

"Good ol' UL," I say, tracing each letter on his backpack with the tip of my finger, flashes of all the shows you and I went to last summer replaying like a greatest-hits reel in my mind. The upset at Battle of the Bands lingers in the background. It might have been hard for you to convince me that random house parties and shopping sprees were worth my time, and it was nearly impossible to get you to go to the library or to an art exhibit with me. But whenever Dante's band had a gig, the only thing we had to decide was who would drive.

I think about Dante and his drums. How he told me once that playing made him feel like he was flying. And I'm about to ask him if he misses it—if he's ever thought about joining another band like I heard Rohan has—but then he grins at some commercial on the radio. I don't want to ruin that smile because it's one of the rare, real ones. So I tell him a stupid joke instead. When he laughs, I blush.

"Are you okay? With coming back to school, I mean?"

Dante puts his arm behind my seat and looks over his shoulder to see where he's going as he backs down my driveway, and I can tell he doesn't want to talk about it. So I don't say anything else. But when we get to the stop sign at the end of my street, I reach out and touch his fingers where they're resting on the emergency brake. It's only for a second, but it sends a chill up my spine, and I hope he gets what I'm trying to say with the gesture: *Thank you.* I hope he hears my heart whispering, *It'll be okay.*

The next time I look over at him, it's because he's pinching the edge of the scarf I'm wearing. "Where's that been?" he asks.

It's the maroon-and-gold one I wore almost every day in winter during middle school. The Gryffindor one you grew to hate. And I haven't worn it in years because you said we were too old for Harry Potter once we started high school. I look down at it, and I almost smile.

"I never stopped liking it," I say. "Even after she sort of banned me from wearing it to school."

I say "she" the way I always do when I talk to Dante about you. I don't ever have to say your name if I don't want to. He always just knows.

He smiles a real smile again, and my cheeks warm at the sight of his brightened eyes.

"She was so damn bossy. But I'm glad it's back."

He must get bored with the music on the radio because the next time he has to stop, he asks me for my phone. He plugs it in and opens my music, and the song that comes on first was one of your favorites. I stiffen, and I think Dante notices, but when he moves to skip the song I touch his hand again.

"It's okay," I say.

He keeps the volume down low while he drives the rest of the way to school. When the lyric "You're the only friend I need" fills the car, I turn toward the window and squeeze my eyes shut, willing tears to come. But they still don't.

If you were in the car with us, you would have started braiding my hair or leaned forward to turn up the music. You would have rolled down the window and stuck your head out like a puppy, even though it was cold. I would have laughed and pulled you back inside, and Dante would have threatened to leave us on the side of the road. But you aren't with us. So my hair hangs loose, and the music stays low, and the car is almost unbearably warm and quiet.

We pull into the lot and find a space. I take a deep breath, open the door, and try again to get your brother to tell me how he's feeling.

"Are you okay? Being back here?"

We're parked, but he isn't moving. His jaw is working, like he isn't okay, but then he nods and grabs his bag. Before Dante even closes his door, Perry's appeared beside me and he's saying your name.

"Tavia loves when the weather is like this," Perry says, looking up at the sky, talking about you in the present tense. It's one of those mornings when the sky is colorless, a blue so pale it's almost a shade of gray. If you were here, you would have whispered to me that the sky looks just like Perry's eyes. And he's right, that you'd love the weather. I don't know why you tried so hard to pretend that you weren't as into him as you were. He's never tried to hide how he feels about you, but I still don't want to talk to him. My hands start to shake.

"Yeah," I say to Perry after a pause that's a little too long. I turn away from him, like he isn't there, and tuck my hair behind my ears the way I always do.

Dante frowns at us over the roof of the car, and he has our question in the blacks of his eyes. *You okay?* they say without him saying anything at all, and I nod once and start moving toward the main entrance.

"Yo, D!" Perry says, like he and Dante are friends, when really, Dante's never liked him. Older brothers aren't supposed to like their younger sister's boyfriends. Plus, angsty musicians and lacrosse bros don't really mix.

Perry keeps pace with us, even when I try to walk a little faster. He looks over my head at Dante and says, "Tavi would love this weather, wouldn't she?"

He says it like you aren't gone for good. He says it like you're out today because you're stuck inside with the flu or away on a trip. He's talked about you like this every day that I've seen him since the accident, and in some ways it hurts more than just admitting you're gone. But it's Dante's first day back, so he isn't used to it like I am.

I stop walking. I stare at Perry's back. He stops when he realizes I'm no longer beside him. Then I look ahead at Dante, who doesn't stop at all. I see that his fists are shoved hard into his pockets and his stiff shoulders are hunched forward, like he's walking straight into thirty-mile-per-hour winds. But he keeps walking, so after a few seconds I allow myself to start breathing again.

Perry glances back at me and then straight ahead at Dante, and he seems torn, like he knows he's said the wrong thing but he doesn't know who to apologize to first. His sincerity is infuriating, and I wish he were more of a jerk so I could hate him the way I want to.

You cried like you were the one who'd gotten dumped the day you broke up with him. You broke your own heart. When I asked why you'd done it, all you said was that you thought you loved him too much. It was the week after we'd applied to all the same schools, so I knew it was probably about college. I'll never forget how you explained it to Alexa: *I want to go wherever I want without having to consider where he'll be. Sometimes loving someone is scarier than leaving them.* Even so, we all knew you'd change your mind about him. We all but betted on it.

I take a step forward, massively grateful that Dante's closer to the door of the school than he is to us. I'm just about to tell Perry not to say anything to your brother for the rest of his life when he mutters something about Dante needing to find a creative outlet for his anger.

"When was the last time he played the drums?" he asks. And before I realize that I can't remember, I hear the thump of Dante dropping his backpack. I look up and he's charging at Perry like they're members of opposing teams on a football field.

Despite his drummer's upper body, Dante is still slighter than Perry, who you called a beefcake for more reasons than just to be funny. But Dante's rage is completely unbridled. They hit the asphalt like a Jenga tower falling hard against a table, and immediately, there is blood.

I stand there, horrified and helpless, as a crowd swarms around them. Everyone watching is shouting and taking videos on their phones, and in the midst of the chaos, I catch a glimpse of Dante's wild eyes. He's flipped his switch, and our Dante—the one who holds my hand, and who cries with his head on my lap, and who used to put you on his shoulders even once you'd gotten way too big—is gone.

I take a few deep breaths, remembering how you always told me that I'm more than the quiet Asian girl everyone expects me to be. I push past the people watching so I can get close enough for Dante to hear my voice. I grab the back of his jacket, and he thinks I'm someone else. When he whips around, his face is contorted and his teeth are bared.

He almost hits me, and if I'm being honest, I kind of want him to. I've been so out of it since the accident; so lost and lonely and numb. *Maybe if he hits me,* I think, *I'll finally start to feel something.* But he sees that it's me, and instantly, his movements slow and his eyes change. Just like when I asked him about school in my backyard, he immediately cools down.

It's like I'm the key to turning the real Dante back on.

So I say, "Please."

I say, "Don't."

And as soon as Dante's fists stop flying, Perry scrambles away, spitting blood and cursing. His shoelaces have come undone, and one of his eyes is starting to swell. When his dark blond hair falls over the other eye, he trips and everyone laughs.

"Fuck you, Dante," he says while picking up his bag from

where it's been pushed under the bumper of a nearby car. Dante doesn't say anything.

I stare at Perry as he stumbles away. I wish you'd made it to his house to tell him you still loved him.

I wish you'd never met him at all.

I grab your brother's hand and pull him back toward his car. He needs to be elsewhere fast, before the teachers start asking questions. I take his keys from his coat pocket and open the back door.

"Get in," I say, without meeting his eyes, because I'm suddenly so mad that I can barely stand the sight of him. I'm angry with Perry for always talking about you, angry that Dante started a fight, angry at the world because you're gone. I get into the car after him, and we just sit there for a minute or two, both of us fuming. I kick the back of the driver's seat over and over. We don't touch each other. We don't say a word.

When Faye taps on the window a few seconds later, we both jump. I didn't notice her during the fight, but I guess she saw the whole thing.

"Oh my god," she says when I open the door. "Dante, are you okay?"

He nods, looks at me, and then looks away. I get out of the car.

"What about you?" Faye asks in her Sympathy Voice.

The fight must have stirred up something mean in me because I say, "Like you care."

Faye looks surprised, probably because I don't normally say stuff like that. But she doesn't say "What's your problem," or anything, for a second. She glances across the parking lot. I follow her eyes to where Alexa and Margo are standing, staring at us.

"Of course I care," she says. She looks genuinely hurt and confused. I remember Willow telling me to show my friends what I need, so I try.

"Sorry," I say. "It just feels like Margo is only talking to Alexa now. And Alexa isn't talking to anyone. And you're talking to everyone except me. I feel like you guys don't even care that I'm here. Or like you don't even miss—"

I stop. I don't want to say your name.

"It's not that," Faye says. She sighs deep and loud and squeezes her fingers together. "Look. Alexa feels . . . like it's her fault. Tavia was leaving *her* party. So she feels guilty, okay? She's hurting. But, I mean, we all are." Faye lowers her voice and steps a little closer to me. "She said seeing you makes her feel worse about everything. She never knows what to say."

It's hard for me to swallow, but I manage it, just barely. I mutter, "I'm sorry I'm such an inconvenience."

Faye touches my shoulder. Her nails are painted a bright shade of white, which makes her dark skin seem even darker. I lace my fingers together and try not to think about the deep purple nail polish that is chipped and falling away from my own nails more and more every day. You'll never paint them again, so against all logic I pray that these small patches of indigo last forever.

"You're *not*," she says.

I glance back across the lot, at Alexa. Margo is stroking Alexa's long red hair, and they both look a little shaken up. When Margo starts typing something on her phone, Alexa puts up her hand in a not-quite wave. She mouths the word "sorry." A minute later I get a text from Margo asking if Dante is okay.

"How long are things going to be like this?" I ask Faye, hating how desperate I sound.

Faye reaches out and pulls me toward her. She hugs me for a long time, the sleeves of her jacket cold against my neck. The closeness makes me think of Willow. And you.

"I'm sorry. I know I've been weird too," she says into my hair. But she's using her normal voice now. She sounds like Faye. She pulls away and holds one of my hands. "How are you?"

I shrug.

"Sorry," she says again, cringing. She tosses a few of her thick braids over her shoulder. "That was dumb. Everything sucks. Of course you're not okay."

"It wasn't dumb," I say slowly. "It was nice."

She smiles weakly.

"I'll try talking to Alexa," she says. "I'll text you tonight, okay?"

I nod, and she hugs me again, and her boots click as she walks away.

In the car, Dante's eyes are watery, and his nose has started dripping blood.

"Jesus," I sigh. I reach over him and open the opposite door, so he can stretch out his legs. Then I pull his head into my lap.

I have tissues and a water bottle in my bag, so I start cleaning him up with that. I wet the tissue, letting the water dribble through my fingers, and Dante stares at the ceiling of the car, at the broken light that should click on whenever someone opens a door. Tears start sliding down the sides of his face and into his ears.

He is so endlessly complicated—gentle one second and brutal

the next. But I can see how he aches, that he rages because he's heartbroken like me. He is so alive, his heart pounding hard and fast even now while he's lying down. He feels everything. But I'm numb, as if some part of me died along with you, and I rarely feel anything at all.

I push his hair back with my shaky hands and dab at a cut on his eyebrow. I wipe away the blood that's still trickling out of his nose.

"I'm sorry," I say. "I'm such an idiot. I shouldn't have made you come back so soon. You should only come back when you're ready."

He lifts one of his hands and catches a strand of my hair between two of his bloodied fingers. He shifts his eyes, letting them follow the length of the hair from his hand up to my face.

"*You're* sorry?" he asks in a voice so soft, it doesn't sound like him. He drops my hair and cracks his knuckles, which are already starting to bruise into a deep shade of red. They'll be purple by morning.

"I'm a fucking mess. I'm sorry. I just couldn't take it—Perry standing there, saying her name, like it cost him nothing. Thinking about him doing that to you every day . . ."

"Well, he probably won't be talking to me again anytime soon," I say. "So mission accomplished?"

I don't mean it like a joke (I'm still pretty mad), but that's how it sounds. Dante bites his lip, and I think he's smiling.

"This is *not* funny, Dante!" I say. I hit his chest, and he grabs my hand. We stare at each other, and he licks his swollen lips, but neither of us says anything else.

I glance through the window. The crowd has cleared, and I

hear the bell ring and I don't care. When Dante lets go of my hand, I look back down at him.

"Let's get out of here," I tell him. And he doesn't hide his smile this time. He unfolds his long body and climbs into the front. I stay in the back and stretch out as much as I can.

He drives. I don't ask where we're going, and I don't really care, but I hand him my phone and tell him to play Unraveling Lovely's album. I think he's going to object, since that's what they found in your car that night. I watched him snap his copy of his old band's EP in half when your parents told us that it was recovered from the car stereo.

Dante stares at my phone for a few seconds, but then he plugs it in. The music fills the car, and I think of the first time I ever heard Dante play the drums. The first ever Unraveling Lovely show was the first time I realized I liked him, and the tour was where the three of us—you, him, and me—all fell a little deeper in love with one another.

I take off my Gryffindor scarf and bunch it up beneath my head. I watch Dante's profile as he drives, and it must be the adrenaline from the fight leaving me all at once because I feel my eyelids getting heavy. After a while, Dante stops the car, and I open my eyes. I'm not sure how long it's been or where we are because I'd fallen asleep.

He turns around and looks at me. Unraveling Lovely is still playing. As I listen to the snare snapping like some kind of complicated magic in the background of the track, I wonder if Dante will ever play the drums again. I know what it's like to need something, or in my case, someone. He needs his music like I need you.

He says, "You okay?"

And for once, I'm honest. I shake my head and look at the bruises blooming across his cheekbones, darker already than they were when we were still in the school parking lot.

"I'm a fucking mess too," I tell him.

I want to ask him about the drums again right now, but he looks over me, out the window. So I sit up and look too. We're at Winnie's, your favorite diner. The one where you'd order banana-walnut pancakes and chili cheese fries, and Dante would always get something off the secret menu. I can't get enough of the pie.

"So you're a mess," he says, and then grins. "But are you hungry?"

We order chili cheese fries and banana-walnut pancakes, and I make a joke about him needing to hit the drums instead of Perry. He laughs and I smile, and my chest hurts a little less than usual.

But it's weird being there, without you.

11

LOGAN

BRAM IS BORED so he makes a survival plan for the
zombie apocalypse.

I'm punching Bram in the face.

I punch him again, and his nose breaks. Blood spills from both
his nostrils and flows over his lips, but I don't stop hitting him.

We're in the locker room, and he's not wearing a shirt, just a
thin pair of Under Armour leggings and football socks. It's fucking freezing. It shouldn't be this cold inside, and I shouldn't be
hitting him, but it is and I can't stop.

I shove him, and one of his broad shoulders hits the row of
lockers closest to the showers. He screams and grabs his arm. It
looks dislocated, and some wicked part of me is glad.

"Logan," he says. He's sobbing, and it's so cold that his voice makes steam puff from his mouth, like there's a fire inside him. "Let me fix this!"

But I don't listen. He trips over a towel someone's left on the floor and falls onto the hard tile of the shower stall. I kick him in his rib cage, even though he's already down and not fighting back. I'm crying too.

He's wheezing. Like something important is broken, or like something is wrong with his lungs, and I'm so mad I can't see straight. I can't remember if he has asthma. I can't remember what I'm mad about either.

I throw a bottle of pills at him. I scream, "Eat them! Eat them all!" And when he doesn't listen, I pick up the bottle, rip it open, and start shoving the pills down his throat. His teeth scratch my knuckles, but I don't stop until the bottle is empty.

Then everything gets quiet. It looks like he's falling asleep. He stops crying. I stop crying. He sinks to the floor and closes his eyes.

"I hope you die alone," I say. The words echo around us a thousand times, even though I whispered them.

When I turn away from him, his heartbeat echoes too. It's suddenly the only thing I can hear. It is so loud. The heartbeat is slowing down, so I start to run through the locker room toward the door. But before I get there, I hear his heart stop.

I push my way out of the gym, and the sun is so bright, it blinds me.

I jerk awake.

When I look around I realize I'm in English class, and everyone is laughing because I completely spazzed out and knocked my backpack (which I was using as a pillow) off my desk and onto the floor. It's not the first time I've dreamed that I'm the one who killed Bram. I'm sure it won't be the last.

"Logan, do you need a minute?" Mr. Hershey says.

"Uh, yeah. Thanks, Mr. H."

I stand up and try to ignore the whispers of "freak" that the jocks sitting in the back row toss in my direction. I never understood why Bram was friends with them, and they didn't say jack to me while we were together. I wonder if he kept them in check or told them not to pick on me. He'd seen me angry, so maybe he was more concerned for their safety than he was for mine.

I step into the hallway and speed walk toward the boys' bathroom while reaching into my pocket for my phone. But before I've unlocked it, before I've even had a second to catch my breath from that dream, I bump right into the last person on earth I want to see: Yara.

Her short black hair is wavy and wet. She's tan and tall, with tender-looking eyes. I mumble a quick "sorry," and she flashes a tight-lipped smile.

She opens her mouth, like she has something to say to me, but then closes it again almost right away. I wonder for a minute if Bram ever talked about me with her. I wonder what she thinks of the asshole who told Bram he hoped he'd die barely six months before he did.

I nod at her, feeling my insides ignite, and I'm burning up as I think about the stupid poem she posted in the comments of his video; as I think about Bram kissing her instead of me. I keep walking because even these hallways remind me that he's gone, and I'd love to have five minutes when he's not the only thing on my mind. I shove my phone back into my pocket, and I'm about to push open the door of the bathroom when I hear Yara's voice ring out like a bell.

"Hey, wait up," she says. "Logan?"

I turn around, my body stiff, my eyelids heavy with the burden of much-needed sleep and a little bit of hate. I look at her long legs, poking out like matchsticks from her short skirt. I stare at her stupid pink Uggs.

"What?" I say, trying not to sound like I'm talking to the bitch who stole my boyfriend, even though I am.

She walks down the hall toward me, and the way the sun is shining through the window behind her almost gives the girl a goddamn halo.

When she reaches me, she says, "I've been meaning to see how you're doing. You know, since . . . it happened."

I bite my lip and look behind her, directly into the light of the sun, because *today is not the day*. I let it burn my eyes for a second so that when I look back at her, she's covered in enough black spots that I can barely make her out.

"Right." I nod again and rock back on my heels, trying to keep the attitude out of my posture. Trying not to think about my recurring nightmare, Gertrude, or Bram. "I'm good."

She looks behind her, down the hall, like she's hoping no one sees her talking to me. She crosses her arms, and I swear to God when the girl looks back up at me, her dark eyes are shiny, like she's working up a cry.

"Good," she says, looking right at me now. "That's good. I'm glad. I, uh, I know he was important to you too."

"You could say that," I mutter.

I hook my thumbs into my pockets and wait. I can tell she has more she wants to say, and I don't know if it's the way her face is getting a little pink or what, but all of a sudden I want to hear whatever Yara Cruz wants to tell me.

"So, I'm not sure if you know this, but Ms. Lassiter's birthday is coming up."

"Okaaaay," I say, because this is random as hell.

Bram always made a huge deal for his mom's birthday. He'd take her out to a big fancy dinner or buy her jewelry he couldn't afford or bake her a fancy dessert. Once, when we were dating, he had me come over really early in the morning to shovel out a messy "HAPPY BDAY MOM" in the snow outside their building so that when she woke up and looked out the window, it would be the first thing she saw.

"It's next week," Yara continues, "and me and a few of the girls . . . we were going to make cupcakes and go hang out with her for a while after school."

She looks really uncomfortable, and I'm kind of enjoying it, so I don't say anything, even though it's clear where this is going.

"I know she likes you, so I wanted to, you know, tell you that we were going, in case you wanted to come."

"Hm," I say.

She ducks her head a little and reaches down to yank at the hem of her skirt. It's short and so tight it doesn't move much, but I can tell that the pulling is a habit. When she presses her shiny lips together and meets my eyes again, her eyelashes are wet, and I feel a little shitty about the way I'm handling this whole encounter.

Then she says, "Well, can I give you my number?" I hesitate

until she smiles. "Just in case you change your mind." She looks earnest and innocent as all hell. I hand over my phone, and she types her number in without a second thought.

"Just think about it," she says. She gives me a tiny wave and turns to head back down the hall. I watch her walk away, trying to decide if the whiskey I stole from Aden, which is sitting in the bottom of my backpack, would feed or snuff out the burning I feel in my chest.

Just as she disappears around the corner, I push my way into the bathroom and reach for the whiskey. But before I left Gertrude's office after my last session, she gave me homework.

"Let's start with this: only drink once a week," she said, and then handed me a card with her cell phone number on it, like she was my AA sponsor or something.

"Text me if something triggers you to drink."

I can't explain it, besides saying that talking to her makes my insides feel less like sharp, hot things that no one should touch. But my phone is still in my hand, so I send Gertrude a text before I can overthink why I want to do it. Maybe I'm just that lonely. That damn pathetic. The message just says, It's Logan. I want to drink.

She texts back almost immediately.

You don't have to tell me why. But think about why. That why is a trigger. Make note of it. Acknowledge it but don't dwell on it. Find something positive to focus on.

I push my way into a stall with the bottle in my hand, and I do the opposite of what she suggests. I dwell on the fucking trigger: Yara Cruz. I kind of hate her. But that's when I realize that I'd just blown off Bram's girlfriend, the person who was probably closer to him than anyone else. Yara spent hours with him every day. If anyone knows what he was like near the end, it would be her. I don't open the bottle.

Logan? Gertrude texts.

I had a bad dream, I tell her, which is partially true. I found something else to focus on.

Did you drink? she asks.

Nope, I send.

Great.

I put the whiskey back into my backpack, at the very bottom. I go to the vending machine and get a Cherry Coke instead.

When I get back to class, I'm still thinking about Yara, her invitation to Ms. Lassiter's, and the things she might know. I message her.

> Hey, it's Logan. Sorry I was such a dick in the hall just now.
>
> You're right—everything's been shit since the day I found out.
>
> If your offer still stands, I do want to come.
>
> But if not, I get it. I can be an ass sometimes.
>
> Anyway, sorry.

She writes back before the end of class.

> It's okay. I get it. I hope you'll still come.

My heart pounds like a goddamn jackhammer as I read her words. Yara has to know what was up with Bram.

Rohan's show is tonight. So I go to Aden's after school and tell my parents I have to do research for a project at the "university library." It's the only reason they're allowing me to leave the house.

But when I knock on Aden's dorm room door, he's not home. His roommate, Connor, swings the door wide and grins.

"Hey. Aden has a study group he forgot about. He'll be back later, though."

"Mind if I hang out?" I ask.

"Come on in," he says.

I kick off my shoes and press my back against the wall beside Aden's bed. I close my eyes because Aden's room has become a safe haven—it's the only place where I feel any kind of distance from all of the Bram stuff.

"Wanna smoke?" Connor asks me a few seconds later.

When I open my eyes, he's standing on his bed wrapping the smoke detector with a red-and-white plastic bag and a rubber band. I grin.

He points to the joint he's already rolled, which is lying neatly beside a bright pink lighter on his pillow.

"Yep," I say, hoping it will spark my creativity, or at least get me out of my own head.

I tell him I'll be right back. I step out of the room to use the bathroom down the hall. After I wash my hands, I dial my mom's cell and press the phone hard against my ear as it rings, and harder still after I say hello and she starts grilling me for details. I walk down the hall with her voice in my ear.

"I'll be back late, but I won't miss curfew. . . . Yes, I promise. . . . No. I'm meeting the other kids in my group right now. . . . Aden's letting me use his ID if I need to check out a few books. . . . Yeah, I know I can't hang out with him."

When she seems satisfied, I hang up and push open Aden's door at the same time.

"See," I say to Connor, "when you want to make shit and you can't, you start to accept that you'll just fade away. And since I want to make music, but I can't write a single lyric, I need to disappear."

This statement made perfect sense in my head, but less sense when I said it out loud. But Connor gets it. He nods, exhales a smoke doughnut, and says, "Damn, brah. That's deep."

I'm taking my fourth or fifth hit off the joint when Aden walks in. I start coughing as soon as the door opens. He looks from me to Connor and back again.

"Hey," he says slowly.

"Hey," I say. "Wanna jam?"

I hand the roach to Connor, who must think what I just said is hilarious. He's cracking up for some reason, and I'm trying hard not to laugh too.

Aden's almost never angry, but I can tell that he's right on the edge.

"Well, it looks like you're having a great time with Connor. Which is awesome considering we still don't have a song, a band name, or a drummer." He squints at me and continues, "I only started this up with you because I thought you'd take it seriously. My friends warned me not to start a band with someone still in high school, but I told them all, 'You don't know Logan, he's legendary.'"

Aden frowns, like he's kind of concerned or suddenly suspicious. "Are you just stringing me along because I'm in college and here you have easier access to this kinda shit?" He kicks an empty beer can and then points at the roach Connor is still holding.

I think about Bram then. About how we would smoke together and how weed turned his fingertips into something cool and smooth against my skin, like he was frosting a cupcake every time he touched me—which is exactly *not* what I should be thinking about right now.

"Logan?" Aden says again. He widens his eyes, and I realize he asked me a question that I haven't answered.

"My bad. I just have a lot going on." I figured out a way to talk to Gertrude about Bram, but I still don't know how to say anything true about him in front of anyone else.

Aden picks up his keys like he's about to leave again, and I'm not sure how to redeem myself. So I lie.

"I have good news," I tell him.

"What?" he asks, sounding like he doesn't believe me at all.

"I found a drummer."

He smiles super wide. "Seriously?" he shouts. I nod and open his laptop to show him some of Nico's videos.

"Holy crap! This guy is amazing! Where'd you find him?"

"Believe it or not, he goes to my school," I say.

Aden lifts me up in a hug because he's so damn happy, and I kinda want to kiss him, but I hold back.

We order pizza because Aden can see that both Connor and I have the munchies. But Aden eats his fair share of the three pies, shoving almost whole pieces in his mouth at once. He invites a couple of kids from down the hall to join us, and an impromptu party starts, just like that. I turn on music and dance with Aden—a continuation of my apology.

I whisper, "Tonight almost makes me want to go to college."

And when he says, "But what about doing music full-time?" I kiss him, his lips still greasy from the pizza, because he's the only person besides Bram and my old band members who has ever taken my music seriously.

I try to sneak away when he and Connor start playing video games. But as soon as I shoulder on my jacket, Aden looks at me and says, "Stay. We can work on the song. I have a few ideas."

I shake my head. "I can't," I tell him, trying to push away the guilt I feel about lying to him about Nico.

"I'll text you later," I say.

"Hey, Nico." I walk from the train station to his car, where he's sitting with his window rolled down, music turned all the way up.

"Logo!" he shouts. I'd forgotten about the dumb nickname he gave me. He jumps out of the car, tosses an arm over my shoulder, and wrestles me into a headlock because Nico is fucking annoying. But I guess that's part of his charm.

He lets me go, and I raise my eyebrows and press my lips together. He has crazy-blue eyes and smooth dark skin, so I get what Bram saw in him. He's wearing a leather jacket that I kind of want to steal. Unraveling Lovely is spilling from his speakers, so the closer I get to his car, the more my voice seems to be everywhere.

"A little show before the show," he says. "Sing to me?"

And as I duck into the passenger seat, I can't help but smile and fulfill his request.

When we get to The 715, it's packed inside. Rohan's band, Our Numbered Days, is one of the first to perform tonight, even though Nico tells me they headlined a few shows last month.

"That's the great thing about Ro," Nico says. "He's unpretentious, you know? He doesn't care about status and all that. He cares about *the music*."

I nod and wonder if Nico knows that he's touching a still-sore-as-hell spot when he asks me to sing Unraveling Lovely songs on the ride over and then tells me how awesome Rohan is. I *know* how great he is. I miss making music with him almost as much as I miss Bram.

But I'm not here to wax poetic about my failed attempt at fame. I'm here to listen to music, to ask Nico about Bram, and, if I can grow big enough balls to do it, maybe even ask him if he wants to join my band.

It's still early, so we stake out a part of the wall closest to the stage. Nico grabs us drinks from the bar—he brings me a Cherry Coke—and I'm surprised by how much fun I'm having already. I thought it would be hard to be around him, knowing that he'd been with Bram, but it isn't. I'd forgotten what it was like to have a friend.

"So I wanted to apologize," I say, because I do, and I also

want to bring up Bram sooner rather than later. They're doing a mike check, and the venue is filling up, so it won't be long now before we're pressed tight against the stage and it's too loud to hear anything.

"I heard about what happened at that party over Thanksgiving break."

Nico looks around and then straight at me, and his eyes are so blue that they feel dangerous in this kind of dark.

"And after I heard," I continue, "I was kinda pissed. Even though I hadn't been with Bram in forever."

I can't read the expression on his face, so I keep talking.

"I know it was dumb," I say, "so I'm sorry. It was shitty of me to disappear."

Nico bites his bottom lip and nods. He takes a sip of his own drink, something bubbly and clear, and he's gone tight around all his edges. The drink could be sparkling water, Sprite, or spiked tonic water, since I know kids sneak booze in here all the time. I lean forward and sniff at the rim of his cup. He grins a little and shakes his head, but he still seems tense.

He says, "I'm driving. Duh."

I swallow. Take a deep pull from my Cherry Coke, and I wish I had brought Aden's whiskey with me. I wish I still had some of my high, but that buzz is long gone.

Nico touches my fingernail where my hand is gripping the can. They're painted midnight blue again, shimmering a little in the low light. Nico says, "They look like the sky."

"How can you even tell in here?" I ask him because it's dim, and details are lost, not noticed, in rooms like this one.

He shrugs. "I just can," he says.

"Were you and Bram hanging out a lot?" I ask, pushing for more while he's still studying my nails. "Or was it like a onetime thing?"

Nico looks away from me, unbuttons his jacket, and drapes it over his arm, and for a second, I worry he's not going to answer at all. I pull up my jeans, and they feel too tight all of a sudden. I slip out of my jacket too. Then Nico levels me with those cobalt eyes, and I resolve to paint my nails that color next time.

"I'll tell you, just to get this conversation over with," he says.

He glances up at the stage, just as the lights get even lower, and everyone around us starts to scream. He leans into me so that his lips graze my earlobe as he says, "He kissed me at that party because he thought we were about to get caught."

"Caught doing what?" I ask.

"We had pills," he says. "A lot of them." The music starts, and I think I see Dante, the drummer from Unraveling Lovely. We haven't spoken in months because of what happened at Battle of the Bands, and I'm not ready to. I move closer to Nico in case Dante turns around.

Nico cups his hand around my ear.

"Bram was my dealer," he says.

12

SHAY

BAMF // SASHA'S SENSES REVIEW . . .
SUNSCREAM

Looks like: GIRL LEAD SINGER!!!

Smells like: a perfect day at the beach

Sounds like: screamy, girl-powered vocals. Powerful
work on the keyboard with lots of synthetic sounds.
Distorted guitar. So basically: ALL OF MY FAVORITE
THINGS.

Tastes like: an everlasting jawbreaker (you don't want
this album to end)

4/5.

I could almost *feel* it.

Dancing is the best medicine.

Maybe only next to listening to music while standing still. Or singing. Singing is really, really great, too. Also kissing. Kissing is good. I've done all these things tonight.

Jerome is beside me, with his hand on the small of my back, and Deedee is right in front of us, her camera lifted over her head. She's screaming and somehow still taking pictures of Sunscream, a band we've been hearing about for a while but have never seen live until tonight. I think Deedee is a little in love with the lead singer, a cute girl with blond hair and an incredible voice, who is wearing combat boots and a tutu. Sasha wrote a review for their album months ago. All night I haven't stopped wishing she was here.

I turn around and press my hands against Jerome's chest, and my bangles slide down to my elbow. He fingers a few of the bracelets as he answers whatever question I guess my body is asking. *Do you want to be closer?* my palms ask him. *Yes*, he seems to say as he grips my hand before kissing me with his hot, soft lips.

"Get a room!" Callie shouts as she squeezes by us, and Jerome laughs at first, but then he leans closer so I can hear him over the music.

"We could get out of here, you know. I've been wanting to ask you something."

I think about where we could go at first—how I could kiss him against the wall in the back hallway of The 715, how we could sneak through the alley behind the club, how fun it would be to take Ro's keys and make out in the Band Wagon. But then what Jerome actually said sinks in. He wants to ask me something. Which is just another way of saying he wants to talk. He might want to define this . . . whatever this is. But I like us as we are: Undefined. Uncomplicated. I pretend I didn't hear what he said and turn away from him, toward our friends.

Callie has two drinks in her hands, and one of them is for me. She's forgiven me for missing the last show because I listened to her podcast, gave her two pages of notes, and told her I'd work the coat check with her to pay back her cousin. Ro's band just got off the stage, and he's posted against the wall with Jo, the drummer. He steals my drink, and I'm glad. I have a reason to step away from Jerome and wrestle the cup out of Rohan's hands.

The song ends. We all scream. And Callie leans toward me and says, "I know Sasha wrote a review of this band already, but we still don't have one up for Our Numbered Days." What she doesn't say, but what's totally implied, is that we *need* to find someone new to write BAMF reviews. But I don't want to think about replacing Sasha right now. So I spin toward Deedee, dancing away from everything and everyone I want to avoid, to see if she took pictures of anything but the lead singer's face.

And there, across the room, near the opposite side of the stage, I think I see Dante, the drummer from Unraveling Lovely.

"Is that Dante?" I shout in Rohan's direction. He goes up on tiptoe and squints. But then his eyes go wide.

"Holy crap, yeah. I think it is."

He pushes past me and Jerome, and as I watch the two pieces of Unraveling Lovely reunite, I think about Logan and the Battle of the Bands disaster. The audience had been screaming for Unraveling Lovely, and all their hard work went down the drain in an instant because Logan showed up drunk. They never played together again, and it was the last show Sasha went to before she

145

got really sick. Rohan's over it (because he can't hold a grudge against anyone), but I'm still pretty pissed about it. The last time I saw either of them, it was Sasha's memorial service, and I wasn't exactly in the mood to talk to anyone about anything. But now, I wonder how Dante feels.

I'm posting one of Deedee's photos on BAMF, and still actively avoiding Jerome, when Rohan comes back over. He has the same look on his face he had that night in Sasha's hospital room.

I move away from Jerome, Deedee, and Callie, with Rohan's hand clutched in mine. I pull him into the narrow hall that leads to the bathrooms.

"What the hell happened?"

"His sister . . . ," Rohan says.

"Whose sister? Dante's?" I ask.

Rohan nods. He finally looks at me instead of the graffiti-covered wall in front of us.

"You remember her, right?"

I did. She came to every UL show wearing something ridiculous: glitter-covered T-shirts, hot pink scarves, light-up sneakers from the nineties.

"Yeah, Tavia. She always came with her quiet Asian friend, Autumn. What about her?"

Rohan looks stricken again. He frowns. Blinks.

"She died," he says. "In a car accident, a few weeks ago."

I stare at him blankly for about two seconds. I try to take a breath, but I can't get any air. I feel like I'm floating away from Rohan, and my eyes fill with tears. The panic is so complete that the edges of my vision go blurry and then turn black. I double over and blink a bunch of times, but it doesn't help.

"Shay?" Rohan says, and it's not so much that I can't talk; it's more like I never learned how. I pull away from him when he touches my back and elbow my way through the crowd until I get outside. The cold helps a little, but I don't even try unlocking my bike. I wish I could go back inside with my friends because it's not even close to curfew yet, but I can tell that's no longer an option. I wipe away my tears and try to block out the thought that is marching through my head, the beginning of what I know will be an awful, endless spiral: *Not her too. Not her too.*

I put on my headphones, the volume as loud as I can stand it, and I run all the way home.

The next morning, there's a new post on Sasha's blog.

After I got home from the club last night, I checked Dante's accounts, but he was never really big into posting online, which explains why I didn't know about his sister—I followed him, not her. There wasn't much to see. I went through Autumn's accounts next, slowly circling closer, and then, finally through Tavia's. The outpouring beneath her photos reminded me of what it was like right after Sasha died. Not that it's been very long. But it's slowed down a lot since the first few weeks. I wanted to text Dante. I stared at his name on my phone for a solid ten minutes. But I didn't know what to say. So I talked to Sasha a little, and since Mom wasn't home, I cried myself to sleep in my sister's bed.

Now Sasha's comments are exploding again. When I went to bed last night, the wilting flowers image she posted a few days before she died was still at the top. But this morning, when I woke up, there it was: a post that said *If you're reading this, I'll never turn sixteen.*

I would think that the blog had been hacked or something, but the message is too painfully true, too on-the-mark. Anyone who would know enough about Sasha to write that would *never* write that. It has a bunch of likes already, because sick kids all over the world follow Sasha's blog. It was where she wrote about her treatments, where she proudly posted pictures of her bald head. She didn't shy away from the hardest parts of having cancer, and people loved that about her.

I look at some of the reblogs the post is getting. One blogger, whose avatar is a photo of a bald girl (her, I assume) with a pink ribbon tied around her head, has reblogged Sasha's post and added the comment, *What a BAMF.* And I know she doesn't mean to reference Badass Music Fanatics, but I like that the acronym works in two ways for Sasha. Another guy has added a reaction GIF of someone crying. A kid who has a character from one of my favorite TV shows as their avatar has written, *I'm working on my queued posts now.*

Queued posts. So the post probably *is* from Sasha. I knew Sasha was afraid of being forgotten, of disappearing without a trace—it's why she wrote so many album reviews, sometimes more than one a day. She wanted people reading her words even after she was gone. So this makes sense. It just makes me sad that I didn't know this about her—that there's more I didn't know about her than I ever realized.

I lie in bed and stare at my phone for so long that I don't realize I'm late for morning track practice until Mom sticks her head into my room. *Crap.*

"You feeling okay, Shay-Shay?" she asks. She started using this nickname for me again after Sasha died. Before then, she hadn't used it in years.

"I think I'm sick," I say. Even though I know I shouldn't be skipping school if I don't want Mom to worry. This queued post is a little too much to handle, but I don't want to tell her about it.

She gives me a look, like *Who do you think you're fooling*, but when she walks into my room, she doesn't say anything. She presses her hand to my forehead and then to my neck. She's wearing a tight pencil skirt and a blazer, and her hair is smoother than usual. She straightened it. She always looks nice when she heads to work, but the blazer and hair make me wonder if she has a big meeting or something today.

"You don't feel warm."

"It's not that," I say. And I look at her. She can tell that I mean I'm the upset kind of sick, not the kind that would give me a fever.

"Oh," she says. "Well, I think we both know you'll only feel better if you get out of the house. Why don't you get dressed and meet me downstairs in twenty minutes?"

"But, Mom," I start, thinking of the queued post, of Tavia. But she puts her hand up, as if she's directing traffic and my voice is a jaywalker.

"Shay, I don't want to hear it. You're not ill. You're sad. And I understand, sweetheart. I do. But the only way to feel better is not to wallow. And you can't really afford to miss another day of classes this year. So get up. You're late, so I'll drop you off. We'll grab breakfast on the way, how's that?" I wait until she walks away; then I scream into my pillow.

The whole time I'm getting dressed, all I can think about is the queued posts. Was this the only one? And if not, how many more of them did she set up? How often can I expect them? I check out the queue functionality, and it looks like I can select a postdate infinitely into the future.

Will the world still be receiving messages from my sister years from now?

In the kitchen with Mom, as I'm zipping up my backpack, I keep thinking about everything Sasha was doing while she was sick that neither of us knew about. Mom's sad music is playing, and it makes me feel bad that I was giving her a hard time about going to school. She's upset about something this morning too.

"Did you get my text about my chemistry test?" I ask, hoping to distract her from her sadness. She turns to look at me.

"I did!" she says. She smiles. "Did I not remember to text you back? I got it during a meeting. I'm so sorry, honey. Great job, really." I press my lips together and nod.

"Did you notice that I haven't missed curfew in a while?" I ask next.

She puts her keys down on the counter instead of slipping them into her pocket. "I had noticed that," she says.

"Oh. Good." I nod again. I'm not sure what reaction I was expecting, but I was expecting *something*. I finish packing my bag, without saying anything else.

When I look up, Mom is walking across the kitchen toward me, and her face looks drawn. She slides her bag off her shoulder and turns down the music that's been playing instead of turning it off, like we're not leaving yet.

"I got a call from your coach yesterday, though. I wanted to talk to you about it. I was going to wait until tonight, but I guess we can do it now."

I freeze. "He called you?" I ask, and she just keeps watching me. "Well, it only happened one time," I assure her. "We don't need to talk about it now. Aren't you running late too?"

She touches my hand. "Shay, I'm just worried. He said he noticed that you've been having a lot of trouble since . . ." She trails off.

I don't know why, but the way she's looking at me, the way her voice sounds, it makes me angry. I've been working so hard to try to make her happy, and it's as if it doesn't even matter. She brings up my only failing, and it feels like a betrayal—like she's ignoring everything else.

"Since I became twinless?" I ask. My voice sounds calm, but I said it to hurt her. I regret it almost immediately.

"Shay," she says. She sounds calm too, but she's shaking her head and frowning. "What a horrible thing to say."

Sasha's post floats through my head. *If you're reading this, I'll never turn sixteen.* That's the real horror here, not anything that I've said.

"It's true, though," I say. "It's what I am. And I'm okay with it. You don't have to worry, Momma."

I'm surprised by how well I'm holding it together. If I can make myself believe it, I can definitely convince her. I take a deep breath, and I hear Sasha's voice in my head. *You're okay.*

"I'm perfectly fine," I say.

"Shay. We should talk about this," she insists. But I ignore her.

"I think I'm going to bike to school," I say. "I already missed practice, and like you said, I can't afford to miss any more classes."

She hesitates, but I think the twinless thing has shaken her up. She doesn't want to talk any more than I do now. "Are you sure? I'll be home late, so I can go in a little later this morning."

What else is new? Sasha says. Though, maybe that was me.

My insides are starting to tense up, but my mouth smiles. I can't get in a car with her. Not now.

"I'll see you tonight."

My phone beeps as I'm climbing onto my bike.

> I know I should be asking if you're okay after the way you ran away last night. But have you looked at Sasha's blog today?

It's a text from Rohan.

Yeah, I send back. Queued post.

Shit. I thought I was losing my mind. Or being haunted or something.

Lol, I send. I thought she'd been hacked.

So are you? Okay, I mean? Between the post and finding out about Tavia, I'm all messed up.

Not really. I tried to fake sick, I send. Then I asked my mom if she'd noticed how much better I'd been doing with everything.

What she say, he asks.

She told me Coach called her and she wanted to talk. She didn't even care about anything else.

The queued post and the nonfight with Mom is stirring something up inside me: a nervous energy I worry might spill over into a panic. I need music or movement, or both, and fast.

Where are you? I ask him.

Still in bed.

I already missed track practice. Wanna run?

YES. Meet you in the usual spot in ten.

When I get there, Rohan is already waiting, sitting on the bumper of his van, like he's been there for a while. He has his black hair pulled back with an orange headband, and he's wearing a gray sweatshirt along with some red fingerless gloves.

"Sorry," I huff, steam filling the air between us. "This backpack filled with actual books slowed me down."

Rohan kinda grins but doesn't say anything; just pushes away from his van and slides the back door open. He puts my bike in, then walks back to me and takes my bag. He doesn't really talk when he's in run mode, as Sasha used to call it. His face is serious, and his normally playful eyes are steady and focused. He lifts his heavy brows at me and tilts his head in the direction of the densely wooded area in front of us—his way of asking if I'm ready without using any words. The entrance to the path is sun dappled and pretty, but it's treacherous once you're in there.

I grin and nod, bouncing on the balls of my feet, a new burst of energy filling me up like pages in a book. Rohan slips in his earbuds because he can't run without music.

We look at each other. We look at the path. Then we run.

"I think I'm gonna skip," Rohan says after we're back in his van and he's driving in the direction of school. He's clenching his jaw, and even though I'd pledged not to skip anymore, something about how Mom was this morning and how wound up Rohan seems, even after a run, tugs at my heart.

"I guess I have to skip too," I say, like it's not a big deal. "In solidarity or whatever."

Rohan lifts his eyebrows, but he doesn't say anything, and I'm glad. He turns the van around.

In his garage, he plays guitar and sings all our favorite songs all morning—music is his outlet too. I strum my air guitar and lip-sync like I mean it. We order lunch with the money Mom left me for dinner, and then he finally plays some Our Numbered Days tracks for me. He stares at me as the first song starts. I stay silent until the last one ends.

"You guys are good, but . . ."

"Don't say it," he mutters.

"You already know."

"Yep."

I stand up and switch the music to an Unraveling Lovely song, and in seconds, Logan's voice swims into the air. UL is just *better*. They had something that's hard to put into words.

We watch *Intervention* the rest of the afternoon. I fall asleep on his couch after the third episode, feeling more relaxed than I've felt in months.

I don't realize I left my phone in Rohan's garage until he shakes me awake and I start looking for it.

"Uh-oh," I say as I climb into the Band Wagon. I literally have eighteen missed calls from Mom.

When we pull up in front of my house, I turn to him. "Regardless of what happens when I get in there, thanks for today," I say.

He nudges my shoulder and says, "Anytime. But I hope it was worth it." My phone buzzes again. It's Mom, *again*. As I climb out of the car, Rohan whispers, "Nice knowing ya" before he drives away.

I try to ease silently into the house, but Mom is standing in the living room, waiting for me. She's still in her blazer. But she's gripping the phone in one hand and holding a Bible in the other.

"Um . . . ," I say.

"I hope you have more to say than that," Mom says. "Where on earth have you been?"

"I thought you were going to be home late?"

"That does *not* answer the question I asked you, Shay Patricia Malone," she says.

I cringe. She only Patricias me when she's *really* mad.

I sit down on the couch and start untying my shoes. I kick them off and keep my eyes on the bit of carpet between my feet because I'm too afraid to look up at her. There's a tiny speck of brownish red, and I know it's probably from one of Sasha's nosebleeds. The sight of it makes my heart beat a little too fast, and I feel the amazing day I had with Rohan slipping through my fingers.

"Start talking," she says.

"I went on a run with Rohan since I missed track practice. And I told you I felt crappy this morning. I just wasn't up for school today."

"Can you *imagine*," Mom says slowly, "what was going through my head when I got a call that you'd never shown up to school this morning?"

When she walks over to me, I notice tears caught in her eyelashes. I open my mouth, but no words came out. This is exactly why I haven't told her the whole truth about the panic attacks.

It's why I've been trying to be better behaved. Those tears in her eyes, and the fight I feel coming, is exactly the kind of conflict I've been trying to avoid.

"If you *ever again* tell me you're going to school or you're going anywhere, and then I find out you're somewhere else, there won't be a discussion. It's not okay. It never has been in this house."

I heave a sigh, and I feel something dark creeping up and out of me.

" 'In this house,' Momma? Seriously? You're hardly ever *in this house*. It's like you don't even notice that I'm here unless I do something that upsets you!"

I'm surprised at myself. I never talk back to Mom. I stand up and kind of back away from her.

She blinks hard, and the tears that were hanging on the edges of her lashes suddenly fall like stones. I expect her to ask who I think I'm talking to or to tell me to go to my room. But something about her has softened. What she says is "How can you say that, Shay?"

I don't answer right away because I thought she'd get angrier, not ask a question. I pull off the beanie I'm wearing today— Sasha's candy cane one—and I look at it instead of Mom while I talk.

"Because it's *true*. I'm sorry, Momma, you know it's true. Sasha got sick. And it was like you disappeared. You were working most of the time, and with Sasha the rest of it. And look, it's fine because she needed you more—believe me, I get it. Sometimes it just feels like now that she's gone, you don't know how to love a kid who isn't dying."

As I say it out loud, I realize it's true. She's just looking at me, so I wonder if she doesn't get it. I keep talking, trying to explain.

"Maybe you're so used to worrying all the time that when I do something good, you don't know what to say. But the second something bad happens, you're all over me."

I look at her again. I hate looking directly at her for more than a few seconds. The mask she always wore to protect her sick kid from everything she was feeling has melted away, and sometimes there's no shield left for me. The raw emotion that's on her face right now reminds me of the way Rohan looks sometimes— like it hurts him to see another person walking around with Sasha's face.

I pull the hat back down over my hair. Even if I'm right about her needing the burden of worry to show love, I still hate that I've failed her again.

"Like I said. You don't need to worry about me, okay? I'm fine." I hear Sasha say, *Shay, you're not. You need her.* But I don't listen.

"I can take care of myself," I mutter more to Sasha than Mom, but part of me hopes they both hear. "I've been doing it for years."

13

AUTUMN

JAN. 27, 7:56 A.M.

I forgot you were dead this morning.

I woke up, and while I was still in a sleepy haze, I reached for my phone and looked for your name.

When I remembered, I couldn't breathe.

Tavia may not be on Hangouts right now. She'll see your messages later.

From: HeCalledItAutumn@gmail.com
To: TaviaViolet@gmail.com
Sent: Jan. 28, 1:56 am
Subject: <none>

I almost chopped all my hair off last night. I was brushing my teeth when I noticed one of my stick-straight hairs coiled in the sink. My hair has gotten so long. There is so much of it weighing me down. I can't get rid of the weight of your absence, but my hair seemed so easy to part with in the wake of everything else.

I was only a few seconds away from doing it when my dad opened the bathroom door. I guess I was in there for a while. He called my name a few times, and I didn't answer. I don't remember hearing anything, but that's why he got nervous enough to come inside.

He took the scissors away and said, "What the shit, Autumn?" He sounded just like Willow. He looked so freaked out, like he thought I might hurt myself or something. Then he called for my mom.

She was totally calm, though. She stepped into the bathroom and then tucked my hair behind my ears. She said, "I'll take you to get it cut tomorrow. Pick out a style. Something different from anything you've ever had. We'll get it cut however you want." So I'm working on it. But I'm not sure how I feel about making such a big decision without you.

Since I can't seem to stay away from your house, your room, or your brother, I'm sitting in your den with my headphones on, looking at celebrity haircuts. Dante's catching up on homework. He's finally come back to school. Every now and then, I tilt my laptop in his direction and ask if he thinks a certain cut would work on my face.

He looks at each photo, and then he looks at me for a little too long, and at first, I wonder if he's trying to match these white celebrities' hairstyles with my Asian features. But then he just says, "Your hair's fine" or "You're distracting me." I keep asking, though, and he continues to look and offer some kind of answer.

After a while, I leave him alone, and I start imagining what you would be saying instead.

You'd change the subject. You'd say something about me needing to become a role model for Korean girls everywhere who might be looking for the right haircut. Like *There aren't enough famous Asian people, Autumn.* Or *You could totally be the first adopted* and *the first Korean Miss America or something.*

After an hour of searching for hairstyles, I start to see what you meant when you said stuff like that. Since I'm not having much luck with celebrities, I pull up Willow's profile because she's always been so much more adventurous with her hair than I am with mine. I wade through her varied bangs and streaks of blond and angled bobs—and the pictures of a few of her Asian friends—looking for ideas. But inevitably, your profile pulls me in like a magnet.

Not for hair, obviously. Mine will never be as curly and wild as yours. But I click on your face and go through the photographs one by one, anyway, for what feels like the millionth time.

I'm looking at a picture of us standing on top of one of those giant boulders in Central Park. I'm trying to remember what else we did on that day trip to the city, quizzing myself on the tiny forgettable facts about our life together—I want to remember everything I possibly can about you. When I go back to my feed and start scrolling, there's a post with your name on it that stops me cold.

Tavia V. Soto and 267 others like Unraveling Lovely.

I take my hands away from the trackpad, like it's suddenly gone hot, and the thought that immediately comes to mind isn't one that makes sense. It is cold and painful, and the truth of it makes me want to double over.

Tavia V. Soto doesn't like anything anymore.

I must say it out loud, because Dante looks up from his screen and pauses for a second, waiting for me to go on. When I don't, he closes his laptop, leans toward mine, and says, "What?"

I feel my chest tightening and my face getting warm. I feel my breath getting away from me. I close my laptop and move it slowly to the coffee table.

"Autumn, what?" Dante says again.

I stand up, and I make it all the way to the door before your brother grabs my wrist. I pull against him, trying to escape, but he holds on until I turn around.

Tears are falling by the time I look at him, a torrent of them, and when Dante sees my face, his looks dark and full like the sky before it rains.

"I've gotta get out of here." I choke out. "Let me go. I can't *breathe.*"

When his grip loosens, I pull away and run out into the backyard without my coat or my shoes.

The air is icy, promising rain or snow, and the ground is

freezing cold under my bare feet. But I hardly feel it. There's a pain in my throat that I've never felt before, like there's something dangerous inside me, clawing its way out.

As soon as I can get a full breath, I let out a tremendous sob. I run across your lawn until I get to the big oak, right beside the fence. Dante's right behind me.

When I collapse against the tree, I grip the trunk and my body won't stop shaking. I need something to hold on to, and I guess Dante decides that thing should be him. He pries my hands away from the tree and pulls me toward him, and for a second, I fall against his chest and bunch the fabric of his shirt in my fists.

"She's gone" is what I say whenever the tears slow enough for me to use my voice. "She's gone, and she's never coming back. How is it possible that she's never coming back?"

I think about never calling you again. About never seeing another movie with you. About how we'll never share another secret. And I look up at Dante, because just like your dad, he has always known how to make things better. But right now, he's just chewing on his bottom lip. I realize then that's why his lips always look so plump and swollen.

When he doesn't say anything, I shove him away from me. I push him so hard and so suddenly that he trips over the roots of the tree and falls into the grass.

"You think you know me, right?" I say, standing over him. "You think you always know what I'm thinking? How I feel? Well, did you know that Tavia will always be more important to me than some . . . *guy*?"

I scrub at my face, and my voice is choked and even crueler when I start talking again.

"I would go back and change *everything* if I could have been with her instead of you that night."

Dante's nostrils flare a few times. He's gritting his teeth, so his jaw is working. Then he surprises me. His eyes fill up and spill over. I thought he was going to yell right back. But he's crying.

"Fuck, Autumn," he says, as if I'm a kid and he has to explain something simple. "She was my *sister*. You don't think I feel the same way?"

He turns like he's about to go back inside, but then he spins back around to face me, fast.

"Why do you think *I* didn't go to that party?" he asks.

I haven't thought about it, but Dante likes parties as much as you do. He closes his eyes and puts his hands into his hair.

"I was going to drive you guys there. But Tavia told me you weren't going. So I stayed home and called to see if you wanted to hang out with me."

"What?" I ask, even though the truth of what he's saying has already hit me hard and knocked me hollow.

"I was going to go to the party, to hang out with *you*. *I* should have been driving. I should have been there . . . ," Dante says in the torn version of his voice.

I can't look at him anymore, so I turn and look at the gate. My toes are almost completely numb from the cold, but before I can stop myself, I'm running to my car without my shoes or coat, backpack or laptop.

And almost as soon as I wrench the door open, it starts sleeting.

163

I sit in your driveway and cry in my car because there's no way I'm driving through a storm, but I can't go back into your house, either. Your brother stands out there in the freezing rain for way too long before going inside.

When the storm passes, I don't go back into the house. Dante eventually comes through the front door a few minutes after the rain stops, wearing a clean white T-shirt, sweatpants, and slippers. He has all my stuff. He taps on my window, and when I roll it down, I can smell your shampoo in his still-wet hair.

I don't say anything when he pushes all my things into my lap. I just toss it into the backseat and reverse out of the driveway as soon as I can get my key into the ignition. I drive fifteen miles per hour all the way home because even though the sleet has stopped, it's almost impossible for me to see through my tears.

I call Willow. I wail and sob, and she asks if I need her to come home. I say that I do, which I normally would not have admitted, and when we hang up, I hear my dad's phone ring. I know it's Willow who's called because he comes into my room a few minutes later. He hovers by the door with a cup of tea and a DVD. I wonder where my mom is, but I don't ask, and I can't tell what movie he's holding because my eyes are so swollen.

"You can come in," I say, and my voice is all scratchy from the crying.

He hands me the mug, and it's still steaming. When I take a sip, the warm liquid soothes my throat. He added so much honey that it hurts my teeth a little bit, but I don't complain.

He doesn't say anything, but he grabs my laptop and sits beside me on my bed. He's looking for the disc drive to play the movie. My laptop doesn't have one.

"How do you work this thing?" he says. He flips the computer over. By now he has to have realized there isn't a place for the DVD, but he always takes things way too far. He closes the laptop and shakes it by his head, as if it's a Christmas present. He taps it like a caveman.

I start laughing.

"Dad," I say. He looks at me. "Just get your computer."

He comes back with it a few minutes later, and inserts the DVD, and when it starts to play, I realize it's a home movie of you and me.

We're in the backyard blowing bubbles and chasing each other, two tiny dark-haired kids we'll never be again. We have on birthday hats, but it has to be my party and not yours because it's just Willow, Dante, and the two of us.

I lean against my dad's shoulder. And even though he knows it's coming, he still chuckles when *you* blow out *my* birthday candles.

Faye texts later that night. She says she talked to Alexa and that she's mostly come around. Margo's still being weird, but Faye's next message reads: The girl is going to have to get over herself. And some small part of me is glad that at least Faye's on my side. She invites me to sit with them again, but something about that—needing to be invited to sit at my own lunch table— feels wrong. I tell her it's okay, that I'll stick to my new table for now, because you dying has changed a lot of things. But most of all, its stirred up something in me that I haven't felt in years.

I've always known that being adopted means that at the very beginning of my life, there was someone who at best couldn't keep me, and at worst, didn't want me. But I never really felt the pain of that rejection because I can't remember a time when I wasn't loved. I had my mom and dad. I had Willow. I had you.

But I have always had this gaping hole in my life where my biological parents were missing. Just this feeling that there was a part of myself I would never know. And you being gone is just another blank space that I know will never be filled. I don't want to let Margo, Faye, and Alexa back in just yet because I'm worried they'll try to fit into the space in my heart that will always belong to you.

Just before midnight, Dante calls. When I pick up and say hello, he hangs up without saying anything back. I think he just wanted to make sure I made it home okay. I'd finally stopped crying, after the tea, the video, and sending you an email, but I stare at his name on my phone and start right back up again.

14

LOGAN

BRAM IS BORED so he sees how long he can stand on his head. (SPOILER ALERT: he passes out.)

6,139 views | 5 months ago

Yara and a bunch of other girls I only kinda recognize are leaning against my locker when I get out of last period, and for a second, I'm really confused. I look behind me to see if it's possible that they're waiting for someone else, but then Yara waves and smiles. I notice Paige, a redhead who's also on the cheerleading team, holding a cupcake carrier, and I remember why they're waiting for me.

"Shit. It's today, isn't it?" I ask as I unzip my backpack and dump all my books into my locker.

"Yep," Yara says. "We're heading over there, like, right now."

She reaches out to straighten my collar, like we're besties; like it's not weird as hell for her to be touching me. But I'm so surprised that I don't move away. She smooths it down with her delicate little fingers.

"Are you nervous? You look like you're *freaking out*," she says, stretching her eyes wide. A few of the girls giggle.

"I'm not fucking nervous," I say, shouldering my bag again.

"*'I'm not fucking nervous,'*" Paige repeats, and it should piss me off, but the impression is pretty spot-on. I crack a smile.

"Bram always said his mom liked you better than anyone he'd ever dated. *Including* me," Yara says, tucking her hair behind her ear. The studs in her lobes sparkle in the sun coming through the closest window. "Don't be nervous."

"Are you nervous?" Paige says to Yara. "This is gonna suck for you too. I mean, you *loved* him. You were with him through everything, all the way till the end."

That pisses me off. But Yara just looks down. Then she changes the subject.

"This is weird, right?" she says as we walk to the parking lot. I shrug, because, yeah, it's weird as hell, but I don't really want to talk about it. I'm still processing what Nico told me, about Bram being his dealer, but I want to take advantage of being here with Yara, too.

We're taking a few different cars, so the girls branch off in different directions, but Yara waves me toward her 4x4.

"You don't drive, right?" she asks. I shake my head. "Do you talk?" she continues with a grin. I nod. I thought it would be hard talking to her, but it seems like it might be really easy. You know those people who are charming without even trying?

Genuine and annoyingly nice? That's Yara. It's like I can't be an ass to her, no matter how badly I want to.

"I talk sometimes," I say eventually.

"Well, don't worry. I won't make you," she teases.

We climb into her truck and buckle up.

"I know this is weird, but we should just try to be there for Ms. Lassiter today. Her first birthday without him? That's bigger than you and me. The thing is—" Yara starts, squeezing her hands together, as if she's nervous. But she doesn't really get to finish because Paige appears out of nowhere and taps on her window. Yara jumps.

"They don't have any space left for me," Paige pouts. "Can I ride with you guys?"

With Paige in the car, Yara doesn't really talk much to me, and I wonder what it was she was about to say. I'm a little upset I can't use the ride over to ask her about Bram, but I just use the time to plan what I'll say when I get the chance.

When we get to Bram's apartment building, I feel goose bumps creeping up my spine like ants. I haven't been inside his place in forever, and the last time I was here was the day we broke up. I remember the way his room smelled, like Axe body spray and hair gel, and the way the couch in his living room squeaked when you sat down on the center cushion. There's a burn mark in the carpet by the window that leads to the fire escape from when I dropped a lit joint as I was climbing back inside one day. And worst of all, Ms. Lassiter is in there, with the same tan skin, curly brown hair, and insanely green eyes as Bram.

I don't want to go inside.

"Let's go inside," Yara says, pressing the buzzer. Her nails are painted a sparkly shade of pink. Seeing her face this like a badass when all I want to do is hide makes me feel like the biggest wuss ever.

"Who is it?" comes Ms. Lassiter's voice, sounding tinny and robotic through the ancient speaker on the door.

Instead of answering, a few of the black girls on the squad start singing the Stevie Wonder version of the happy birthday song. I join in, only because it's the Stevie Wonder version.

Other than Aden and Nico, I haven't sung in front of anyone since last summer, so I think I forgot how much I love an audience. About halfway through the verse, the girls stop singing one by one, but the change is so gradual, and I'm so into it, that I don't notice until my voice is the only one left.

When I open my eyes (I hadn't even realized I'd closed them), everyone's staring at me.

"What the hell?" I say to them, and a few of them start fanning their faces or pretending to faint. Like I'm Paul McCartney or something. Yara smiles at me.

"I forgot you sounded like that," she says, and I wonder how the hell she knows. She doesn't seem like the type to go to shows, but maybe I prejudged her.

I look away because, dammit, I feel heat creeping up my neck. I can't believe Yara Cruz of all people is making me fucking *blush*.

Ms. Lassiter's staticky voice comes through the speaker again.

"Well. I'd know that voice anywhere. Come on up, Logan. And whoever else is with you."

Yara smirks. And Paige looks at me, like I'm her best fucking friend. She links her arm through mine and pushes me through the door when it buzzes long and loud. I swallow hard and step into the building.

When Ms. Lassiter opens her door, she's in pajamas. The cute kind that have a matching top and bottom, but it's still depressing as hell to see her dressed like that at three-thirty in the afternoon. Especially since it's her birthday.

"Happy birthday," the girls say, their voices a chorus of squeals that make me flinch. Yara's holding the cupcakes now, which she places on the coffee table. When Ms. Lassiter sees them, she smiles a sad smile and pats her hair nervously, as if she's only just realized what she looks like.

"Girls," she says, like I'm not standing here. "I can't believe this!"

The cupcakes are red velvet, her favorite, and I know from the ride over that Yara's mom made the cream cheese frosting for her because after three tries, Yara still hadn't gotten it right.

Ms. Lassiter looks at me and purses her lips. She looks even more like Bram than I remember. I walk over to her because she's a magnet, just like her son was. Before I even realize what's happening, she's hugging me really tightly.

"Thank you for coming," she mutters into my ear between sniffs. She says this only to me, even though her house is full of pretty girls in short skirts with cupcakes and ice cream. People who actually did remember it was her birthday, when I didn't, because I was too preoccupied with watching her late son's dumb videos.

"Of course," I say. I hug her a little tighter. She doesn't know this wasn't my idea, but maybe that doesn't matter.

"So," Yara says. "What have you been up to today, Ms. L?"

While they talk, I make my way through the apartment. I stick my head into their extra bedroom, and I see that she hasn't gotten rid of any of Bram's books. I pour myself a cup of coffee in the kitchen, and Bram's last report card, a mediocre mix of Bs and Cs that's pretty similar to my own, is still stuck to the fridge, magnetic poetry pieces for the words "chocolate" and "sky" holding it in place. I try and fail to ignore the fact that this is where Unraveling Lovely got its name.

He and I were messing around with the magnetic poetry on his fridge one day, giggling like little kids at our shitty attempts at art. As we stumbled through perverted poems and stilted stanzas, we somehow lined up the words "unraveling" and "lovely."

"That would be an awesome name for your band," he said, even though I didn't have my own band at the time. Bram was the only person other than my parents who had ever heard me sing. In every band I'd ever been in before UL I just played guitar and stayed quiet. After he found some crappy, scribbled lyrics on a napkin I left behind at a lunch table, he pulled it out of me that my dream was to become a famous singer-songwriter.

With him egging me on, I started Unraveling Lovely. We entered Battle of the Bands and were selected to play live, and after all that, he dumped me right before the concert. I showed up late and wasted because I couldn't imagine singing songs about him sober. We were disqualified when I puked onstage, and the BotB officials figured out it was alcohol related and not just a stomach bug.

The memory makes my heart beat like crazy, so I stumble away from the fridge. I go into the bathroom to take a piss before heading back to the living room. But before I even catch my reflection in the mirror, I spot something on the sink that stops me dead: Bram's green toothbrush. It's still in the small glass cup beside his mom's. It's leaning against hers, like it can't stand up on its own, and it makes me feel sadder than anything else in this apartment has. I stare at it for a while, feeling torn up and reckless, forcing away the urge to put it in my mouth and taste it. To put it in my mouth, hoping to taste *him*.

Another memory comes out of nowhere, and it's so vivid that I almost choke: Bram used to let me borrow his toothbrush. Whenever we drank or smoked and I needed to cover the smell; if ever I fell asleep and ended up spending the night. He'd give me one of his wrinkled T-shirts or put his gel in my hair, or spray me with too much of his cologne. And he'd lend me his shitty toothbrush and kiss me hard and long while my mouth was still foamy.

The bristles are smashed to hell, as if he'd kept it for way too long. I step farther inside the bathroom and close the door and keep watching the toothbrush; like if I look away, it will disappear. I put down the lid on the toilet and sit. I pick it up, and as I hold it in my hand I start to cry. Because . . . *Fuck.*

Before I leave, I flush the toilet, even though I didn't piss.

After the toothbrush, I rejoin everyone else in the living room, afraid of being destroyed by another random thing he touched or owned or used.

I want to leave.

I can't leave.

Almost the whole cheerleading squad is here, and the girls are spread out around the small living room, sitting on the arms of the couch, the floor, the windowsills. Ms. Lassiter is in the kitchen making more coffee and hot chocolate and boiling water for Yara, who only drinks herbal tea, because of course she does. I lean against the wall closest to the stove and watch Ms. Lassiter's small, steady hands while she fills the kettle with water.

She hands me a cupcake right away, like she knows I was just crying in her bathroom over a toothbrush. I shove more than half of it into my mouth, eating it the way Aden eats everything.

"It's so good to see you, Logan," she says again. "I was hoping you'd come around."

I take another big bite from the cupcake and nod because I don't trust myself to say the right thing. I smile around the food in my mouth and lick the icing from my fingers.

"Do me a favor and grab a few mugs out of that cabinet, would you?" she asks me.

She points to a door near my elbow, so I open it and start pulling down cups.

"There's, like, a million girls in there," I say, peering through the doorway and counting cheerleaders and then counting out mugs. Ms. Lassiter smiles.

"That was Bram," she says as she twists her hair into a bun and sticks a chopstick from the counter through it; easing back into mom-mode without even realizing it.

"He always drew a crowd. Everybody loved him."

"Especially cheerleaders," I mutter, and she laughs a little, but a second later, when I look back up, she's staring at me kind of seriously.

"You and Yara seem like you're in a good place," she says.

I shrug. "We're okay, I guess. She seems like she wants to be friends or something."

I tell her about her inviting me to come over with them. Then I ask, "Is Yara this . . . handsy . . . with everyone?"

"I think so," she says, kind of laughing. "She braided my hair the first day I met her."

I'd forgotten how easy Ms. Lassiter is to talk to. It's hard to forget that she's where Bram got his looks, but after hanging out with her for fifteen minutes, I remember that she gave him all his infuriating charm, too.

"I'm glad you and Yara are becoming friends. You guys knew him better than anyone," she says, ruffling my hair a little. "I was a little worried that you'd blame her."

I frown and stop fiddling with the mugs. I was lining them up according to color: reds and oranges, then greens and blues.

"Blame her? For what?"

"For what happened," she says. Ms. Lassiter lowers her voice and glances over her shoulder. The cheerleaders have switched on the TV and are watching *The Real Housewives of Somewhere.* "With Bram," she almost whispers.

"Why would I blame Yara?"

"I thought you might think . . ." Ms. Lassiter trails off when Paige comes into the kitchen. I hand her two mugs with coffee and one with hot chocolate. The other girls trickle in to grab hot drinks, and the whole time my insides are screaming because I want to know what the hell Ms. Lassiter is talking about. We finally hand Yara her hot water, and then she takes forever picking out a flavor of tea.

When she leaves, I look back at Ms. Lassiter. She hands me a mug, but I just put it down on the counter and wait for her to say whatever she was about to say.

"He had so much going on," she says. She cradles a cup in her own hands and then sits down at the small kitchen table. There are only two chairs. "There was that tape and all the awful messages people were sending him. He lost his scholarships. Did you know about that?"

I shake my head. I didn't even know he had scholarships. Ms. Lassiter stirs her coffee and then clears her throat the way Bram used to.

"There was a random drug test at school. And I guess he failed it," she says. She shakes her head. "I should have known. His behavior was a little off, but I never would have guessed that he was . . . on drugs. A mother should know these things."

I shrug because I don't know what I can say, but she probably doesn't know he was dealing, either.

"I know that losing the scholarships was bad—he desperately wanted to go to college. And I know that he was probably so embarrassed about that and everything else that was happening. But it was a rough patch. It would have been fine if he'd given it some time—I tried to tell him that. Money was tight, but we could have figured out how to pay for school."

"But wait—what does any of that have to do with Yara?"

Ms. Lassiter sighs. "Well, I thought you'd think this all happened because Yara broke up with him, but I just wanted you to know there were so many things piling up. And you know Bram. It was like he didn't understand that there are some things that are out of his control. He was so stubborn. He refused to ask for help."

She shakes her head again and looks out the window. She's crying a little. A pigeon is perched on the ledge, and it shits right there while we're staring at it.

I hand Ms. Lassiter a napkin from the dispenser, but all I can think is: *When did Yara break up with him?*

"Do you mind," I ask her before she can say anything else, "if I go to his room?"

She presses her lips together. "No, of course not, honey. Do whatever you need to. If there's something of his you find in there that you'd like to take with you, just let me know."

I nod and head to the back of their apartment. Bram's room is at the end of the hall. I wonder if Yara broke up with him because of what happened at the party with Nico or for some other reason, because they were definitely still together after the sex tape was released. Yara either believed all the rumors—that I was behind it, that it had been recorded months before—or she just forgave him.

So they stuck it out for a while, but I guess at some point they didn't. And since everyone is still treating her like the grieving girlfriend, I bet no one knows they broke up. I guess everyone has secrets, even sweet little Yara.

I start to see how Bram could have been unraveling with all the things that were going to shit. His life was collapsing in on itself. Imploding. It's not hard to imagine all the little pieces adding up like Ms. Lassiter said. Throw drugs into the mix, and yeah—a person you think you know well can easily become a stranger.

I ease my way through Bram's bedroom door more slowly than I entered the bathroom; then I slowly glance around.

The bed is stripped, and the dresser is cleared off almost completely, and it smells wrong—like cleaning chemicals and artificial lemon instead of Axe body spray and hair gel. The hardwood floor is shiny, and his rug has been vacuumed clean—no food crumbs or random socks in sight.

I suddenly realize that the police were probably here at some point going through all his shit, looking for clues. Maybe Ms. Lassiter cleaned because they dusted for fingerprints and touched his stuff. She had to wipe away most of the traces of *him* to get rid of the traces of *them*. It's depressing as hell to think about.

Even though the furniture and floor are pretty sterile, his walls seem mostly untouched. There are posters of a few crappy Top 40 bands that I hate, and one small framed picture of Bram and his mom. There's one of those strips from a photo booth stuck into the edge of his mirror. When I get closer I see that it's him and Yara smiling, him and Yara sticking out their tongues, him and Yara . . . making out.

I turn around, and there are black-and-white photographs of graffiti and street art decorating almost half of the north wall. And I can't help but grin. Because of course Bram was a goddamn secret hipster.

There's one street art photo in particular that catches my eye, new since I was last here. It's of a big piece of paper that's been plastered on a brick wall. In the middle of the white is a single sentence in typewriter font:

> For the sensitive among us,
> sometimes the noise
> is just too much.

I pivot again, and I see the image of the headstone from *Slaughterhouse-Five*: "Everything was beautiful, and nothing hurt." It looks like he ripped the epitaph right out of the book. I run my fingers over the letters of the quote, missing his corny, happy-go-lucky attitude like crazy. But apparently, he hadn't been that person in a long time.

I hear a noise, and when I turn around, Yara's standing in the doorway watching me. And I feel strange. Not mad. Not sad. Just weird.

She steps into the room and closes the door behind her. She looks around, and her chin starts trembling, and before I can say anything, Yara is crying.

I'm not one of those people who melts at the sight of a girl crying, but Yara is *such a girl*. Something about her standing there, in her pink Uggs and polka-dot leggings, just rips me up. She looks too . . . innocent.

"Hey," I say. "Don't cry." I feel like such a cliché, but I point to the bed.

"Want to sit?" I ask her. She sits down. I stay standing and shove my hands into my pockets.

"I know Ms. Lassiter told you," she whispers. "I was talking to her, and she said she was so glad we were getting along, and I knew."

I nod.

"I kinda freaked a little bit when I realized. Luckily, no one else was in the kitchen. I asked her not to say anything to anyone else. And I know you hate me, but no one else knows so you can't tell."

"It's not that I hate you," I say, realizing it's true. "I just—"

179

I'm not sure how to finish, so I go with "Look, I won't say anything, okay?"

"I don't want them to blame me," she says.

I tell her I get it, because I do.

She mostly stops crying and wipes her eyes with her sleeve, and I feel more relieved than uncomfortable when she stands up and hugs me. She walks over to Bram's mirror and fiddles with the photo strip.

"He talked about it sometimes. He talked about it the night we broke up," Yara says.

"What? Dying?" I ask, and she nods. "Shit, Yara."

"I know," she says. Her eyes are full again, and her voice is shaking. "We broke up. He basically said he wanted to die. Then two weeks later he was gone. I should have told someone," she says so softly that I barely hear her. She takes a deep breath and looks at me. "I have dreams where he's still alive because I told someone."

Maybe it's the room, or Yara's tender eyes, but I say, "I have dreams where I'm killing him. Where I'm the reason he's dead."

I look at Yara, wishing I could blame every bad thing that happened to Bram on her. And part of me does blame her. But no more, I guess, than how much I blame myself or the guy in the video. The trolls, the drugs, or Bram himself.

"If it's anyone's fault," Yara says, "it's Nico's."

I pull my hand away from hers. At some point she started holding it.

"Wait . . . what?" I ask.

"Yeah. He's the one who got Bram started with the drugs. He's the only reason Bram was using."

180

She sees how shocked I am by this information. "He told me Bram was his dealer," I say.

She rolls her still-wet eyes. "It was the other way around."

I'm having a slight problem keeping my shit together. I was going to try to be Nico's friend again, maybe even ask him to play in my band, and he lied to me? But I don't have any time to digest the news because Yara keeps talking.

"I've been seeing someone; like, a therapist or whatever. And part of my treatment—God, I feel so stupid saying that—is that I'm supposed to figure out a way to, like, say goodbye. Since I didn't go to the . . . funeral."

I look over at her again, wondering why she would skip the funeral, wondering why I didn't notice her missing. The church was packed, filled with everyone from geeks to jocks, but I bet the absence of someone as high-profile as Yara—one of the most popular members of the cheerleading team and his fucking girlfriend, as far as everyone there knew—probably didn't go unnoticed by most.

"So I'm having this thing at my house next Saturday. It was my mom's idea, but I basically have to go along with it. It's a candlelight vigil, where me and a few friends will, like, talk about him."

She walks back over to the mirror, so that her back is to me, but her reflection is looking at mine.

"I'm really glad you came today. It's honestly a relief to have someone who knows about the breakup besides me and Ms. Lassiter."

She sits on the bed beside me again.

"I was going to ask you this in the car, but do you want to

come to the vigil? My parents won't be there or anything; it's more for us to try to get over what happened. To, like, deal with it in a way that makes it less scary or whatever."

We hear music playing a few minutes later, and Yara and I look at each other. We want to see what's going on, so I don't really have a chance to answer her question. She dabs at her face in the mirror for a few minutes, and when she's ready, we walk into the living room. Ms. Lassiter, Paige, and a few of the other girls have pushed the coffee table against a wall, and they're having a dance party in the middle of the floor.

An EDM song is playing, one of Bram's favorites. So when Paige grabs one of Yara's hands, and one of mine, I hesitate, but only for a second. I can't do anything about the Nico news here, and this is a damn good song. I strut to the middle of the room. I bust a few of Bram's signature moves, and Ms. Lassiter laughs. I dance with Yara and Paige and then all by myself, until my feet ache, and later, after I hug Ms. Lassiter goodbye and we all head for the door, I tap Yara on the shoulder.

"I'll come to the vigil," I say, thinking of Gertrude. She'll eat this up. "I want to say goodbye to him the right way too."

But first, I need some answers from Nico.

15

SHAY

**BAMF // SASHA'S SENSES REVIEW . . .
TIDY DARK PLACES**

Looks like: idk, homework? Lots of big words in these
lyrics.
Sounds like: the pretentious a-holes you hear at coffee
shops, tbh
2/5

"Come somewhere with me after school?"

Jerome doesn't use question words like "will" or "can" or
"do." He just starts with the part of the sentence that counts
most, and I kind of love that about him.

He's wearing a blazer with elbow patches today. I wonder

where he gets these clothes—if they're hand-me-downs or if he picks them out at thrift stores or consignment shops just as they are.

I don't ask him, though. I don't ask Jerome much of anything because I'm worried that if I start asking questions about him, he'll start asking things about me. But I do feel like I can't avoid the conversation he wants to have about "us" for much longer.

I pluck the front of the shirt he's wearing under the blazer, and the fabric is surprisingly soft between my fingers. Something about the way he's looking at me makes me want to press my cheek against his chest. He takes my wrist in his hand and pulls me closer, like he knows or something, and I settle my face there right against his heart.

"Where do you wanna go?" I ask him. "I'm kind of grounded."

"Nowhere far," he says. "Trust me."

And even though we've only been kissing for six short weeks, I do.

I leave my bike locked up outside of school and we hop on the bus as soon as the bell rings. And I close my eyes and kiss him for most of the twenty minutes it takes the bus to go seven stops, hoping I can delay the inevitable.

"We're here," Jerome says, and when I open my eyes, we're at the stop closest to Rohan's house.

"But why are we *here*?" I ask him as he takes my hand and leads me off the bus. Jerome doesn't answer. With his fingers curled around mine, I wonder if this is what it would be like to be officially his. For him to be mine. And because I'm so distracted by the question of what it would be like if we were boyfriend-girlfriend and not just make-out buddies that I forget about my question until we get to Rohan's.

"J," I say when we're standing outside of Ro's garage. "What's going on?"

"It's kind of a surprise." he says, and since we're still holding hands I allow myself to be led forward.

They're all in Rohan's garage.

Callie is sitting on the floor, her long, denim-covered legs twisted into a pretzel. Deedee is leaning against the far wall with her earbuds in, her thick hair wrestled into two adorable puff-balls, one on either side of her head. Rohan is sitting on a milk crate, strumming his acoustic guitar.

"Hey, guys. What's up?"

No one says anything for a few seconds, which is super weird, but they look at one another, which is weirder. Deedee takes her earbuds out, and her and Callie's eyes meet. And Rohan looks right through me, at Jerome. That's when I see Deedee's eyes get a little shiny. I look around at my friends, and the whole setup, with everyone hanging around awkwardly, not quite looking at me seems all too familiar. Then it hits me, where I've seen this exact scenario dozens of times before.

"You guys. Oh my god. Is this an intervention?"

I start laughing. I know from the show that this is supposed to be a serious moment, but I don't think it needs to be. And I want to keep the mood light, keep everyone happy. That's what I've wanted all along.

"Dee, you don't need to cry," I say.

But then Jerome's deep voice sweeps around from behind me like a warm breeze, and his words are so gentle that they immediately make my smile disappear.

"My granddad died last year," he says.

I turn to look at him. His eyes are misty, and he looks like he needs a smoke.

"I know he was old, so it's different from Sasha. But it messed me up for a while."

This is the most I've heard Jerome talk (maybe it's the most I've let him talk), and I stare at him, feeling sad that I'm learning something so important only now. "I didn't know that," I say, looking up at him. "I feel like I should have known that."

Jerome shrugs. "It's cool."

But it really isn't. Every person is a well, and everything I know about Jerome could fit on a leaf floating atop the dark depths of him.

"I couldn't take it, you know?" he continues. "He lived with us near the end, so after he died, I would do weird shit, like stand in his room for hours not doing anything. Just staring. Then I started getting nervous about stuff that never made me nervous before."

My palms get sweaty in crowded spaces now. I can't misplace anything of Sasha's without losing my cool. I nod.

"I had a few panic attacks after that."

I'm staring at Jerome, wondering how he could kiss me when he knew exactly what was up with me. But then I start to think that maybe that's why we started kissing in the first place. We kissed for the first time after one of my track meets, when I just kept running past the finish line and out of the gym because someone called me Sasha by mistake. I remember bumping into him in the hall and noticing that he was wearing bright red suspenders, and he coached my breathing back to normal. I'd known him for a while, but in that moment, I wondered why I hadn't ever noticed how kind his eyes were. I wondered why I hadn't talked to him more at shows. Then I kissed him.

Something just clicks inside my head. I look at his blazer. At his hand full of vintage rings. All of his hats and overcoats, his oversize old-people clothes.

"You started wearing his clothes," I say, thinking about myself and Sasha's beanies.

Jerome nods. "My folks, they think therapy is only for 'crazy people,' whatever that means. A lot of black people think that." He looks down and smiles a little. His eyes come back up and stay steady, stuck to mine. "What's worse, though? Telling someone that sometimes I miss my granddad so much I can't breathe? Or dressing like a seventy-year-old all of junior year?"

Everyone in the garage laughs a little bit, in that awkward way people laugh when they're not sure if it's okay. But my eyes are filling with tears.

"It's a distraction." It's Rohan talking now. He sets his guitar down on the concrete floor, stands up, and walks over to me. "Pretending that you're okay, that you're better than okay? 'Look at my great grades!'" He puts air quotes around that and everything he says next. "'Look at me! I quit smoking!' and 'I never miss curfew!' And yeah, I mean . . . Those are all good things.

But you're still sad, Shay. I don't know how you wouldn't be. *I* am. And everyone sees right through the rest of it—you pretending to be fine."

I swallow hard and look around at them.

"You're freaking out all the time, and that can't be good. It can't be healthy, and I can't . . ." He licks his lips and shakes his head, making that face he always makes, like it hurts him to look at me. "I don't know how it works exactly, but I know panic attacks are a sign of depression. I looked it up, and I found some pretty scary stuff."

"Stop looking at me like that," I say to him, almost pleading. But he keeps his eyes on mine.

"I know you think I look at you some weird way or something because you look like Sasha. But that's not it. It's hard to look at you sometimes because I don't know what I would do if something happened to you too."

Callie comes over next. She hugs me and whispers in my ear, "You haven't called me since she died. Not even once." As soon as she says it, I'm shocked. I hadn't thought about it, but I know without a doubt that it's true.

Deedee's crying when it's her turn. She pulls out a piece of paper, and I let out a weird half sob, half laugh. "You wrote something down?" I ask.

"So I wouldn't forget when this happened!" She points to her wet eyes. I laugh again and walk over so I can clean off her tear-streaked glasses.

" 'Shay,' " she reads once I've handed them back. " 'I miss going to shows with the old you. I miss making playlists for each other and sharing them. I miss showing you my other photos—

188

stuff not related to BAMF. And I miss doing BAMF stuff with you, too. When was the last time you stuck it out through a whole show? When was the last time we had a meeting to talk about content for the blog?' "

I know I've been neglecting BAMF. But Sasha was so on top of everything that I didn't want to feel like I was replacing her. I was hoping no one noticed. Well, I didn't think Deedee did. Callie definitely did.

Deedee keeps reading.

" 'I started dating Olive, the lead singer from Sunscream, and you don't even know about that. Because you ran out of their last show, when Callie introduced us. You didn't answer my texts when I invited you over last weekend. And the last time I tried to tell you about her at lunch, you disappeared.' "

She continues, " 'I know losing a sister is a horrible thing to have happen to you, but me, Callie, Ro, and everyone—we lost her too. We just want to help. We think it might be better for everyone if we figure out how to get through this together.' "

Everyone's crying now. And everything in me is dying to run, to get away from them because it's all too much. It hurts *too much*.

Just when I'm ready to push my way out of the garage, Jerome hugs me. His soft shirt is against my cheek, and I can hear his heart beating. Then I feel another pair of arms around me: Rohan. Then Deedee is there, her bushy hair tickling my ear, then Callie. I'm completely surrounded by them in the best group hug I've ever been a part of, and we're all ugly crying—big, gulping sobs.

"So will you get help today?" Rohan asks, borrowing a line from my favorite show. And just like that, we're all laughing.

I still want my sister desperately. I think I always will. And though the weight of this kind of love won't replace her, it might just make it so that I'm a little closer to okay.

When I get home, I work up the nerve and text Dante. Talking to Jerome about his granddad had actually opened up the part of me that wasn't willing to share my hurt because I thought that no one would get it. But if Jerome can understand what it's like to lose a sister after losing his grandfather, I think Dante and I might be able to help each other even more. It's weird that I don't know what to say even though I just went through the exact same thing. But I guess talking about losing someone you love is never easy.

I'm nervous, so I just send Hey.

He hasn't texted me back when Mom gets home, and I'm so surprised to hear her enter the house before eight that I head downstairs right away, with my phone in my back pocket.

Mom glances up when I step into the dining room, but she doesn't say anything, though she's brought home takeout from our favorite Italian place. This is the first time she's been back early enough for us to have dinner together in forever, and we haven't really talked since I told her I could take care of myself. I feel like I should apologize for what I said, so I speak up first.

"Rohan just *Intervention*ed me," I say.

She looks up from the pasta she's spooning out onto two plates. "What in the world does that mean?" she asks, and I'm relieved that her face doesn't look tormented, the way it did when we last talked.

I walk over to the table and take the plastic utensils out of the bag. I put a fork on each of our plates. "All my friends, they had an intervention for me. They said they're worried about me. They think I'm depressed and having panic attacks and not talking to anyone about how I'm feeling about Sasha." I sit down and look up at her. "So I wanted to say sorry for how I reacted the other morning when you brought up Coach's call. What happened at the track meet was exactly why they were worried too."

Mom sits down and nods along to everything I'm saying. But when I apologize, she shakes her head, just once. "No, Shay. You were right, at least partially, about what you said. I do think I'm used to feeling anxious—to being worried all the time. I've been holding on to that. So I wanted to apologize to you." She twirls some spaghetti with her fork, but then she puts the fork down on the side of her plate without eating any pasta. "I'm sorry that I've ignored the positive changes you've been making. I *have* noticed them, and I am proud of you. But worrying is kind of part of the mom job description."

I smile. I feel my phone vibrate, but I can't look at it now.

"So," she continues. "I've been trying to figure out if there's anything else I can be doing for you. To start, I'm going to make an effort not to leave you alone so much. And when you said that word the other night, 'twinless,' I looked it up."

My eyes go wide and I sit up straighter. It's weird to hear Mom say the word that's been tormenting me for weeks, so casually.

"I found something that I think might help."

She picks up her phone from the table and taps around the screen for a second. Then she places it back on the table between

191

us. It's an email, and at the top, I see that word from my search. The heading says: *Twinless Twins Support Group. Once a Twin, Always a Twin.*

I feel the weight on my chest almost immediately, and it's suddenly harder than it should be to get air into my lungs. Spots appear in front of my eyes, like some kind of bad magic trick, and I'm almost certain I'm going to faint. But I try to stay calm. I try to talk to Sasha, to get her to tell me I'm okay. With her voice inside my head, we begin to talk my body out of this quickly descending betrayal of itself. Mom has never seen this happen to me, and I don't want her to see it now.

She notices what's happening anyway. She stands up and comes over to my side of the table.

"Look at me," she says, but her face is full of pain, so I want to close my eyes. I want to run away from the table. I push my chair back.

"No, Shay," she says. "Look at me." I do. She takes my hand and presses it against the base of her neck. Just like Jerome did that day in the hallway, she tells me to breathe with her. I try to. And it helps.

My heart is still pounding, but my breathing is a little more even by the time she says, "I'll go with you, if you want. But I think this is something you need to do."

I go to my room after dinner and take out my phone to see who was messaging me while I was talking to Mom. Dante hasn't texted me back yet. The vibration I felt was a message from Rohan.

I hope you're okay.

I am and I'm not, I guess, but I don't text him back. I message Dante again. It hurts to think that he's going through the same thing I am, but I still don't know what to say. So I just start with something simple.

I heard about Tavia.

I'm so sorry.

I think of Rohan's message, and send the same thing to Dante.

I hope you're okay.

Working on it, he replies suddenly, and those three small words make me feel so much better, so much braver. I'm working on it too.

"Shay?" Mom says. She's standing at my bedroom door. "Want to watch TV for a little while?" I smile and look down at my phone. It gives me an idea.

"Sure. And I was thinking: would you mind if I went to the support group with someone else?"

16

AUTUMN

JAN. 29, 1:23 P.M.

I haven't spoken to Dante in days. I miss him.

Tavia may not be on Hangouts right now. She'll see your messages later.

From: HeCalledItAutumn@gmail.com
To: TaviaViolet@gmail.com
Sent: Feb. 1, 9:34 p.m.
Subject: <none>

I think the crying was a mistake.

Ever since that scene at your house in the yard with Dante, I've been losing it constantly. I've gone from feeling hardly anything at all to feeling everything all of the time.

If my parents were worried before, they're really worried now. Willow too. She came home for the weekend. She's trying to pretend she's here because she has a cavity and needs to see Dr. Chen. But I know that she got her wisdom teeth taken out by some random dentist in New Hampshire, right near her school last year. I texted her after I got myself together the other night and told her she didn't need to come home, but then, I think my mom called her. She might have even told her about the fight I had with Dante.

Willow asks me to go with her to get bagels on Saturday morning. I really just want to lie in bed, eat pistachio ice cream, and listen to UL, but I agree, hoping it will make my family stop being so weird. It's not until we get to the bagel shop that I realize the last time I was here, I was with you.

"You mind if I chill in the car?" I ask Willow. I lie and say, "I kinda just want to listen to some music." The line is a nightmare, so Willow pouts for a minute or so about me keeping her company, but I'm more stubborn than she is, and eventually, she gives up. I wave to her while she shivers in the cold, and feeling like a bad sister is the only thing helping me hold it together. As soon as she gets inside, I lose it, and my hands are shaking so badly that I can't even text her back when she asks if I want an everything or a sesame seed bagel.

She didn't tell our parents about how upset I got in the car, but she's been hovering around me ever since we got back to the house. My mom noticed, though, and now she's hovering too. To convince my family that everything really is fine, to try to make everything *be* fine, I decide I want to go to a beach party Saturday night.

It's the kind of thing you would have dragged me to. The kind of thing I would have done anything to avoid. But instead, I'm the one begging Willow to come with me. I'm almost certain I'll only talk to her the whole time, but my mom doesn't know that. She says, "Go ahead, girls. You two haven't hung out together in a while."

When I'm putting on my coat I hear my dad say, "It'll be good to get her out of the house." And Willow says, "No shit."

I wish they'd stop talking about me like I'm a little kid.

As soon as we park, I realize your brother's there. It's cold and foggy, but I spot his dark hair, his green army jacket, and his particular stance from where I'm standing, about a quarter mile down the flat, gray beach.

"You hate stuff like this," Willow says as she pulls her hood up and steps out of our SUV. "And the weather's gross. Are you sure you don't want to go do something else?"

I shake my head and force a smile.

"I want to make it up to you, for standing in that long line for bagels this morning," I say.

"By making me stand in the cold more?" she asks.

I don't laugh, even though I should. "Yeah, I guess. But this time, there's booze." I waggle my eyebrows.

"You don't even really drink. And I can't drink because I'm driving," she says.

"Oh yeah. I guess that's true. But look—" I point across the beach, grasping for anything that can save my not-very-well-thought-out plan. "Aren't those some of your friends?"

I stand beside her in my puffy black jacket, the Gryffindor scarf twisted tightly around my neck, and I watch Dante while Willow stands on tiptoe and tries to spot her "high school friends" in the crowd. That's what she calls them, and I can't imagine what that will be like—to separate my friends based on where I met them. You were my first friend. For a long time, you were my only friend. But I don't want to think about that.

Dante's laughing and touching some senior girl on the shoulder, and when my eyes fill with tears, I don't know if it's about you or him. I roughly wipe my face before Willow sees.

My sister's right about me not really being a drinker. You know I've steered clear of the kegs and coolers for most of high school. But something about your brother or the weather or just being at a party without you makes me want to grab a red cup.

So I walk straight toward the fire where the keg is and pour myself a beer.

About twenty minutes later, I'm dizzy with relief or pleasure or *something*. Willow's ready to leave, but I beg her to stay a little longer. I'm starting to get a head rush, the good kind that makes everything seem better, and I know my cheeks will go ruddy soon if they haven't already. If you were here, you would be teasing me about my "Asian glow."

So I ask my sister, "Am I *glowing*?" because that's what you'd always say on the rare occasions when I did have a drink—that I was glowing, like I was a firefly or a star. Willow doesn't get it. (Or maybe she does.) She rolls her eyes, and I laugh.

Willow runs into some guy she used to date and asks if it's cool if she hangs out with him for a few. Since I'm giddy with beer, I'm hoping he'll distract her from wanting to leave, so of course I say, "Sure." A few minutes later, I see Faye climbing out of her car. Margo's sitting shotgun, and Alexa's in the back. If I were sober, seeing them would make me want to hide since things are still weird between us. But since I'm not, I wave.

Faye sees me and waves back.

"Oh good. I was hoping you'd be here," she says when she walks over. I smile, and my mouth feels weird making the shape.

Alexa looks buzzed already. Her hair is a little messy, and her eyes are glassy and unfocused. Margo's sober, I think, but she's always staring at her phone, so who knows.

"Hey, Autumn," Alexa says. And Margo looks up, surprised.

"Hi," I say.

Faye looks at us. "I was telling them on the ride over that I'm sick of this. You're our friend. Things are crappy, and we shouldn't be splitting up. We should be, I don't know, like constantly hugging or something." She looks over at Margo, who licks her lips and crosses her arms.

"What's your deal?" Faye asks Margo.

I think Faye forgets sometimes that she's the glue that put us all together. That before her, it was you and me, and Margo and Alexa. We were two separate sets of friends. I don't know if Margo likes me in the specific ways that friends are supposed to like one another. Her allegiance lies with Alexa the way mine is always with you.

Margo goes, "I don't have a *deal*. I just want to be there for Lex."

"That's just it, though. You make it sound like Autumn's the problem," Alexa says. She kind of trips in the sand, and I wonder how many drinks she had before she got to the party. "It's not Autumn, not really."

Alexa comes over to me and pulls me into a hug. We both stumble a little as she does it.

"I'm sorry I've been weird lately, okay?" Her breath smells like peppermint, so I know she's had a lot of schnapps. I nod against her shoulder.

"Me too," I say. "I miss you guys." I feel my eyes stinging with tears, and when I look at Faye, she smiles at me and joins our hug. I look at Margo and wave her forward with my free hand.

Faye says, "Margo, get over here!" And after a second, she smiles a little and tucks her phone into her pocket. Alexa pulls her into the center of our group hug so roughly that all four of us almost tumble into the sand.

After that, even though you're still gone—I still don't know where I fit without you, and we're all still sad—everything feels a little better.

I have another cup of foamy beer with the girls, and we talk about music. Alexa puts a fishtail braid into my hair, and Margo shows me a couple of photos she took at the last show they went to together. Faye pushes one of her earbuds into my hand, but I pass it to Alexa instead of listening myself. I don't know when I'll get back into that scene. I can't imagine going to see a new band and knowing you'll never get to hear another song.

A little while later, I start playing tug-of-war with one of Perry's friends from the football team. He brought me another drink and then started tugging at one end of my scarf. It's starting to feel like a real party because the music's been turned all the way up and the girls are giggling and yelling things at us. "You can take him, Autumn," they shout, as if he and I were putting on a show just for them, and it feels better than I want to admit to be a part of the group again. The guy is trying to drag me closer to the water, and I'm laughing hysterically and resisting. He's laughing too, which makes me keep yanking, but suddenly, his whole face changes.

He drops my scarf so fast that I fall backward into the sand. He winces and mumbles, "Sorry, Autumn. I gotta go. I'll, uh, see you at school or something." It seems like he's looking at someone just behind me as he walks away. When I turn around, Dante's standing there, with his hands stuffed into his pockets, and he looks pissed.

He reaches down to help me up, but I move away from his hands, shake my head, and stay in the sand.

"It's better if we just don't. Don't you think?" I say, thinking about him touching that other girl.

Your brother looks at me like I'm a stranger. But before he can say anything, Perry materializes from somewhere. I'd forgotten that this part of South Shore is basically his backyard. He has to be buzzed if he's willingly coming over to me and Dante after their fight. That fight is probably why his friend dropped my scarf so quickly.

"Hey, dude, no hard feelings, right?" Perry says.

I look over at Dante. Your brother shrugs. Nods.

"Cool," Perry says.

It's taken two weeks for Alexa and Margo to apologize to me when I hadn't even done anything. Dante tried to kill Perry, and they're just, like, *I know you punched me a bunch of times, but it's cool.* Boys are so weird.

Perry looks down at me.

"Okay, A?" he asks.

I want to talk to him even less than I normally do, so I nod too and pray that he'll just leave. I probably haven't thought of you for more than an hour, but then he says your name.

"Parties are more of Tavi's thing than yours, aren't they?" he asks me, stooping so that we're face to face. And there it is all over again: your name and the present tense. The memory of you going to Alexa's party without me. And now, Dante's face in the yard when he told me he didn't go to the party with you because *I* didn't go. I look away from Perry, knowing that if my face hasn't turned red from the beer, it's probably flushing now from me trying so hard not to cry. I puff out my cheeks and scan the beach for Willow. I can't remember where we parked the car.

When I turn around, Dante's still standing there. Seeing him is the end of any hope I had of holding it together. The way I feel must be evident on my face because Perry reaches out to me and says, "Hey, what's wrong?"

He's wearing a stupid fitted baseball cap with the sticker still on the bill, and it's barely propped on top of his head. And just as I look up at him, a big gust of wind blows it away. But he barely even flinches. He just keeps watching me.

Crappy beach parties in winter would be better with you here. Everything was better with you. And I can't talk to Perry—I can't even look at him—without feeling like you'd still be here if you'd never fallen in love with him.

When I start sobbing into my gritty hands a minute later, both Dante and Perry try to help me up. Instead of reaching out for either of them, I crawl away from your brother and scream at your ex.

"She was coming to see you!" I shout to make Perry get away from me. I don't say your name, the way he always does, but I can tell by his face that he knows I mean you. "She wanted to get back together!" is what I yell next.

"Autumn, don't," Dante says. But I don't listen. We're all at this stupid party as if everything is normal, so I might as well tell the truth. Perry looks at me with something close to hope in his eyes, and it just makes me angrier. I don't want him to feel hopeful. I want him to hurt too.

"She wanted to get back together," I say again, anger seeping into my low voice. "And she died on her way here, to *your* beach. To *your* house."

I'm drunk, so I'm not even close to being done, but Dante pulls me up out of the sand and brushes off my clothes, like I'm a kid climbing out of a sandbox, even as I try to pull away from him.

"Did you drive here?" he says to me.

I roll my eyes. "I'm not an idiot."

Faye runs over and says, "She came with Willow." Alexa and Margo are still by the log where we were sitting earlier, but they're watching us, too. I'd forgotten they were even here, and their faces are full of some mix of sadness and concern. Alexa looks like she might cry, and it just makes me angrier.

I'm stumbling, and still kind of sobbing, and by then, other people start to notice. Dante picks me up and throws me over his shoulder when I won't start walking on my own, and I hit his back, but he won't put me down. As he carts me away, I look back at Perry one last time. In a voice that sounds nothing like my own I screech, "She's dead because of you!"

Dante finds Willow. He puts me down right in front of her and says, "I think you should get her out of here." His jaw is working hard, and my hands are shaking like crazy.

I'm crying so hard that I can't even say what I want to say to him. But I look behind him, at the girl he'd been flirting with, and I choke out a "Her?"

He must understand, even though I'm coughing and crying and sniffing. I'm sure my face is covered in sand, and I probably look terrible. But Dante just frowns at me, and I don't know what his frown means. When Willow sees the state I'm in, I don't have a chance to figure it out.

Before, it was like I was drowning. The water looked smooth, but I was thrashing around under the waves, struggling to breathe. Now I've broken the surface, and people can see me. But I'm too far away from the shore to be rescued.

I curl into a ball in the backseat while Willow drives us home. She sneaks me up to the bathroom, and I shower until my whole body is pink with heat and my head is a little clearer. I let her tuck me in.

17

LOGAN

BRAM IS BORED so he sniffs a kitten (even though he's allergic).

Yara and I have talked and texted almost every day since Ms. Lassiter's birthday. She seems to feel as guilty as I do about Bram, and I can't hate her, knowing that's true. I walk down the halls at school, and it feels strange to see people and want to talk to them. I'm no good at having friends, but I guess I'm trying.

"Hey, Yara," I say. I walk over to her, and Paige is there too, so I wave. Yara slaps my arm and says, "Oh my god, I thought you were skipping or something. Where have you been all day?"

I shrug. I was hiding out in the nurse's office because they reopened the gym. Until today, the doors had been crisscrossed with caution tape since the gym leads to the locker rooms—the scene of Bram's suicide. I had phys ed fourth period, and there was just no way I was stepping foot in there. So I immediately claimed I had a killer migraine. The nurse's office was pretty comfortable, so I just stayed in there till fifth. I have a feeling I'll come down with a headache every time phys ed shows up on my schedule for the rest of the year.

"The gym opening back up is super depressing, right?" Yara asks.

"You could say that," I agree.

"I know," Paige says. She smacks her lips together. "We're going shopping after school. Retail therapy. Wanna come?"

"He can't," Yara chimes in. "He has to go into the city for actual therapy today. Right?" She looks back at me to confirm.

I nod, trying to remember when I told Yara my therapy schedule. Paige knocks her hip into mine before the three of us start down the hall together. Yara grabs my hand. If she touches you once, the girl doesn't stop.

"Maybe we can just get ice cream real quick?" Yara says. "Since you can't shop."

"It's twenty fucking degrees out," I mumble.

"So what?" she says.

"It's *ice cream*," Paige agrees.

My phone rings as Paige impersonates me. "*'It's twenty fucking degrees,'*" she mutters, and Yara laughs. When I pull it out and look to see which one of my parents is calling (because they're the only people who ever call me), it isn't either. It's Nico.

I've been trying to figure out what to do about him. I've been texting him about music stuff, like everything's cool between us, even though whenever I see him at school I want to kick his ass. Still, I'm surprised to see him calling me. I know I need to talk to him about Bram again, but I've been putting it off.

Now he's on the phone, and I can't exactly ignore that. I untangle my fingers from Yara's, and I tell both girls I'll be right back.

"Nico?" I ask as soon as I'm alone, and he laughs. The TV is on way too loud in the background, and I'm just about to tell him to turn it down when he does.

"Hey," he says, like we call each other on the phone all the time or something.

"Uh, hi?"

He laughs again, and then I hear slurping and the unmistakable sound of ice hitting glass. Nico's pulling desperately at the last bit of a drink.

"You wanna come over?" he asks me, and his words are slurred. It's the middle of the day, Nico's drunk, and he's inviting me over, like it's not a Tuesday, like he shouldn't be at school right now.

I'm already in trouble for skipping classes, so I hesitate for a minute, but only for a minute. Because even though things are a little better at school, I still can't stop thinking about Bram. I need to find out what was going on between the two of them, because I know from Yara that he lied to me. And I haven't forgotten that Bram was beat to hell when he was found. I want to know the truth about that night, and drunk people tell the truth. Nico lied to me once already. I know he knows more than he's saying.

"Sure, I'll come over," I say. "Send me your address."

Nico hangs up hard and fast, like he has another call or somewhere else he has to be. I shoot Yara a text and tell her something came up so no ice cream for me, and Nico's text arrives with his address a minute later. As I exit the building, I wonder why I didn't just leave school the second I saw the open doors to the gym.

When I get to Nico's, he wrestles me into a headlock and laughs at how my hair is sticking up all over the place when he's done. I have to try really hard not to hit him the second he backs off, because he's always fucking annoying, but it's harder to let it slide, now that I know he's also a liar. He pours an inch of whiskey for me into a short water-stained glass and says his dad won't miss the booze. I mix it with a warm Cherry Coke that I pull from my backpack.

"Cheers to us changing clothes where a kid fucking *died*," Nico says, lifting his glass. I guess he *was* at school this morning, and he had the balls to do what I didn't—leave. He's smiling, but his eyes are a little glassy, and he's wasted, so the gym being reopened is obviously a big deal to him. I wasn't expecting him to be so emotional. It turns my anger with him down to a simmer. "It's pretty messed up, don't you think?"

I nod and take a sip of my drink, trying not to think about how disappointed Gertrude would be. I silently convince myself she'd be cool with me drinking, considering the gym drama.

"I hid in the nurse's office all afternoon," I tell him.

Nico thinks that's hilarious.

I try to find my footing in this room, in this relationship. Is Nico—the guy who kissed my ex, the guy who introduced him to drugs—a drummer, a dealer, a liar, or my friend? Or is he somehow all of those things at once?

Nico stands up and stumbles a little as he walks over to a record player in a far corner of the apartment. He pulls out a record from his parents' pretty extensive collection and presses it into the player with more care than I've ever seen him use with anything else.

When the music starts, it's a song I love and one that demands all your senses. I close my eyes for the first few bars. When I open them, Nico is holding out his hand. "May I have this dance, Logo?" he asks with a grin.

I swallow what's left in my glass and then oblige because I hope dancing will be a way to open him up, to ease into asking him more about Bram. I was pissed when I got here, but it's funny how quickly booze can make bad feelings float away.

We start out with just our fingers intertwined. And almost immediately, Nico twirls me. Neither of us knows what the hell we're doing, but it's kind of fun, anyway. I laugh when he pulls me close after the spin. We both hum and keep swaying to the music. Even though I'm shit at keeping friends, I'm bad at being alone, too. So it's so nice to be close to someone and not want something more, and to know he doesn't want anything from me, either.

"You miss him?" I ask Nico. And as much as I'm asking him to get to the truth about him and Bram, part of me honestly wants to know.

He nods and sniffs. I can't see his face, but shit, he must be crying.

"I thought he was just your dealer," I say because people don't cry when their drug dealer dies. Almost immediately, Nico's body stiffens.

He looks up at me with his wet too-blue eyes.

"I never said he was *just* my dealer."

The song ends, and we back away from each other. Whatever bubble we were in thanks to the music has burst.

"I invited you over here because I wanted to talk to someone who understood," Nico says, as if I'm betraying him.

"So talk," I say, like a dick. Because fuck him for making me feel bad when he's the one who lied. Whatever softness I'd felt for him a few seconds ago is gone. Funny how booze can make good feelings disappear, too. "But how about this time, you lie a little less."

Nico is normally all jokes and laughter; roughhousing and rough hugs. But now he sits on the floor. He looks different— older or something—when he looks up at me.

"What does *that* mean?"

"I know you were Bram's dealer, Nico. Not the other way around. Yara told me."

He shakes his head, like I'm wrong, and I'm gearing up to argue with him when tears start falling from his eyes. Seeing that shuts me all the way up.

"I didn't lie," he says, "But I also didn't tell you everything." He traces a circle on the floor beside him. "So here it is: I do deal. But Bram? He was dealing too. Yara just didn't know. She assumed when she saw him with me that he was buying. But that wasn't the way it was going down. He told me he needed to make some extra money, so I hooked him up."

I shut up and walk over to the whiskey, which is still on the coffee table. I don't mix it with Coke this time—I just swallow it straight, and when my chest burns, I feel like I deserve it. Nico might have lied to me before, but I know he's not lying now because Ms. Lassiter told me they were broke and that Bram was trying to fix things the way he always did.

"The party over Thanksgiving weekend was only, like, the third time I'd hooked him up with a supply, but he was burning through everything so fast. I was mostly selling at shows, and he did house parties since he got invited to most of them, anyway. He was worried what he was doing would get back to Coach, so he'd organize these drops and then text people to pick up their shit and leave their money instead of doing hand-to-hand exchanges. He asked me to help him set up a drop at that party. That's what we were doing when he kissed me. He thought someone was coming into the room, and he wanted to cover it up. Then he kind of . . . kept kissing me. Said I gave him a rush."

That sounds like the truth too—like something Bram would definitely do. I could see him getting a taste of someone (Nico), or something (the drugs, the money), and deciding that he liked them regardless of the consequences.

Nico keeps talking. "We made that video for fun the second or third time we hooked up. I didn't plan to do anything with it, but then he broke things off with me out of nowhere. Said he couldn't sell anymore and that he didn't want to hook up anymore, either."

"Wait. What video?" I say. But it's like Nico doesn't hear me.

"God, I was so pissed. He came over here, and we got into this huge fight. But I tried to tell him—"

"Wait, Nico," I say, my voice dropping. "You're the guy in the sex tape?"

Nico's drunk, so he looks up, clearly confused. He wipes away the tears that are left in his eyes and says, "Duh. Everyone knows that."

"Um, *I* didn't."

"Oh, well. Yeah."

"And you uploaded it?"

Nico nods. "I did it to get a reaction out of him, but he kept totally ignoring me for, like, weeks after. I think he was trying to work it out with Yara. Whatever. When he finally showed up, I guess he'd been thinking about it for so long that he wasn't even mad I'd uploaded it anymore. I think he actually felt bad."

"Jesus," I say. "When did that happen?"

"That's the screwed-up thing," Nico says. "We fought the night he died, and fuck, dude." He looks around for his glass, and when he finds it, he downs the remains like it's water. "It messed me up."

The news report said Bram was so badly beaten, they thought that was how he died at first. I'd dreamed that I was the one who'd beaten up Bram, and I'd just danced with the guy who actually did.

"So, what? You beat the shit out of him in that locker room and left him for dead?"

Nico blinks a few times, then furrows his brow and looks at me as if I've just spoken to him in another language.

"What?" he says. "Do I look like I would win in a fight with Bram Lassiter?"

I look at him a little closer, at his skinny arms and legs. And damn, he's right. I run my hand through my hair. "So what the hell happened?"

"Ugh. Look, I'll tell you what I told the police, okay? He

texted me to say he wanted to talk. It had been about three weeks since I uploaded the video, and as far as I was concerned there was nothing left to say. He was still with Yara, and I'd already gotten him back for dropping me like I was nothing."

Nico pours himself more whiskey, as if he needs it to get through this. I want another drink, too, but I feel like I can't ask for the bottle right now.

"But he shows up, and he's all, 'Let me fix this. I still want to be friends.' He kept saying that. And I just said, 'Dude, you can't. Too late. Go make out with Yara.' Whatever. I was pissed. He came toward me, like he wanted to hug or kiss me or something, and I don't know. I lost it."

Nico looks toward the stairs, and I know how that feels, to be back at a time and place in your head and for it to be so real, like it's happening all over again.

"We were in the hall, right up there. I just wanted him to leave, so I was telling him to, but he kept coming toward me." Nico starts crying again. "I shoved him, just to keep space between us. And he slipped on a pair of my fucking drumsticks, which I'd left on the floor like an idiot. He fell down about half the stairs. He was all banged up, busted lip, probably broken ribs and who knows what else, but then he started crying and saying this stuff about how his life was shit and he didn't deserve to live. And then, I was the one apologizing, but he wouldn't stay. He wouldn't let me take him to the hospital to get checked out or anything."

I sit on the floor across from Nico, not sure what I'm feeling. I thought I knew what happened to Bram, but it seems like the more I find out, the deeper the rabbit hole goes.

"I found out he was dead the next day. And look, I know you guys dated for forever, but you hadn't talked to him in months," he said. "He's been into a lot of different drugs for a while. Recreational *and* prescription stuff. He was pretty depressed," Nico says, and smiles sadistically at his feet. "It was why we got along so well."

I realize Nico and I . . . We're the same. We got hurt by Bram, so we did something to hurt him back: Nico with the video. Me with my last words.

I'm not expecting him to say anything else, but Nico speaks up again a minute later.

"We were only hooking up for a month, but I think I was starting to love him."

"You weren't the only one he had that effect on."

I get up and grab the whiskey bottle. It travels from my hands to his and back again, as if we're preschoolers sharing blocks. We don't have Bram, and we can't have his forgiveness, but at least, right now, we have each other. The same dark regret is hanging over both of us; a storm cloud we can't outrun. So, to lighten the mood, I say, "This is going to sound random as hell. But have you ever thought about joining a band?"

When I get to Gertrude's office, I say, "Trudy, you're not going to believe this shit."

I start with the trip to Ms. Lassiter's on her birthday. I tell her I've been tracking down the truth about how Bram had changed and what really happened the night he died. I mention making friends with Yara and reconnecting with Nico. But I still don't tell her what I said to him the day we broke up. She might think I'm a fuck-up; an angry, grief-stricken kid. But she doesn't know I'm a straight-up asshole who wished for someone's death. I'm not ready for Gertrude to see me the way I already see myself.

I thought she'd be into my story—especially the parts where we danced at Ms. Lassiter's and when I confirm that I've been trying to cut back on my drinking—but even though she nods as I talk, and writes in her little notebook, something about her seems uncomfortable.

"I'm glad you spoke to Ms. Lassiter again. And I'm glad you're reaching out to some of your old friends. It's great that you and Yara have made a connection, and it's honestly not something I was expecting when you wouldn't even say her name during our first session. But, Logan . . . you haven't exactly been doing the work we talked about," Gertrude says. "You know that, right?"

I look at her. Then I look out the window. *What the hell does she want from me?*

"I'm talking to all these people I never wanted to talk to," I say to her, and she nods, agreeing with me. "People who were close to Bram, like you said."

"But I wonder if you're talking to them for the right reasons. What was your intent when you went to Ms. Lassiter's for her birthday? Were you there to try to be open with someone who was close to Bram, or were you . . . I don't know, investigating? Were you using your head or your heart?"

So maybe she does already know that I'm an asshole. I don't answer her questions, so she tries a different angle.

"It sounds like Bram and his mom were both having a really hard time," she says.

I shrug, and Gertrude shifts in her seat.

"And what about your boyfriend? I don't think you ever told me his name."

I had been staring at my shoes, but I look up at that. She's talking about Aden.

"He's not my boyfriend," I say.

"Oh. I'm so sorry. I thought you hung out with him all the time and that you were starting a band together?" She flips back in her notebook. "From the way you spoke about him, it seemed like you two were . . . close."

"Well, yeah," I say. "I guess. But he's not my boyfriend."

"Okay, my mistake. So, have you spoken to him about how you're feeling? About what you've been going through the past few weeks?"

"You want me to tell a guy I met a month ago that my ex-boyfriend is dead and that I'm all fucked up about it?"

Gertrude looks at me for a beat too long.

"Is he your friend?"

I shrug again. "I guess."

"Is there a reason why you don't want to be honest with him?"

"Secrets are safer," I say.

Gertrude takes her glasses off, like by having blurrier vision, she can see the real me more clearly.

"You seem to have some guilt over Bram's death. And I don't know exactly why that is. Maybe you don't either. But I think reaching out—speaking to other people who loved him, as you've been doing a bit, but also speaking to people who love *you*—can only help you process this loss. You're allowed to be upset."

I must shake my head because Gertrude says, "*Yes,* you are. Give yourself the space to feel whatever you need to feel."

I don't say anything else to Gertrude, but I'm a little worried. I may have become too used to the pain to feel it.

18

SHAY

BAMF // SASHA'S SENSES REVIEW . . .
SWEET SUITE SUIT

Looks like: The Beatles . . . at a gala? Idk. They're so damn well-dressed.
Smells like: clean laundry
Sounds like: an eargasm
Feels like: a warm towel when you take it fresh from the dryer. If you don't know what that means, I guess you'll have to listen. And if you do know what that means, you'll be *dying* to listen.

4/5

"My name is Shay," I say. "And my sister, her name was Sasha."

Dante is sitting right beside me. We're in a rec-center community room, and we're surrounded by much older strangers. Turns out most twinless twins are older than sixteen. But everyone's been really nice to me so far.

When I first asked Dante to come to this support group with me, I thought for sure he'd say no. But when I called him after we'd been texting about sisters and what it was like to lose one, he said, "I punched my sister's ex-boyfriend in the face, just because he was talking to Autumn. So it might be good for me too."

"This is my first time," I say, "so I'll keep it kind of short."

There's a woman with curly black hair, a guy with watery brown eyes, Dante, and twelve other strangers who have lost their twins.

"My sister, Sasha . . . She died in November of last year from leukemia. She'd had it since we were ten, and . . . even though I'd known she could die from it for five years, I've been having a tough time. Panic attacks and stuff like that. So my friends wanted me to talk about it—about her—with them. And I did, a little. But then my mom . . . she told me about this."

I look around at them all. I look down at Dante.

"This is my friend. He lost his sister really recently, and talking to him made me feel a lot better because I felt like he understood even more than my other friends. So I guess I thought coming here would be a good next step."

The chairs were arranged in a circle, so I can see everyone at once. And they're all nodding and smiling. Some of them have tears in their eyes, but there's something I feel from being in this room—a kind of gut understanding. Losing a twin is like losing a leg—you forget how to stand on your own because you never needed to. Everyone in this room is missing a piece of themselves in the same unbearable, unexplainable way that I am.

When some of the others stand to tell their stories and talk about their twins, they all say versions of that—the impossible loss I've been trying my hardest not to feel—like half of them is gone, like no one gets it, like their friends and family can't stand to see them because they look so much like the person who died.

We cry when the curly-haired lady talks about her sister having a heart attack out of nowhere, and how she's now on medication for anxiety because she's constantly terrified she's going to have one and die too. We cry when the tall guy with watery brown eyes tells us how his brother was stabbed in a bar fight and how the guy who stabbed him was just released from jail early.

I don't expect Dante to say anything, but he stands up near the end of the meeting.

"I'm Dante. I'm not a twin, but my sister looked a lot like me, and we weren't even a year apart. Irish twins, some of our older relatives called us. I know it's not the same, but . . ."

We all nod. We all get it. There's no way to measure grief; to know if mine is bigger than his. Dante probably spent way more time with Tavia than I spent with Sasha, just because she was sick for so long. I cry hardest when Dante says that he had been planning to drive Tavia to the party, but that he changed his mind to hang out with a girl and how that choice haunts him.

We tell him it isn't his fault; it isn't anyone's fault.

I bump his shoulder when he sits back down, and he almost smiles. But there are tears in his eyes too.

"The universe is unpredictable," the guy leading the group says right before we leave. He makes a globe with his hands, by touching his fingertips together.

"As much as we might think that our twins' fates reveal something about our own, the world is too random for things to be that simple. And as much as we want to think we're at fault or that we're in control, we aren't."

When we walk out of the rec center, the Band Wagon is parked right by the door; Rohan promised to pick me up. Dante and I walk over to the van together.

Rohan rolls down his window and sticks his hand out to greet Dante.

"It was really cool of you to go with her," he says. They do a boy-hug through the window; clasped hands, hard pats on the back.

Dante shrugs. "I'll do anything to get out of my house, so I'm glad she invited me." He points to the side of the van. "Still, huh?" he asks, and the name of their band almost glows in the darkness.

Ro nods and kind of laughs. "My current band is so pissed that I won't paint over it."

"You never told me that," I say.

"Oh, yeah," he says. "Pooja's been threatening to leave Our Numbered Days if I don't paint over it by the summer."

After what happened at Battle of the Bands, Rohan, Dante, and Logan started fighting constantly. The grand prize from the competition was studio time and the possibility of recording a full-length album. So I called everyone I knew to try to get them into a studio, hoping it would save them. But even once I secured them a few free studio hours and a few more at a discount, they couldn't get along enough to record.

Then Sasha started getting sicker, and Rohan went a little AWOL from the band because he refused to leave her side. Dante stopped caring since Rohan wasn't around, and Logan hadn't written anything new in a while. They never recovered, and I wonder if he keeps the band name there to hold on to what they might have been.

Dante turns and looks back at the building. "It was weird," he says, "just imagining doubles of all those people. But it was good. Let me know the next time you want to go."

On the drive home, I tell Rohan about the group, and then, once I'm home, I tell Mom, who's already at the table with take-out when I arrive.

"You were right," I say. "It helped."

The next day, I call the first BAMF staff meeting in months. Deedee shows up with chips, soda, candy, and ice cream. Callie comes with a list of all the BAMF things she's been wanting to talk to me about, and a content calendar.

"The archive link is broken," Callie says. She makes a check mark on her list of concerns.

"I think that's something that we need to fix ASAP because we get tons of traffic through people hearing about a band and then coming to search the archive."

"That makes sense," I say. I write "archive link" down in my notebook and bite into a gummy worm. It stretches out and bounces back up to my lips as I turn back to Callie.

"What's next?"

"You haven't uploaded any of the pictures from the Sunscream show yet," Callie says.

"I was going to do it," Deedee pipes up. "But I know there's a format you like, and I didn't want it to look weird next to the other posts."

"It's okay," I say. "I've been slacking. I know I have, but that's the point of this meeting, right? To get back on schedule with everything." I write down "upload sunscream photos" and "teach Deedee how to format photos."

"What else?"

Callie and Deedee look at each other. Deedee gets a little misty-eyed.

"Album reviews," they both say.

"We can discontinue them," Deedee offers right away.

"But I don't think that would be smart," Callie says. "From a business standpoint. I mean . . . People quote Sasha's reviews. And I know you've been reposting them when it made sense to, and that she had a bunch we hadn't posted yet, but we're going to need new content really soon. Sasha didn't review every band in the world. And, like, I know Our Numbered Days doesn't have an album yet, but they have a ton of listens on the songs they have available to stream. Don't you think we should have something posted about them besides that one photo?"

Deedee nods. "It's Ro," she says, like I don't know that already.

I bite the insides of my cheeks. They're right, but I'm not ready to recruit some new random person to do this. Whoever follows in Sasha's footsteps has to love music as much as she did. And they have to have a voice that fits the tone of BAMF.

"Let me think about that one, okay?"

Callie starts to say something else, but Deedee noisily opens a bag of chips and asks if either of us want any.

They hang out for a while after we finish the official BAMF business. I put on an episode of *Intervention* to play in the background while Deedee tells us about Olive.

I fix the archive link. I post a couple of photos of Olive, because she's mostly who Deedee took photos of during Sunscream's performance. I look through all of Sasha's most recent reviews, and when I think about her not ever writing another one, the panic bubbles up in me again. I look at my friends, who are riveted by the actual intervention part of the show and not paying much attention to me, and I try to control my breathing by myself. I think about Mom placing my hand on her throat, where I could feel the air moving in and out of her, and I place my hand on my own chest.

Instead of running out of the room, I stay in my seat. I breathe slowly, thinking about Jerome next. There's something comforting about his soft voice; his too-big sweaters and shiny gold rings. I think I do want more with him. Maybe.

I focus on all the other people I love; on all the beauty that remains. I'm grateful that I still have so much left, even though Sasha's gone. Thoughts of loud, beautiful music; banana splits; Mom and Rohan; and Callie and Deedee help me fight my way back to calm. It doesn't work completely, but it also isn't totally useless. My breathing evens out. The hot, bad butterflies go away. I touch my Sasha tattoo until I feel brave enough to pick up my phone.

I text Jerome, Can we meet after school on Monday?

He texts back, Yep.

I text him again. No kissing! Just talking.

When he doesn't answer right away, I get a little nervous. But then the bubbles that tell me that he's typing pop up, and all I can do is wait. They appear and disappear, and he doesn't text back, and I start freaking out.

"I told Jerome I wanted to talk and not kiss, and he's not texting me back," I say kind of frantically to Callie and Deedee.

Callie rolls her eyes, but Deedee reaches for my phone and reads our exchange. She looks like she's thinking for a second, but then she grins.

"He just texted," she says. She hands the phone back to me.

Cool.

19

AUTUMN

FEB. 1, 1:25 P.M.

I wish you had shown me how to do fishtail braids.
You did teach me how to do a handstand, and every
time I flip my body over, blood rushes to my head along
with images of how we balanced on opposite walls
and laughed until our faces turned purple.

*Tavia may not be on Hangouts right now. She'll see your
messages later.*

From: HeCalledItAutumn@gmail.com
To: TaviaViolet@gmail.com
Sent: Feb. 2, 7:23 a.m.
Subject: <none>

Lately, it takes almost an hour for me to get home from
school because I can't drive past the overpass where
it happened. Someone posted a picture of the street
a few days ago, so I know that the shattered glass is
gone, but they haven't repaired the guardrail yet.
I also know that the street is littered with teddy bears
and balloons, flowers and letters, photographs and
candles. And I'm not ready for that either. Even thinking
about it makes it hard for me to see straight.

It also doesn't help that I kind of lose it every time I
have to get on any kind of highway—or any street,
really—with more than two lanes. I have to pull over or
call Willow or type out a desperate message to you to
calm down enough to start driving again because
I feel so out of control.

So I take the long way home because it helps me to
stay calm. I put on some good music, and I just settle in,
taking back roads that zigzag through the town next
to ours, making almost a complete circle, stretching the
trip from ten minutes to almost fifty. I realize this isn't
normal. But nothing has felt normal for a while.

When I get home at my new normal time today, a cop cruiser is
in my driveway, and Dante's pacing in front of his car, yanking
at his hair.

My heart stops when I see him and the cops. I run toward

Dante instead of the house, certain something else horrible has befallen someone I love, and afraid to face whatever truth might be inside alone.

"What happened?" I shout before I even reach his car, my hands already shaking. I'm thinking of Willow, who always takes the kinds of chances I won't; of my mom, who drives more than an hour to work every day; of my dad, who got off early today and should be home by now, but I don't see his car. I can't stop thinking that someone else might be dead.

But when Dante sees me sprinting toward him, he doesn't answer. He kicks his front tire and won't look at me. He leans his head against the roof of his car and starts cursing under his breath. At first I think that he doesn't want to have to tell me some new, awful truth.

So I take a deep breath and start to walk past him up the driveway toward the house. He reaches out and takes my hand, though. He pulls me to him, but still, he stays silent.

"God, Dante," I say. "What is it? Just tell me. I can take it."

But he doesn't say anything. He stares at me. And when I say he stares, I mean he looks at my face, then his eyes travel down to my elbows and my forearms and my wrists, my thighs and my knees and my ankles.

His eyes change, onyx melting into molasses, and he touches my shoulders and hair and face with the tips of his fingers, like he's making sure all of me is there.

"I thought . . . We thought . . ."

He takes a breath without looking away from my eyes. He steadies himself and starts again.

"You left school so long ago. I saw you leave. Your dad called me when you didn't answer your phone. And I told him when you left. We . . . couldn't figure out why you weren't back, and you weren't picking up our calls or answering any of my texts."

And then I understood.

I haven't told anyone except Willow about my new route home, and with her back at school, no one else had any idea. Not even Dante.

My parents couldn't tell themselves that I was fine—those buttons inside their brains are broken now because of what happened to you. The nightmare has already come true once, so they know the worst-case scenario can turn out to be real. Your death gave us all an unshakable faith in that, if nothing else.

Dante swallows slowly as I pull out my dead cell phone.

"The battery died," I tell him.

He shakes his head. "Dammit, Autumn."

He doesn't hug me. But something about his face makes me feel like he has. Then he blinks once and holds his eyes closed for a little too long, like he's making a hard decision.

He leans forward and puts his hand on my cheek. We've touched so much since you left us, but never like that. I stiffen because I'm surprised, not because I don't like it.

He asks me if it's okay, for him to touch me like this; for him to touch me the way he had started to the night you died.

Slowly, I nod.

"I hope this is, too," he whispers, and squints his eyes, like I'm the sun.

He only kisses me, but it feels like something else is happening. I'm instantly more grounded and less broken. At once, I feel less empty and more real.

It's only a kiss, but somehow it makes me newly aware of every part of my whole body. Dante's kiss makes me realize, without a doubt, that I'm alive.

But noticing so suddenly the rhythm of my own heartbeat, my own breath—and his—has its consequences. It makes me remember that everything about you has stopped completely, even though everyone you left behind is still going strong.

When he pulls away, he doesn't look sheepish the way every other boy would after a first kiss. He isn't looking down, or grinning, like he's nervous. He doesn't kiss me again. He just looks pleased; like he had finally confirmed something he'd always known was right. His eyebrows are even, and he's standing so still. He almost looks . . . proud.

I start crying then, blinking too fast and shaking my head.

"I can't drive by where it happened. I have to go all the way around. I should have told you," I say. "I should have charged my phone."

He just nods.

I wipe my face with my jacket sleeve and let out an unnatural laugh. "I'm so sorry," I say, and I can tell he knows I mean I'm sorry for everything: our fight in the yard, the scene at the beach, today.

He chews his bottom lip and nods again, but he looks at me, like he can't believe I'm real. I kind of can't believe he is, either. I go up on my tiptoes, grab the back of his neck, and kiss him again, because whatever is happening between us feels like the only thing I'm sure of.

My dad must have looked through the window because a minute later, he runs from the house. He grabs me roughly and pulls me to him. He starts to yell at me, and you know my dad almost never yells, but then I think he sees my chin trembling.

"I thought you were with him, not answering your phone on purpose." He shoots a look over my head at Dante. "I almost had a brawl with him, right here in the driveway," he whispers into my ear.

We all start up toward the house together. My dad's arm is draped around me, but I reach out for Dante without looking back at him. He grabs my hand, squeezes, and doesn't let go.

Once my dad calms down and sends the cops away, I call my mom to let her know I made it home too. Then I walk Dante back out to his car. We kiss again, slower this time. Less like our lives depend on it and more like it's a choice we're making together.

When I pull away and look up at him, his black eyes are filled with tears and all the words I know he won't say. He tucks a thin strand of hair behind my ear with his still-bruised fingers before he gets into his car and drives away.

Inside, I finish up the sketch I'd started of him. I can see him so clearly that I don't need him here to know the shape of his dark eyes, the slope of his long nose.

Then I close my eyes tightly for a long minute, open them, and start a portrait of you.

20

LOGAN

BRAM IS BORED so he tries to knit a blanket.

3,810 views | 7 months ago

"I'm a genius," I say as I walk into the basement of Aden's dorm. Aden texted and said we could practice down here and that no one would mind. When we walk in, he looks up from where he's sitting tuning his guitar, and grins.

Nico is right behind me, and this is the first time all three of us have been in a room together, though we've been texting all week. Nico and I came up with the perfect band name on the ride over, but Aden has to sign off on it.

"More like we're both geniuses, wouldn't you say, Logo?" Nico says, and then he extends his hand in Aden's direction. "Hey, I'm Nico."

Aden's grin widens. "Yeah, I kinda figured." He stands up and crosses the room, grabs Nico's hand, and claps him on the back. "Damn good to meet you. Been watching your videos. Your drum skills are sick."

"Thanks, dude!"

"How long have you been—"

"Enough getting to know each other. You guys can make out later if you want to." I realize as I'm saying it that the statement doesn't have as much bite as I planned it to, for one very specific reason. It must hit Nico and Aden at the same time because they both start laughing: our band is made up of three gay guys. I get even more excited than I was a second earlier because, *holy shit,* that's awesome.

"What do you think of calling the band Undying Light?" I say to Aden. I'm a little bit buzzed, but I don't think they can tell. I was just so nervous about us all being together for the first time. We're so good on paper that I'm terrified we're not going to have that magic—whatever magic it is that makes bands work—and I fucking need us to. I need it like air. So I just had a little to take the edge off.

"Love it," Aden says, barely even hesitating. "It's perfect."

"Told you," Nico says to me, grinning.

"Fuck yeah," I say. "Let's play some music."

We start by practicing a bunch of covers, classic songs that we, and everyone, knows. I throw out a line or two, and Aden picks it up right away. He starts strumming, and it's like magic— *that* magic—the way my voice mixes with the notes he plays. And then Nico comes in out of nowhere and fills in Aden's melodies with some crazy-complicated rhythms that seem to be made for the songs some of our favorite artists wrote years ago. We sound damn good together.

Next we play some more up-to-date tracks—singles that could be on the radio or MTV right now if we tuned in. These work too, and even when we have to stop for me to figure out what key to sing in or for Aden to grab a clamp or for Nico to decide what rhythm fits best, we still fall back into sync quickly.

I've missed this. Feeling the heady vibration of bass in my chest. And even without the heat of the lights on my face and the ecstasy of a fifty or a hundred strangers screaming words I wrote from memory, I suddenly remember that the stage was the one place where I felt powerful. Once I knew without a doubt that I was gay, I also knew there wouldn't be many places where I could feel like that: like I could do anything.

Bram was right to love that shitty Vonnegut quote. Everything is so fucking beautiful, and absolutely nothing hurts. If you don't let it. And with music coursing through me like the very blood in my veins, I take Gertrude's advice, and I let myself feel it all.

When we're about five songs in, Aden starts strumming out a melody that I recognize right away as an Unraveling Lovely song, and everything in me that was full of light turns stormy. I spin to look at him, and over the music, he shouts, "We're doing tributes to our favorite bands, right?" He's flirting, but now is not the time.

Nico's into it too. He says "Hell yes" and hops onboard, kicking it up a notch with quick snaps from his snare and big booms from his bass drum. And I feel like I'm back in Rohan's garage or worse—back at fucking Battle of the Bands, and Dante is pissed at me for missing his cue and Ro is desperately mouthing back to me the first line of a song I wrote.

Nico and Aden . . . They don't know that this song is about Bram. That almost every song I wrote for the Unraveling Lovely EP is about him. They don't know that I wanted to call this band Undying Light because Bram is like a flame inside my belly that won't go out. They don't know that I pounded three beers before I got into Nico's car and that I chewed gum to cover the boozy smell. So they don't know that these few bars of music are crushing my heart, like it's in a garlic press.

"Cut it out," I say, but they don't hear me because they're playing so loud. I say it again a little louder. "Guys, cut it the fuck out." They keep playing, and I am not okay. I'm the least okay that I've been in a while. I don't want to still feel like this; I thought I was *done* feeling like this. I don't want them playing a song that belongs to me, Rohan, and Dante. That song being played live reminds me too much of all that I've lost. I kick the mike stand, and it slides across the floor. They finally stop playing.

"Jesus, L. What was that about?" Aden is walking over to me, and puts his hand on my shoulder. I'm so pissed, but apparently, I'm gassy, too. Before I can tell him to get the hell away from me I burp, and it tastes just like beer. I know it smells like beer, too. Aden gets a faceful.

"Whoa," he says. He backs away, rights the mike stand, and picks up the mike from where it rolled across the floor. He looks at me, then back at Nico. "We'll be right back," he says.

Aden takes my hand and pulls me away from Nico, toward the door that leads outside. The sky is the perfect ombre shade of twilight blue, but my nails are cobalt like Nico's eyes. The city seems quiet for once, as if it knows I can use a little bit of peace.

"Are you drunk?" Aden asks as soon as the door closes.

"Huh?" I say to him.

"L, it's our first rehearsal," he says. His voice is soft, the way it always is, and he sounds like he's talking to someone he loves. But that someone shouldn't be me. "Why are you messed up? What's going on?"

I don't want to talk about it. I just want to keep jamming out, feeling the music inside me. I want everything to be beautiful. I don't want to deal with what hurts.

"Can we talk about this later?" I ask, and when it comes out of my mouth, I can tell right away that it was the wrong thing to say.

Aden sighs, so hard that I feel the air travel across the space between us and hit my face. His breath still smells like toothpaste, and it makes me want to kiss him. Because I'm an ass, I actually pucker up and try.

Aden backs away from me so fast, he almost trips and falls. He rubs his elbow, which banged into the door we'd just come through, and shakes his head.

"No, Logan. No. I can't just kiss you and pretend like everything is okay. This band . . . it's important to me. When I came to New York for school, I thought it would be easy to find people who took music seriously. But a lot of people who go here are so damn pretentious. When I met you, I was like, *Yes.* Here's a guy who wants what I want. Wants it for real. But you're not making the music your priority. Something is going on. And I think it has something to do with your old band."

I blink. Once, twice, three times. With each blink, I realize something new.

I'm ruining the one potentially good thing in my life by being a total asshole.

I don't deserve another chance, but he's giving me one, right now.

I should probably tell him about Bram.

"I, uh," I say. "I, um . . ."

Aden presses his lips together and opens the door to go back inside. He swings it wide and is about to step through, and in that moment, I feel the weight of what his walking away will mean: no band means no music. But then it hits me that what I'm most afraid of losing in that moment is *him*. Not as a band-mate or even as a guy who I enjoy kissing from time to time. Aden, I realize, is my *friend*. When he turns away, it feels like he's cut me open.

"Aden, wait," I say.

I start crying. And Aden's eyes go wide because I've lied to him so much that he's never seen the way I really feel about anything. Including him.

"I'm sorry, okay? Can you close the door? I'm sorry. I'll talk. I'll tell you everything. Just let me. Please?"

He moves his hand so the door slips shut. He walks back over to me, and we walk toward the street to sit down on the ice-cold curb. He bites his bottom lip. His eyes are so dark, and we're sitting so closely together, that I can see tiny reflections of myself in them.

I swipe my arm across my face, and try to blink away the tears that are left. "You know that kid from my school who died? The one who was all over the news?" And when Aden nods, I take a deep breath and begin.

By the time I get to the part of the story where Nico told me what really happened the day Bram died by suicide, I'm sobbing so hard, I'm hiccupping.

"It's so *hic* messed *hic* up. I'm so *hic* messed *hic-hic* up. And you," I say. I look at him, and I can barely see him because the tears are coming so fast and furious. "You're *hic* always so fucking *hic-hic* nice *hic* to me, even when *hic* I'm being a *hic-hic* dick, and I don't *hic* deserve it."

Aden crosses his arms again. I can't read his expression, and I'm terrified about what will happen next. But he just drags his hands down his face and reaches out for my hands, which are trembling where they're tucked between my thighs.

"Take a few deep breaths," he says softly. "This happens to the kid I babysit, and that's how his mom tells me to calm him down."

I start trying to, but it kind of hurts to breathe. I didn't even know that Aden babysat, which is just more proof of how awful a friend I am.

"That's good," Aden says. He looks down at his shoes, which are brown leather boots with bright red laces.

"Logan. I'm really glad you told me all that. But what I don't get is why you felt like you couldn't tell me in the first place." He looks over at me, and his eyes seem sad. "I thought we were friends."

My head aches, so I hold it in my hands. My eyes hurt, so I close them. My throat feels like I've been screaming for hours. But I still manage to say, "We are."

"I'm sorry you feel . . . responsible for what happened to Bram. And it sucks that he died," Aden says. He pauses for a beat, and when I open my eyes, he's staring at his hands.

"But you're drinking all the time. And even with the amazing rehearsal we just walked away from, I'm worried you don't care about this band, or anything, very much. It's fine that you're still in love with him—"

"What?" I say, standing up. "I'm *not.*"

"Yeah, you are, Logan. I can tell by the way you talk about him." Aden shakes his head and meets my eyes again. "You should see your face right now."

I think about the last few months. How consumed I've been. My life has revolved around Bram's death like the duller planets revolve around the sun. Everything about Bram was like an undeniable force while he was alive. Even now he still has a hold on me like gravity.

I've been trying to stop myself from picturing Bram's eyes, from imagining his smile, from wanting every piece of him. But I can't—I never could—so Aden must be right.

This kind of longing has to be love.

I'm in love with a boy who hasn't been mine to love for half a year. A boy who belonged to his mother and Yara, Nico and no one, all at the same time. A boy who left a gaping hole in my life when he dumped me and who carved an even larger one right through everything when he died.

What the fuck am I supposed to do now?

"I think we should break up," Aden says, and his voice cracks on those very words. "That came out wrong. Not *us.* I mean, we probably *shouldn't* hook up anymore. But what I really mean is the band. I think we're in different places. And I'll be honest—I stuck it out because your voice is amazing. It also helps that you're hot as hell. But being a part of a band is the most important thing to me right now. With people who are as focused and serious about this as I am."

Even though he doesn't say anything else, I can see what he's thinking in his eyes: *In the meantime, maybe you should try to get your shit together.*

It looks like he wants to kiss me, but he doesn't. "Let's tell Nico that Undying Light is no more."

I nod, but when we get back inside, before Aden can say anything, I speak up.

"Why don't you two just look for a new singer?" I say.

Aden looks at me as if he doesn't know who I am. And I'm not sure where the idea came from, but something about it feels right.

"What?" Both he and Nico say this at the same time.

"You heard me. You guys sound good together. Good as hell." I swallow hard, and my eyes start to sting again. I try not to think about how blotchy my face must be.

"I don't want to be responsible for another band falling apart."

Nico nods because he knows I'm the reason Unraveling Lovely broke up. Aden gets this weird, sad look on his face. "Are you sure, Logan?"

He's using my full name, so I can tell he's all business. I hesitate for a second, but then I say, "Don't look so upset. You'll be fine."

"Maybe," he says. "But will you?"

I smile. "I'll survive. I swear."

Aden comes over and hugs me, hard. "I'll miss jamming with you," he says.

"Jesus, Aden. We can still jam," I tell him.

"Stop being so damn adorable," Nico says, and Aden laughs.

I say goodbye to both of them. I tell them I'll definitely be at any shows they play. I wish them good luck.

When I turn to walk away I don't look back, but I can hear when they start talking and laughing, strategizing and comparing notes on who might be able to take my place in a band I started. Before the door closes all the way, I hear them start to play music.

I grab a coffee and then sit on the steps of one of the university buildings to drink it. I watch the cars for a while before I pull out my phone to add Undying Light to the Battle of the Bands website, something I was planning to do anyway as soon as we came up with a name. I go to the band description. I hesitate for a second, and then I cry a little as I type in Aden Brooks as the guitarist and Nico Aronson as the drummer, leaving the line for lead singer blank. It's only now, staring at the page, that I realize Undying Light is another failed band of mine that begins with the letters *U* and *L*. "Motherfucker," I say to myself. The subconscious mind is a bitch.

I upvote them, even though there's no music on the page yet, and I feel cleaner somehow—like the tears washed something away or, at least, like telling Aden about Bram and sacrificing myself so that Undying Light could continue wasn't a mistake.

I check the time on my phone. It's 9:34 p.m. Ironically, as soon as I don't have a band, I'm able to type out a line of lyrics that I don't hate. The familiar swirl of words and music starts to fill me up like sadness, and I finish the song I've been trying to finish for so long. Then I get the urge to write another one.

21

SHAY

BAMF // DEMO REVIEW . . .
OUR NUMBERED DAYS

It would be easy for me to say that Our Numbered Days is awesome. The lead guitarist, Rohan Malik, is one of my best friends. I could call their single "Relatively Speaking" "inspired," and because I've known her for years I could mention that Jo Rollins kills on the drums. I could also praise Pooja Patel, for her work on the bass, because she and I bonded while UL was on tour last summer. And Marc Black on the keyboard takes all of it to the next level. But I won't say any of those things. I'll just say this: all they have is a demo so far, but you can bet your ass they're gonna make waves.

—Shay (Sasha's sister)

I'm not ready to find someone else to write reviews for BAMF, but I'm pretty sure Callie will kill me if we don't stay on the schedule she created and laid out in the content calendar. So I write a review of Our Numbered Days's demo myself.

It's not as good as Sasha's reviews were—she had this great way of distilling a whole album into a few sentences. (*People are lazy,* I hear Sasha say in my head. *They like it short and sweet.*) But it's a start. I read over the review, making sure I don't have any typos, and I post it with a photo of Rohan that Deedee took, since their demo doesn't have any album art.

I go downstairs to Sasha's room, and when I push the door, open, Mom's in there, lying on Sasha's bed. Her sad music is playing. And she's crying, looking straight up at the ceiling.

"Mom?" I say because I've never seen her cry except during sad movies. She turns her head and just opens her arms to me. And it's weird that it doesn't feel weirder when I walk over and fall against her. I can't remember the last time we were close like this.

"I couldn't remember what she smelled like," Mom whispers as one sad song ends and another one starts.

"It's like a mix of flowers and laundry lint," I say, and she laughs.

"Well, yeah. It's kind of impossible to ignore in here."

"Momma?" I say.

"Hmm?"

"I'm sorry for that stuff I said, or I guess, the way I said it. I'm glad you're here now."

She squeezes me tighter to her, and I feel like a little kid. I wish I could stay here in Sasha's bed, in Mom's arms, forever.

"I'm sorry it was true," she says.

She shifts around, and my sleeve slips up a little. She sees the tattoo. I try to yank it back down, but I'm too slow.

"Is that a . . . ?"

Crap. "Don't be mad," I say, sitting up and crossing my arms.

She sighs. "Let me see it, Shay."

We only just got to a good place, and I don't want to ruin it. But I guess being in a truly good place includes being honest.

She puts her hand out, and I sigh and place my wrist in her palm.

"It's a little red," she says. "Are you moisturizing it correctly? Make sure it doesn't get infected." She twists my wrist from side to side. "Is that her handwriting?" she asks. I nod. She bites her lip and nods, too. Then she drops my arm.

I look at her. "That's it?"

She shrugs and then sinks back down into Sasha's bed.

"I mean, don't get me wrong. I'm mad. You should have asked me first, and I don't even think I want to know how a sixteen-year-old got a tattoo without parental permission. But mostly, I'm surprised. I would have guessed you'd be too scared."

She doesn't say it, but I know what she's thinking: Sasha was the gutsy one.

"Maybe needles scare me less because I had to give so much blood to Sasha."

Mom looks at me for too long and then stretches her arms out again.

Once I'm tucked against her, the fabric of her shirt making soft sounds in my ear, I whisper, "It was pretty scary, though."

She chuckles.

We read the words written across Sasha's ceiling to each other, and Mom asks me where each quote is from.

"That one's definitely from a song," I say, "and I'm pretty sure that one is completely made up." Mom laughs.

"No, Shay. That's poetry," she says. "*'Do I dare disturb the universe?'* I remember that from college."

"Sasha was so much smarter than me," I say.

"Nah," Mom disagrees. "She just had a lot of time to read."

When she turns on the TV, *Intervention* is on.

"What in the world?" she says.

"No, Momma, I swear. It's so good. This is a really good one—she's addicted to those lollipops pregnant people use to help their morning sickness."

Mom looks at me as if I'm speaking French, but she watches and keeps watching, and when she says, "Oh Lord, this one is about meth? Should you be watching this? I feel like a bad parent. . . ." she pauses. "Maybe just one more."

In my head I hear Sasha say, *See, you guys* do *have something in common!*

My phone vibrates from where it lies between us on the bed, and it makes us both jump. We'd fallen asleep, cuddling, wrapped up together, the way Sasha and I used to. Mom starts laughing while I rub my eyes and pick up my cell. It's a group text with Callie and Deedee.

CALLIE: Your review has so many likes!!!!

SHAY: How many is so many?

DEEDEE: EVERY TIME I REFRESH THERE ARE MORE.

SHAY: Like more than a thousand?

CALLIE: More than 5,000 ;)

SHAY: No way.

DEEDEE: I'M TAKING SCREENSHOTS.

I go to the BAMF blog. And there are 5,381 notes, and more are pouring in. I read over my post. There's nothing exceptional about it. I click through to look at some of the reblogs. But (not) surprisingly, no one is really talking about my review. They're talking about Rohan, Unraveling Lovely, and Sasha.

Hey, it's the guitarist from Unraveling Lovely!

I miss UL.

I miss Sasha's reviews.

His new band is called Our Numbered Days, and his gf died???

OMG, this is SO SAD.

So I guess it was the combination of Rohan's photo and saying I'm Sasha's sister that pushed the review over the edge. I miss UL too.

I tell the girls.

SHAY: Looks like people just fangirling over Rohan.

DEEDEE: And people sad about Sasha . . .

CALLIE: Yeah.

None of us say anything for a while. I read a few more comments and then send another message.

> SHAY: What if we got Unraveling Lovely back together?

> CALLIE: If that were possible, wouldn't you have tried it by now?

> DEEDEE: Not necessarily. How would she have had time to organize a reunion show?

> SHAY: Dee, you're brilliant. An Unraveling Lovely reunion show needs to happen!

> CALLIE: In loving memory of Sasha!

> DEEDEE: OMG. YES.

I think about Dante then, and his sister. To my friends I send, In loving memory of Sasha AND Tavia.

They both send clapping emojis.

I ask Callie to find what nights The 715, our favorite venue, has open in the next couple of months and then tell Deedee to make sure she stays quiet about this so Rohan doesn't find out, because she's horrible at keeping secrets. I want to surprise him as a thank-you. He organized the intervention, and it's changed everything.

I know Rohan will be into the idea, so I just have to win over Dante. Since Logan was the one who ruined everything, I have a feeling he'll like the chance to make amends, but Logan's a real wild card. I message Dante first, since I've spoken to him so much more recently. Dante told me he's always looking for a reason to get out of the house, and the show will be for his sister too, so I hope he'll be into this plan. Logan is a lot scarier than Dante.

Is Ro in? Dante sends minutes after I message him.

He will be, I send back. You know Ro can't stay mad at anyone for very long.

I'm still pretty pissed, Dante sends. But I guess I'm in.

Cool, I send, trying to sound less excited than I actually am.

I think we're done, but a second later, my phone chimes again.

The real question is, will Logan even show up?

He better, I text back. Then I hold my breath and send a message to Logan.

Jerome is wearing his tweed blazer when I find him after school the next day. He's posted up near an empty classroom at the end of the hallway where my locker is. I follow him after he looks at me and steps inside the room.

"Hey," I say. I hug him, but I'm immediately not sure if it's the right thing to do.

"Hey," he says, against my ear. I want to kiss him so badly, but I bite my bottom lip so I won't. I tug on one of his lapels, to put a little space back between us.

"You look like a college professor with this thing on."

Jerome grins and slips the blazer off. He walks to the front of the classroom and drapes it over the teacher's chair.

I sit in one of the desks in the front row.

"So," I say. He levels me with his shiny brown eyes and bats his thick eyelashes, but he doesn't say anything. He's waiting for me to do all the talking.

"I guess I like you," I say. He smiles pretty widely, so I put up my hand. "Wait! I'm not done. I like you, but I don't know you very well. I want to get to know you better," I continue. "And I want you to get to know me, too. When we're kissing, we don't do much talking."

"That's true," he says. He looks a little uncomfortable for a second, and I'm worried he was only in it for the make-out sessions—that he doesn't like me enough to just want to hang out. But then he says, "So you want to be just friends?"

"For now," I say. "But don't say 'just friends.' Friends are really important to me."

He nods. "I get it," he says, and then gets quiet. "I, uh . . . I don't usually say too much."

"Only during interventions, huh?" I ask, smiling.

He grins. "I speak up when it counts," he says.

"I still can't believe you guys Interventioned me."

"But you're better?" he asks in that way of his.

I think of Dante. "I'm working on it."

22

AUTUMN

FEB. 4, 5:39 P.M.

Are you angry that Dante kissed me?

. . .

Because Dante keeps kissing me.

Tavi, I don't know what to do. I keep kissing him, too.

Tavia may not be on Hangouts right now. She'll see your messages later.

From: HeCalledItAutumn@gmail.com
To: TaviaViolet@gmail.com
Sent: Feb. 4, 11:17 p.m.
Subject: <none>

On the way to school, Dante kissed me again. Like we've been dating for months. Like it isn't weird or

the kind of thing that normal people talk about. It's
like yesterday I was your best friend—someone he
wasn't even speaking to. But today I'm his girlfriend,
without ceremony, without the question of us even being
discussed. And oddly enough, I'm mostly okay with
it. But some part of being with him still feels like I'm
betraying you.

As soon as I climb into Dante's car, he kisses me. And afterward,
we smile, but we don't say anything. It's like we've come to an
understanding. Or like we're finally acknowledging that, behind
the veil of our grief for you—our anger about what happened
and how—we've been sinking into something like love, falling
for each other slowly this whole time.

But God. I want to talk to you about it so badly. I want to tell
you how he makes feel, the way I always told you everything else.
I want, more than anything, to know what you'd think.

When he reaches across the space between our seats a minute later and lays his wide palm on my knee, I jump a little. Not
because I don't want him to touch me—because believe me, it
is quite the opposite. But because I'm so deep in thought about
how you'd feel or what you'd think about us that I'd forgotten
where I was. Dante pulls his hand away.

We both say sorry quickly, like we're strangers on a blind
date. Like I didn't hold his head while he cried a week ago, or like
he hadn't carried me across a beach against my will last Saturday.
And then we both say, "What are you sorry about," speaking at
the same time all over again.

We laugh and look out of our windows. Then I think we both feel badly about laughing, so we look at our laps. If he thinks anything like I do, I bet he still feels a little guilty having any kind of fun without you.

"You first," he says.

I sigh because I don't know what to say or where to start. I pull my sleeves over my shaking hands. "I didn't mean to jump; you just surprised me, that's all."

I want to tell him that he can touch me whenever he wants. I want to reach out and put his hand back on my leg.

"It's just that . . . that night—" I say. And I stop. In my mind, the truth has been spinning since I woke up this morning. *I was with you when I should have been with her. I want to kiss you, but something about it feels . . . not wrong. But not right, either.*

He says, "Autumn, I know," as if I said the thought out loud. Then he actually looks a little nervous.

"I feel the same way, but whatever this is . . . with us? It isn't going away."

We're still sitting in my driveway, and if we don't leave soon, we were going to be late for school. The car's running, but instead of shifting into drive, Dante turns the keys the wrong way and kills the engine.

"I'm shit with words" is what he says next. "But you know how things have been. You know probably better than anyone, and I don't want you to think that this"—he moves his hand back and forth in the space between us—"is just some fluke like that fight with Perry. Just something I'm doing because my head is fucked. I like you. I've liked you for a while. I liked you before . . ."

I look up at him, and he's looking at me, like he's never seen me before. The tops of my ears go all hot, and I'm terrified that I'm blushing like an idiot on top of having just jumped out of my skin when he touched me.

He drums his fingers on the steering wheel, and I watch them fly up and down. I still haven't said anything, and I think my silence is getting to him. He lets his hair fall over his eyes and cheekbones, so that when I look back up, I can only see the lower half of his face: a bit of his nose; his square jaw; black stubble; pink lips.

He looks at me again with those molasses eyes, and because I don't know what he's going to say or do next, my heart beats so hard that I can hear it in my ears.

He reaches out again and tucks some of my hair behind my ear, and he leaves his hand there, in that soft place right behind my jaw. But this time, even though I know he can probably feel my racing pulse, I don't move away.

"It feels kind of freakishly right, doesn't it? Us?" He says, "It feels like it should have been this way before now."

I feel myself nodding, and I feel my hands growing as warm as my face, and I feel like I need to kiss him or cry.

"We can take it slow," he says. "I just . . . I don't want to make you do anything you're not ready for. Or anything you don't really want to do."

I bite my bottom lip. "Have we met? I never do anything I don't want to do," I say.

When he grins, I put one of my hands over his and unbuckle my seat belt with the other. I lean across the emergency brake and then kiss him with my eyes screwed shut so tightly that I can't see anything that might make me hesitate, like his cheek-bones, which are insanely high like yours, or the still-bruised skin below his eye, or like my house, which is just beyond the window, where my parents could have been watching.

When I pull away, I keep my hands and eyes busy with my seat belt and then, once Dante starts the car again, with the radio. I can barely look at him because I can't believe any of what's happening.

You know that I've only ever kissed two other boys, but I've never felt what I feel when I kiss Dante.

By the time we pull into the school parking lot, my breathing and heart rate have slowed down to something closer to normal. And when I sneak a glance at Dante, he's watching me already and grinning a real grin. I reach for my bag, and he kisses my cheek, but I turn toward him, hoping he'll kiss my lips instead.

I zip up my puffy jacket and try not to catch my reflection in his side-view mirror. Even now I don't know what he sees.

I've never felt very pretty. Next to your strong Latin features—your bronze skin, your wide brown eyes, your plump lips and wild hair—everything about me seemed too subtle. I was always beside you, so I got used to it. And I was all right with fading into the background; with letting you have the spotlight because more often than not, you shared it with me. But when your brother looks at me, with the same skin and eyes and lips as you, part of me wants to be beautiful. I want to be curvier and brighter and lovelier in any way I can.

But at the same time, the other part of me—the part that's looking back at him? That part feels like what I look like doesn't even matter because, for whatever reason, Dante sees *me.*

I'd like to say that when he looks at me I feel like the prettiest girl in the world, but something about him makes it so much more than that. When Dante looks at me, I feel like the brightest star in the sky. And I don't know what to do with a feeling like that.

"Will I see you at lunch?" I ask him, even though I don't want to wait that long.

"I'll meet you at your locker after first period," he says. I guess he doesn't want to wait either.

I grin. I feel my lips curve up, and I can't believe I'm smiling.

"She smiles," Dante says. And he touches my hair before he walks away.

I guess I do, I think. But then I want to tell you what's just happened and remember that I can't. I stop smiling and start talking myself out of crying.

I text Alexa to tell her about the kiss, and she texts right back and says everything I want to hear: a few "OMGs," that Dante is "soooo hot," that you would have been so happy for us. But I still stay in the parking lot until it's empty. I type out a message to you.

Then I walk to first period, the soundtrack to our last summer together playing in my ears, and I try not to miss you. I sit next to Faye, and I pass her a note about the kiss and try not to wish I were pressing the folded secret into your palm instead. I try not to count the minutes until I can see Dante again.

When I turn the corner after my first class, Dante's waiting for me, like he said he would be, smiling.

That's when he asks if I want to go to Winnie's after school.

I say yes, thinking it will be just like every other time we've been there.

But it isn't. I don't realize until we're three blocks away from school that his car smells a little different. I sniff the air, then lean over and sniff him.

"Why are you wearing cologne?"

He kind of blushes. Tavia, *your brother blushed*. Then he says, "I borrowed some, since this is our, um, first date."

I look down at myself. I'm wearing a bright purple Alice in Wonderland hoodie with the creepy, grinning Cheshire Cat on the front, and he's wearing an adorable, baby blue polo and *cologne*.

He looks at me and smiles a little. He says, "I want to take you to this show after, if that's okay."

"Can I think about it?" I ask him. Going to shows still feels like something that belongs to you and me alone.

"Sure," he says.

At the diner, I feel awful. I keep patting my unwashed hair, and I pick at my food but can't really eat it. I keep thinking that if you were here, you would have known that he was asking me out. You would have warned me, and maybe I would have told him that usually, you give girls more of a heads-up about this kind of thing. Then you would have helped me pick out a cute shirt to wear, and I might have even let you put makeup on my eyes.

I excuse myself from the table, go into the bathroom, and call Willow. She picks up on the first ring, and at the sound of her voice, I unexpectedly feel like I want to cry.

"Hey," she says. There's noise in the background, so I wonder what she's doing. College seems so far away to me right now, like it's some country on the other side of the world that I can't be really sure of.

"Hi," I say, and there must be something pathetic in my voice, in that one word, that gives me away. I hear her telling people that she'll be right back, a door closing, and then, suddenly, her side of the phone is as quiet as mine.

"What's wrong? Are you okay?"

I stare at myself in the mirror, unsure of where to start.

I feel like a terrible sister because of the way I'm always calling and texting her now. We talked a few times a week before, but I never called her this much when I had you. I don't think she thinks about my calls like that, like she's my substitute best friend. But I do.

"Um, yeah. I'm fine," I tell her. "It's just that I'm on a date with Dante and—"

She doesn't let me finish before she says, "Wow, he's not wasting any time, huh?"

I don't know what I was expecting her to say, but it wasn't that.

I try not to sound offended when I ask, "What does *that* mean?"

"I'm just worried, dude. Seems like things are moving kinda quickly. I mean, you weren't even speaking to him the last time I was in town. Plus, you both just experienced a pretty major trauma."

She sighs when I don't say anything.

"Don't you think you should ease into things, just to be safe?

Just to make sure what you're feeling is real?" But she doesn't know that Dante and I were flirting with the idea of us before you even died. She doesn't know that while you were at the last party you'd ever go to, I was holding your brother's hand in his dim bedroom moments away from doing more.

She doesn't know, and since I can't tell you first, I don't want to tell her at all.

I want to get angry with her. I even feel the heat start to creep up the back of my neck, the way it always does when I get upset. I want to tell her that I trust my heart, that I know my own feelings, that I'm not some lovesick little kid. That even though she's a psych major she doesn't actually know anything.

But then I think about how fast this has all been happening. That I didn't even know this was a date. I start to think my big sister might have a point. So I stay quiet.

I wonder what you would have said.

"I've been meaning to ask you about something," Willow says, changing the subject. I lean against the sink and wait for her to keep talking. I'm slightly worried that Dante will think I left the restaurant, but I want to hear her out.

"I'm going to travel this summer," she says. "I'm going to Europe: London, Paris, and maybe Brussels and Amsterdam. Ten weeks altogether. I think you should come with me."

"Really?" I ask.

"Mm-hmm," she answers. "It could be good to get away, don't you think?"

I'm not sure. Right now, I like being surrounded by your things and your family. I like your brother, a lot. And since I don't have you anymore, I can't imagine going somewhere where I wouldn't be able to see your room or your clothes or your parents if I wanted to.

"I'll think about it," I tell her. But mostly, I'm thinking about Dante. It's only been a few hours of us being this new thing. But being away from him doesn't really seem like something I'd want . . . ever.

"But what do I do now?" I plead. "We're at a diner, and he has on a polo and I have on a freaking hoodie."

Willow laughs. "Autumn, I know you're, like, really into him and everything, but it's still just Dante."

Oddly enough, her saying that actually helps.

When I get back to the table, Dante's almost done with his burger. And with Willow's words floating through my mind—*it's still just Dante*—I look at him and see someone else entirely. I still see the gorgeous boy who I've dreamed of kissing for months, but I also see the goofball who threw water balloons at us when we were ten. I see his dark, dreamy eyes, but the awkward twelve-year-old whose feet grew to a size eleven before the rest of his body caught up is also there. I see the sexy drummer from Unraveling Lovely shows last summer, but I can't ignore the sweet-faced, tough kid—who chased away anyone who made fun of me in middle school—peeking out at me too.

"Hey," I say to him. "Sorry." I sit on his side of the booth, because, yeah, I'm wearing a hoodie, but this is Dante. Our Dante. Maybe even *my* Dante. He likes me, and I need to trust that.

He takes my purple hood and pulls it over my head, and I start laughing because I feel so ridiculous.

I look down at my sweatshirt. At the creepy cat smiling back up at me. When I look back up at Dante he says, "I like your shirt."

"Cheshire Grins would be a pretty good name for a band," I say to him.

He smirks. "If I ever join another one, I'll tell them my girl has the perfect name already picked out."

I try not to float away from the table because he called me his girl, but I am a balloon full of air barely tethered by a too-thin string. I grab my plate, dump ketchup on the edge of it, and take a huge bite of my burger while Dante grins and watches me.

I tell him I'll pass on the show. That if he wants to go, he can go without me. But he shakes his head. "I'd rather hang out with you," he says.

We go to my house instead of yours and watch a movie in the basement. We throw kettle corn into each other's mouths, and we steal sweet, salty kisses that make my heart work like it never has before. By the time he goes home, my cheeks are sore from smiling.

If I could call you right now, I'd only want you to answer one question:

"Does dating always feel like flying?"

23

LOGAN

BRAM IS BORED so he shaves his head.

Yara's house is dark when I turn on to her block the night of the vigil. And as I approach her door I think I've made a mistake coming here tonight. I'm cool with Yara and Paige, but I don't know these other kids, and I'm sure some of the jerky jocks I hate will be inside. But as I get closer I hear music.

My music. Unraveling Lovely is blaring through speakers that I can't see, and it's loud as hell. My voice is filling the dark air like thunder during a storm. I frown for a second, wondering if I'm gonna be the butt of some popular douchebag's joke. But Yara's expecting me, so I knock anyway. A bridge and half of the chorus plays while I wait. And I can't help it—I start singing along. I'm belting out the longest, loudest note ever when Yara opens the door. She's grinning like a little kid.

"You're late," she says in a flirty voice that tells me she's definitely under the influence of something. I immediately want some of whatever it is she's had, and that's when I realize I haven't had any alcohol since Undying Light's first rehearsal last weekend.

"I like to make an entrance," I say, and she laughs. I want to drink, but I know I shouldn't. So instead of asking where the booze is, I say, "You're playing my song."

Yara nods without saying a word, reaches through the door, and pulls me inside by the hand.

"Logan's here!" Yara shouts as she turns and starts down a short hallway. She keeps hold of my hand, like I'll get lost if she doesn't. I keep my head down, part of me wondering what the hell I was thinking coming here tonight. Part of me drinking in the music that I still can't believe is floating through the house.

All the lights are off, and candles are everywhere. They glow from the tops of bookshelves and mantels, and there are a shit ton in the center of her dining room table. I look around and notice guys from the football team sitting in one corner, away from all the candles. Their faces are the brightest things in the room, lit up by the screens of their phones. They nod at me as I pass instead of calling me a freak. It's kind of nice.

I see some of the other cheerleaders—pretty, bitchy girls I kinda remember being friends with in middle school, when we were all in the drama and glee club together, when people cared less about having the right kinds of friends. I see a few other kids who I wasn't really expecting to be here: Bram's nerdy tutor, a guy from the debate team, Nico.

"Wait, Nico's here?" I ask. Yara barely glances at him.

"Yeah," she says. "I know, I know. I should hate him, right?"

"Um, yeah," I say, not sure how much of the story she knows. But any one piece of it—the drugs, the sex tape, the night Bram died—should be more than enough.

"Bram is the one who decided to take pills or whatever. I can't hate Nico for a choice Bram made."

I don't think "everyone" knows Nico is the guy from the sex tape like he said. And of course the only two friends I have in school would be two people who have every reason to hate each other—two people whose secrets I know and have to keep.

Surrounded by all these candles and all these people, I feel a little like it's the end of the world, and by some fucked-up twist of fate, we're the only ones left.

"I think you know everyone, right?" Yara asks as she leads the way through the flickering rooms and into the kitchen.

"Mostly," I say. I squeeze Nico's shoulder as I walk by him. I'm about to ask her what the plan for the rest of the night is, but I get distracted. Because as soon as I open my mouth, a new song starts to play. It's called "Unknown." It's another one of mine.

It's cold in the kitchen because there's a window open. I'm guessing that's why I could hear the music from outside. We stop in front of the fridge, and Yara finally releases my hand as she flings the door open. The hard rims of the dozen or so beer cans that line the door ping against each other.

I point into the air because it's the closest I can get to pointing to the music. I actually say "no thank you" to a beer when she tries to push one into my other hand.

"Why are you playing UL?" I ask her. Something like nervousness is fluttering against my chest while I wait for her to answer.

She keeps the beer for herself, and instead of opening it she grabs a knife from the dish rack next to the sink and jabs it into the side of the can. It sprays across the front of her shirt a little, and she laughs.

She puts the hole to her lips, pops the top, and I watch as dainty Yara, in her fucking pink Uggs and miniskirt, shotguns the whole twelve ounces in less than a minute.

She burps. Loud as hell.

I would never admit it out loud, but Yara's a little badass.

"You didn't know?" she says. "Bram was your biggest fan."

She walks out of the kitchen without saying anything else, and I open the fridge again and pull out a Coke. It's not cherry, but it'll do. I hop up onto the granite counter, which is ice cold with the window open, but I don't mind.

Bram liked my music.

It shouldn't be a surprise. He loved the stuff I wrote while we were together. But it's different to hear that he listened to it, even after I broke his fucking nose.

I sip my soda and let the lyrics swell inside me, and I feel like a cracked vase that's just been filled with expensive roses: broken but beautiful. When I finish my drink, I reach into the fridge, grab another one, and head back to the family room, where everyone else is sitting, feeling like a goddamned rock star.

"Remember that time he jumped off the roof of the rec center and into the pool?" Kole Roberts is saying as I walk in. I guess this is the storytelling part of the evening. A bunch of the other guys, mostly from the football team, laugh. Yara snorts.

"He got banned for that, you know," she says, and everyone laughs louder. "Not just from that pool, but from, like, every public pool in the city."

"Oh! But what about when he put on that fake British accent to get out of speeding tickets?" a girl with blond hair, whose name I can't remember, asks.

"How many times did he use that?" somebody else says, but I can't see who.

"Pretty much every time he got stopped," Dexter Lee, another guy from the team, answers.

I smile and look down at my can of Coke. I'd heard Bram's accent. It was damn good.

I stay quiet while a few other people talk about funny or crazy or awesome things Bram had done or said. They talk about his stupid videos and how they can't believe how many views he'd started to get. They talk about the time he shaved his head, just because he wanted to see the shape of his skull. The team talks about great plays he'd made in games, and the girls talk about how hot and sweet he was. And even though I remember the Bram they're talking about, they aren't remembering all of him. Maybe I've been trying to forget the dark parts of him too, or maybe, like them, I just didn't want to admit that the bad side of Bram existed now that he's gone.

"Sometimes Bram could be an ass," I say, thinking about how he'd flip out at me for dumb things—forgetting to return a DVD to him, not texting him back quickly enough. Or the way he'd act like I was his bitch sometimes in front of his friends. He never let them say shit about me, but sometimes, he'd do it for them. The whole room goes silent, the way it did when we were all kids and someone used a curse word for the first time, but it feels worth it—to make sure we remember him as he was, not just as we wanted him to be.

Everyone is staring at me, but then Yara grins lazily.

"Yeah. But he was only like that to the dumbasses like us, who actually loved him."

And I can't help it. My eyes find Nico's.

Yara's eyes go glassy, even as she keeps the smile on her face, and she's looking at me as if I'm the only person here who understands her. And it should be a nice moment. I should smile at Yara and agree with just my eyes as the music I wrote plays in the background, like we're in a shitty, sentimental TV movie or something. But I look away because, even though we're becoming something like friends, part of me hasn't let it go.

I loved him *first*.

Yara gets up and walks over to me, even though I'm clearly trying to avoid making eye contact with her. She sniffs and then touches my hand in a way that makes me feel younger than I am. Hers are fingers used to touching people; soft and warm and steady. I look down at our hands. I'm almost used to the way hers feel on mine.

"I never really said sorry about the way the whole thing with me and Bram went down," she says. "I didn't know he was, like, *with* you—with anyone—until you guys had already broken up."

I always knew that Yara was a transfer kid—that she met Bram during the summer before our senior year. She wouldn't

267

have known about me unless someone told her. And apparently, no one, not even Bram, did. But it was so much easier to keep her, and everyone else, at arm's length.

If she had said this to me a few weeks ago, I know I would have said "bullshit" and walked away from her, no questions asked. But the lighting or the music—or maybe the way she's been so nice to me every day for no reason at all—have made me feel differently. Her words make something in my belly unknot.

I don't have a smart-ass comeback. I don't know what to say. Bram told me that I would like Yara if I got to know her. And he was so right.

"Thanks," I say, and I'm not exactly about to cry, but all of a sudden it's a lot harder to swallow.

Yara nods and sniffs a few times as she walks back to the table. Paige pats her on the shoulder as Yara passes in front of her. Then Yara picks up one of the candelabras from a shelf.

"Grab your coats," she says. "Time for the main event."

I'd never taken my peacoat off, so I grab a small tea light candle sitting in an old-fashioned copper holder. I stand by the door waiting, looking for Yara in the dark.

Nico walks by. He grabs my hand, and I slap his back, and we nod at each other but don't say anything. I want to ask him about Undying Light—if they found a singer yet, if they've written a song—but this isn't the time or place. Even though I kind of gave him and Aden my blessing to move forward without me, if and when they do, it'll still sting.

I squint and spot Yara at the end of the long line of kids. She's blowing out all the candles that got left behind. Dozens of tiny spirals of smoke spin up into the air behind her, and by the time she reaches the door, the tears that have been pooling in her eyes are falling.

This time, I'm the one who reaches for her hand.

She looks past me at the kids gathering in her small backyard. If we lived anywhere else in the world besides Queens, there would probably be a fire pit or kindling or at least something akin to a bonfire. But Yara just has a charcoal grill set up in the center of the ten by ten square of grass, and with the way everyone is standing around it, they almost look like hobos crowded under a bridge.

Yara kind of dissolves at this point. Two of her friends materialize out of the night and come to where we're standing in the doorway. Each one takes one of Yara's arms, and they walk her over to the grill, but she doesn't let go of me, so I'm kinda dragged along with them.

Standing there, in the center of it all, I feel weirdly closer to everyone, the way you can only feel when a crazy or impossible thing unites you with a group of half strangers. Nico comes over to me.

"I'll tell her, I swear," he says, like he knows the position his secrets put me in. "When she invited me, I knew there was no way she knew about Bram and me. So I'll tell her. Not tonight, though."

I'm surprised nobody else has told her yet, to be honest. But I just nod and put my arm around his shoulder, thinking about how everyone is so much more complicated than we think they are.

Take Bram. His mom was broke. He was dealing drugs. He was *using* drugs. He failed a drug test and lost his scholarships. He dumped Nico the same day he died—but only after Yara dumped him first. I loved him. Maybe I still love him, but I didn't really know who he was anymore. Maybe I always imagined him a little too simply. I made him into who I wanted him to be and ignored the person who was right in front of me.

Someone grabs the lighter fluid and matches that are on the ground beside the grill and lights the wood chips stacked inside. A few minutes later, everyone starts walking up to the fire and dropping pieces of paper into the flames.

Nico hands me a stack of Post-its and a Sharpie, and then he steps closer to the flames, his own Post-its already scribbled on and crumpled in his hand.

"They're memories," a guy from the football team says, explaining what's happening because I'm frowning. "Everyone's writing down their best and worst memories of Bram, and that's what they're throwing in."

"Oh," I say. "Right."

A lot of people are crying, and some are even kissing the papers or looking at the sky before tossing them into the flames. It's a little melodramatic for my taste, but I can get behind the sentiment.

Writing down my memories is the easiest part of the whole night. Watching them burn is the hardest.

> BEST: the first time you kissed me.
> WORST: the day we broke up. The day you died.
> And just about every day in between.

24

SHAY

BAMF // SHAY'S ALBUM REVIEW . . .
FOUND OBJECTS

When I say that this album was transformative, I mean
that I am literally a different person after listening to it.
The haunting lyrics and synth sounds come together for
something that makes me feel like I'm floating through
space and tripping on acid at the same time.
I think Sasha would say, *Sounds like: kinetic energy.*

—Shay (Sasha's sister)

At away meets, I'm used to running with no familiar faces in
the audience. Track meets are boring enough as it is, and when
they're far away, my friends don't come. Most of the onlookers

here are holding signs in black and gray—the colors of the team whose gym we're in. I glance over at the girls warming up on the other side of the track, wondering who my biggest competition will be once we're out and running.

As I approach the starting line, my eyes sweep across the crowd, and there's no one holding a sign with my name, though I do see a few people wearing my school colors: bright blue and green.

A queued post from Sasha arrived just before I started warming up. It was a photo of the two of us doing yoga, because Sasha never really had the lung capacity for running. The caption read *Keep Calm and Carry On*—nothing more. It felt like a message from her, just to me. So as I warm up, I try to breathe a little more deeply—to clear my head of everything: BAMF, Mom, even Jerome, and I just "keep calm."

As six girls line up beside me, I shake my hands and jump up and down. This is my favorite part—the anticipation. The not knowing exactly what's going to happen. The indoor track should be a piece of cake since I've been running and riding my bike out in the cold all winter. So I'm not worried. I'm actually feeling a little cocky. I'll make good time, and I might even place.

We all take our marks, and I look at my shoes. Then I stare straight ahead at the track. When the buzzer sounds, I propel myself forward, and the track unspools in front of me. I become the rhythm of my feet as they hit the floor, the rhythm of my heart as it crashes around in my chest, the rhythm of my own breathing. I have tunnel vision, and nothing can break my focus.

There's only one other girl in front of me as I round the corner to start my last lap. I know I can pass her. But that's when I see a flash of green and blue unfurl in a way that makes me turn my head. I see a pair of brown hands holding up a sign that says YOU CAN DO IT, SHAY!

I grin because Rohan didn't tell me he was coming, and I put my head down and try to run faster. The smile on my face widens as I lean forward, and even though I still finish in a close second, Ro is here, and it makes me feel like I finished first.

I rush toward the sign, panting and laughing. And just before I'm about to say, "Why didn't you tell me you were coming," the person holding the sign lowers it, and it's Mom's round face staring back at me instead of Rohan's.

My smile falls away faster than the drips of sweat sliding down my back, mostly out of surprise.

"What are you doing here?" I ask, and immediately wish I'd said something else.

Mom smiles a small smile and shrugs. "I got out of a meeting earlier than I expected, and this school is actually on the way home, so . . ."

Mom licks her lips and looks back behind her. She picks something up from her seat, and then she's handing me a bouquet of yellow roses. The flowers seem to be exploding from the white paper they're wrapped in, and I don't know what to say or do.

"Great job out there," Mom says awkwardly. "You've gotten faster since I last saw you run."

I nod. I take the flowers and press my nose into them, and the smell reminds me of Sasha. I look back up at Mom, and I want to cry.

"I can't believe you're here," I say, because I can't remember the last time she came to a meet. I reach out to hug her, and the spray of bright petals gets a little crushed between us. A few fall to the floor as I step back, and I think about picking up each one and slipping them into my pockets; drying the whole bouquet the way Sasha used to so I can keep them forever.

"Me neither," Mom says, laughing.

She takes me out for ice cream. We go to my favorite diner, and I order a banana split piled high with every possible topping. Mom gets an apple turnover and a vanilla milk shake.

And it's weird, but we talk. Mom asks me about school and Rohan's band and boys. When I tell her about Jerome, she asks how much I like him, then giggles at how much I grin. When I explain the Unraveling Lovely reunion show I'm trying to organize, she claps. She asks about running and what training in winter has been like, and if I like off-season track and field as much as I love cross-country. She wants to know about the beanie I'm wearing today: a sky-blue one that Sasha knitted herself.

But we don't talk much about Sasha. Just the occasional "She would have ordered this" or "She would have said that." When Mom gets quiet after we finish our desserts, though, she asks if I'm planning to go back to the Twinless Twins Support Group.

"I think so," I say. "Even though most of the people were way older than me, I just felt like they got it, you know? In a way that even my friends, even you, don't."

She nods. She looks nervous then, which is strange because she's normally so confident. She takes out her phone and starts typing something, then pushes it across the table a minute later. The heading reads *There's No Word for Us*. It's a website that lists support groups for parents who have lost a child.

Mom says, "It's weird to think about, but the name of the site is really true. You're a widow or a widower if your spouse died. You're an orphan if you lose your parents. Even you . . . You're—"

"Twinless," I say.

"Right. But I'm not childless, thank God. I have you. So what am I? There's no word for it, and I don't know why, but something about not being able to say 'I'm a *whatever*' makes this harder to talk about. To even think about."

I realize how many times I've had the thought *I'm twinless,* and I totally get what she means. Then I think about my mom for a second. I think about Sasha. I push my spoon into the soupy remains of my banana split.

"You're Sasha-less," I say, and my heart starts thumping in a way that feels dangerous. Mom smiles, but she doesn't look happy.

"Yeah, I am," she says. "We both are." She reaches across the table for my hand. "Will you come with me to the first meeting? There's one next Thursday. And since you've been to one of these already, I figure you could, you know. Show me how it's done."

I swallow hard and push away the ache in my legs that always makes me run away from too-hard conversations; the urge inside me to push people aside. Maybe it's time to be brave. Mom needs me.

"Yeah, of course. We can go to one of mine first, if you want."

She nods again. Mom looks scared but kind of relieved by my suggestion. "Yeah, that sounds perfect. Let's do that."

She raises her hand to get the waitress's attention. And I hear Sasha whispering in my head. But it's not really words this time. It's like I can hear her smiling at us.

25

AUTUMN

FEB. 5, 7:22 A.M.

Lately I've been thinking you'd want me to go on this trip with Willow—to see this stuff because you never got the chance to.

Is that a crazy way to feel?

FEB. 6, 8:37 A.M.

Your birthday is tomorrow, and just knowing that makes me want to rip a hole in the universe. That day shouldn't exist if you don't.

Tavia may not be on Hangouts right now. She'll see your messages later.

From: HeCalledItAutumn@gmail.com
To: TaviaViolet@gmail.com
Sent: Feb. 7, 10:57 p.m.
Subject: <none>

July fourth was your favorite holiday, which makes sense, as extravagant as you were. You liked the explosions. You liked the crazy clothes. You liked that it was a celebration of freedom, even though you weren't very patriotic at all.

So we bought sparklers for your birthday.

On Tavia Eve, as you called it, I'm at your house. Dante and I go out with the sparklers as soon as it's dark enough to use them, and we write your name in the air a hundred times with light. I laugh as we spell out other words that are yours alone, like "Sunchild," something you always called yourself, even though you were born in winter, and "mother of Pearl," something you've been saying all the time since you swore off cursing last year.

After, we go to your room. Your mom is more and more like herself these days, so I don't think the closed-door privacy I've enjoyed with Dante for the last couple of weeks will last much longer. But for now, we still have it, and I'm glad. We decide to stay up until midnight like we've done with you almost every year. Even two years ago, when you had to be up super early the next morning to get ready for your *quinceañera*. Even when you sobbed all night last year because your parents refused to *also* throw you a sweet sixteen.

So it's just the two of us, sitting here casting long shadows, waiting for the alarm I set on my phone to go off. We play cards on your floor and watch a few of your favorite movies, and we drink a few beers that Dante sneaks from the kitchen, even though you loved champagne best. But when there's only a few minutes left, we just kind of sit there looking at each other.

It's 11:47 p.m.

"What do you think she would have wanted?" Dante asks me.

I smile and picture the birthday version of you in my head: wearing a tiara and fancy clothes and makeup, even when we were six. Even that year when you had the flu and you were feverish and sick.

"Probably a sequin-covered dress. Or red glitter-covered shoes. Or a new keyboard," I tell him. "But she would have said, 'I need a gown that looks like the stars' or ' the shoes that Dorothy wore on the yellow brick road' or 'I want to make music,' and she would have made me or you or your parents figure it out."

Dante grins and touches the end of one of the braids I put into my hair. I never did get it cut, so his hand and the end of the braid are hovering near my elbow. After I cried the first time, my hair didn't bother me as much anymore. Plus, this is the last way you ever saw me. I feel like too much is changing. I don't want to change that just yet.

I rub the side of Dante's face. It's getting scruffy because he hasn't shaved in forever. His eyes are still so bright and boyish, but we haven't been kids for a while. I kiss his cheek despite the stubble, and it's rough beneath my lips.

It's 11:51 p.m.

"What do you think she would have wanted to do?" he asks me next. I twist my shaky hands together and squeeze my own fingers.

"Probably go ice-skating to show off," I say. "Or go to karaoke to show off. Or go to a play and reenact the entire thing once it was over because she'd think she could have done the whole production better."

I pause and drum my fingers on his knee. Look up at him.

"Or maybe she would've just watched a movie with us. Eaten some ice cream. Gotten drunk and covered us with kisses. Fallen asleep spread across our laps like a kitten."

Cats grow out of the overly affectionate habit, but you never did.

He nods and nibbles on his bottom lip, and I start to miss you in that sudden way that always makes me lose my breath. I audibly inhale and exhale a few times, and Dante grabs my hand.

It's 11:55 p.m.

A tear slips out of my eye before I can stop it. And when I look up, Dante's crying too. He clears his throat, though. And smiles one of his sad smiles. I press my lips together and nod, even though he hasn't said anything.

"What do you think she would have said about us?" he asks next, scooting closer to me on the bed. We're sitting cross-legged, face-to-face, and he moves forward until our knees are touching.

I have to swallow a few times before I speak so my voice will come out right.

"Probably something funny. Probably something like 'You

guys can never procreate because I'd love that kid more than anyone has ever loved anything.'"

I don't look at him when I say, in a smaller voice, "Or maybe she'd think it was weird."

This is what we don't talk about. It is our biggest fear. Because if you were alive, your brother would never have asked me out without asking you first. And I'd never have fallen for him without your permission. The first time we hung out without you, you died. It haunts us.

We need your blessing, and you can't give it.

So we sit there with wet eyes, and Dante leans in close to kiss me. His lips are soft, and his big hands are warm where they rest on either side of my wet face.

"I don't think she'd think it's weird," he says, stooping his head and looking up at me through his thick fringe of lashes. "We were her favorites."

And being one of your favorites has always been one of the things I liked most about myself. To be loved in a special way by someone like you, who was loved by everyone so much, was the best part of being your best friend.

You could have had anyone you wanted. But you picked me.

My alarm sounds softly, a tinkling piano version of the happy birthday song, and Dante pulls me toward him and then down, until we're lying side by side.

We stare at the ceiling. We hold hands. We stay quiet and listen to the song.

On the fourth or fifth loop, I shut off my phone. I'm weeping, but in the quiet kind of way, even though my insides ache for you at a frequency so shrill, it would be deafening if anyone could hear it. And Dante's crying again too. He's shaking and covering his face with his hand, so I press my shoulder into the vacant space below his lifted arm. I press my wet eyes against his quivering neck.

When we're done crying, it's 12:14 a.m.

Dante brings the yellow cupcake with vanilla icing that I bought earlier into the room from the kitchen and sits on the floor with it. I climb down from the bed and sit across from him as he pushes a tiny violet candle into the frosting. It takes me six tries to light it because my hands are trembling so badly. We blow it out together. Neither of us wants to eat the cake, so we decide to save it until morning.

"Happy birthday, Tavi," I say.

And Dante says, "Wish you were here."

He turns out the lights and then curls around me, right there on the floor of your bedroom, and even though I wasn't planning on sleeping over, it feels like he won't be letting me go anytime soon. I don't want him to. I text my mom and ask her if it's okay for me to stay the night. She calls me, and when I answer, I don't even let her say anything. "It's Tavia's birthday," I whisper. *"Please."*

She sighs, and hesitates, and then she says, "Okay. I love you."

I'm sure she would have said no if she could see the tangle of limbs Dante and I are right now. If she could see your brother, with his arms wrapped around my torso.

If I'm being honest, I'm almost as worried as my mom is. I'm worried that I'm starting to cling to him the way I clung to you; that I'm becoming more important to him than I want to be. When you died, I got lost, and I'm still finding my way back.

As good as it feels to have someone I need and who needs me, I don't want our lives to become so wrapped up in each other's that we'd be broken if anything were to happen. I have to know that I can live without him. And he needs to be okay without me, too.

But I can't think about that for too long without feeling like I'm going to cry again. So I close my eyes and imagine you in a sequin-covered dress, and sparkly red shoes, with a brand-new keyboard. I imagine you as I know you would have been at seventeen: a glamorous show-off. A misfit performer.

A beautiful mess.

When I close my eyes, I dream that it's fall. Your voice fills my head all night.

Everywhere I look, all I see is you. This one's that milky-tea color, like your skin, you say. You're holding light brown leaves in your hand, collecting them as we walk home from school, and we're ten or eleven or twelve.

You pick up a few more leaves. *This one's sunset pink like your lips. This one's purple, but it's almost as dark as your hair.* You hold them up to my face, like nature is a palate for all the parts of me.

No wonder your name is Autumn, you say, giggling, and I knock the leaves from your hands and start running so you chase me home. I don't worry that you won't follow me, and you know I'll never leave you too far behind, even though I'm faster.

Then it's summer, and it's raining. You show up at my door drenched and laughing in your pink bikini and yellow rain boots. *You coming?* you ask me. Your bronze skin shines, even though it's cloudy, and of course I'm coming, so I run to get dressed. I step out of the house with a big T-shirt over my swimsuit. I'm barefoot because I like the feeling of the gritty water and wet grass beneath my toes, and we hold hands and jump into the puddles in my front yard.

The scene changes again, and it's spring. You're picking flowers and then making crowns out of the smallest ones. You place a crown of buttercups on my head while I bundle together bouquets for both our mothers, and the petals tickle me just above my eyebrows. We wade through a field of wildflowers and weeds, and you say, *Dandelions will always be my favorite flower. They change like costumes.* You pick a yellow one and tuck it behind your ear. I pick a white dandelion puff and close my eyes. I make a wish: that we can be together like this forever. I blow the cloud of seeds out in front of me, like I'm blowing a kiss to you. I wake up.

I turn to look through your bedroom window, and it's bright white outside because we slept well into the afternoon. Dante is standing there, with his finger hooked into the curtain, pulling it aside. It's snowing, and it's your birthday, and I feel so close to you after that dream. There's only one way I can feel even closer.

"Let's go to the bridge," I say.

Dante turns around and stares at me for a long time before he answers. He chews his bottom lip and then rubs the back of his neck. "Okay," he finally says.

Dante drives and I stare through the window at the snow, thinking about you. My hands are shaking, but I squeeze them into tight fists so your brother won't notice.

Before we left your house, he asked if I was sure; if I was

ready. I told him yes, even though it wasn't true. But I can't keep driving dozens of extra miles every time I have to get on the freeway. I felt closer to you this morning than I have since you died, and you've always had a way of making me feel brave.

"You okay?" he asks, and I nod. But he sees my eyes, even though I try to look away quickly.

"We don't have to do this today," he says, reaching one of his hands across the emergency break to lay it on my thigh. I want to cover his hand with my own, but I don't want him to see how badly I'm shaking.

"I know," I tell him. "But we have to do it eventually. So why not now?"

We're almost there. My throat throbs, but I try to keep it together, at least until we get to the mile marker. Even if we have to leave right away, I want to see the place where you died. I know that if I can't stay calm, Dante will turn the car around. And I don't want him to do that when we're so close.

Dante looks nervous, too. He has that wrinkle in the center of his forehead; you know the one I mean. And he's holding the steering wheel with both hands now, so tightly that his bronze skin had gone taut across the knuckles.

I look through the windshield and stare straight ahead. I can see it. I can see the outlines of the teddy bears and balloons, flowers and photos and cards. They're all still there beneath the dusting of snow, a few red rose petals and yellow plush fur poking out through the wet white blanket. I don't know why, but I thought the gifts would be gone by now. I wonder how long the authorities will leave them there. Maybe they think it will serve as a warning. Maybe they hope it will make people slow down.

Do you even know how it happened? You were speeding, going too fast, in a rush to get to Perry to make your dramatic declaration of love. They think you hit a patch of black ice, lost control, and hit the guardrail, which, on any other day, with any other car, might have stopped the forward motion. But the angle was wrong or the car was too heavy. Physics or maybe the universe was not on your side.

Or you were just going way too fast.

We pull up short, and Dante turns off the car. He's the one breathing heavily now, and I reach over to peel his fingers from the steering wheel. I grip his hand in mine.

"Want to get out?" I ask him, hoping this won't turn into a total disaster like when I asked him to take me to school. He looks out of my window at the pile of lumpy snow. I want to uncover it all to see what's there. I want to know who came here before me.

He nods, but he doesn't move to open his door.

So I let go of his hand and open mine before I lose my nerve. I step out into the snow, and it crunches a little under my boots. I don't go around to open Dante's door. He'll get out when he's ready.

I kneel in the pile of snow that's been pushed away from the road by a plow. Only a few inches fell last night, but here along the side of the road is where it's deepest. With my gloved hands, I push away the thin layer covering the gifts and lift the first thing my fingers uncover to get a closer look.

It's a big sunflower stiffened from the cold, and a small note is wrapped around the stem. The paper is wet, so I unroll it carefully. I recognize it right away as a few lines of Shakespeare, and even though the words are a bit smeared, I can still read what it says.

> *"Death lies on her like an untimely frost*
> *Upon the sweetest flower of all the field."*
> *You're gone too soon. I'm so sorry. I'll miss you.*

It's from Alexa. I can imagine her small hands laying that flower in the snow, and a few minutes later, I uncover things from Margo and Faye, too. It feels wrong that there isn't something here from me.

I walk down the shoulder a little farther. I dig out a tiny stuffed dog and a large stuffed bunny. I grab a handful of flowers and pictures of you with the drama club and the choir. And by the time I hear Dante open and close his door, my hands are full of everything everyone left behind for you.

"Should we take this stuff?" I ask Dante when he gets close enough to hear. But when I look up at him, I can tell he isn't okay. He looks scared.

I reach out for him, but he flinches away from me. I know what's going through his head. Because the second I looked at him, I realized that for the first time in a long time, it *wasn't* going through mine.

"If I had been driving, this never would have happened," he says. He squats down beside me and clenches his jaw, his fists. "If I had been driving—" he starts again, but I cut him off.

"If I had gone to the party. If you had gone to the party. If she *hadn't* gone to the party. If it hadn't been icy. If she'd taken a back road . . ." I stand up, and even though I've felt so strong since I woke up this morning, tears are falling like heavy stones from my eyes all of a sudden. But maybe this is strength. Maybe holding on to all the circumstances I couldn't control was the weak thing to do.

"If she'd been listening to something else on the radio. If she'd looked up a second earlier. If she hadn't been going so fast!" I yell. I keep going. "If she and Perry hadn't broken up. If they had never dated. If Perry had been at the party. If she had just waited until the next day, or called him or called you or called me!"

The number of ifs and what-ifs are infinite, and I keep listing them—trying to convince myself or Dante, or maybe you, that I'm sorry; that life and death are random; that we can't control anything except how we deal with it all now—until Dante stands up too. Because I dreamed about you all night, and something about hearing you again so clearly has assured me that this is true: It wasn't my fault or Dante's or Perry's. Or even yours. Your brother grips my shoulders so I'll stop, and I do. He swallows hard, then nods like he gets it.

"All right. Okay." He wipes my face with his gloved fingers.

"Don't do it again," I beg, blinking, and shaking my head. "We've both done it enough."

I kneel back down and pull a vanilla-scented candle out of the snow. I place it in front of his feet. I wrap my arms around my knees and just stare at everything else. He walks over to the railing and looks down at the road that runs below the one we're standing on.

"She landed down there," he says softly. I barely hear him. The sun's just starting to set, so his shiny black hair is reflecting the light at an angle that makes it look almost white on top. The snow looks orange and pink and yellow. And the sky is every color in between. I stand up to look over the edge with him.

I'm holding the small stuffed dog in my hand. The ears are black and the body is white, and he's holding a tiny red heart that says I MISS YOU. There's no name and no card, but I just assume it's from Perry. Both of you were obsessed with beagles, and the dog kind of looks like Snoopy. I look over at the wooded area on either side of the empty road. It looks so ominous in this light, and I know that this was what you saw when you broke through the guardrail.

You must have been so scared.

"I wish she died right away, you know? That I could know for sure that she didn't know what was happening to her, that she didn't have time to be afraid," Dante says, and it's as if he's reading my mind. He looks straight ahead, and the failing light makes his eyes shine more than normal. Or maybe the shine is from the tears, but I can tell by the set of his jaw that he isn't going to let them fall.

I drop the dog back into the snow. I slip my arm around his waist and take a deep breath. I'm not used to touching him like he's mine just yet.

"This place . . . ," I say. "It almost feels sacred." Dante nods.

I reach into his coat pocket. I have a feeling he'll have a lighter, and he does. I walk back over to the pile of gifts, looking for the candle. When I find it, I try to light it, and at first the wick is too wet. But Dante sees what I'm trying to do, and he dries it with the bottom of his coat.

I set the candle atop a small mountain of snow, and after a

few tries, the flame catches. It flickers and moves a bit as small breezes try to blow it out, but we block the wind with our bodies and stare at it in a weird kind of reverence.

Dante keeps watching it burn while I read the rest of your cards and look at the photos and arrange the flowers in a way I know you would have liked. And when I blow out the candle, my eyes are stinging, but I feel more hopeful than I have in weeks.

"Maybe I can drive us home," I say, looking up at your brother. His eyes are wet, too.

Dante puts his arm around my shoulders and kisses my temple. He presses his nose deep into my hair, and it feels like the most natural thing in the world.

"Yeah," he says. "Sure."

But we don't leave until it's almost completely dark.

26

LOGAN

BRAM IS BORED so he sees how long he can hold
his breath.

"Aden and Nico found a singer for their band," I say to Gertrude.

"Anyone you know?" she asks.

"No, thank God. Some girl from Aden's school. Her name's Constance Lo, and get this, she goes by *Lo.*"

Gertrude laughs. "So it's like you're still there, kind of."

"Only if Aden calls her L and Nico calls her Logo. I just take it as a sign that they miss me," I say.

"Who wouldn't?" Gertrude agrees.

I clear my throat. I study my reflection in the mirror behind her head. My hair is sticking up all over, now that it's all grown out, but I still look better than I have in months. There are no dark shadows under my eyes, and there's a bit of color in my cheeks. I've actually been sleeping, and it shows.

Gertrude gets a little more serious all of a sudden. "So you seem like you're feeling a little better about things."

I nod.

"How are you feeling about Bram?"

I shrug. "Aden said I was still in love with him."

"What do you think?"

I shrug again. "He was just my ex," I say, but even I don't believe those words.

"I think he was a little more than just that," Gertrude says.

She's right. Bram was an arrogant bastard with a gorgeous smile, a big heart, and a loud laugh. He was a jock and a hopeless romantic and everything in between. He was kind of an ass sometimes, but unbelievably sweet when you least expected it. But that was just Bram. Moody, goofy, brilliant, beautiful Bram.

I loved him.

I still love him.

"Yeah," I say, and when I look up, Gertrude's face is wide open. "Trudy," I say, and she rolls her eyes a little, but she smiles. "I guess I'm ready to tell you about him now."

I stand up and walk to the window. Gertrude turns to a new page in her notebook.

We both take deep breaths, and I begin.

"When Bram and I broke up, I told him I hoped he'd die alone. And when it really happened, I didn't want it to be true— that he was dead, that he'd died all alone. I regret what I said, and I never told him I was sorry. And now I know it doesn't matter how or why he's gone. Just that he is, and I have to figure out a way to be okay with it or I'm gonna ruin everything good in my life, if I haven't already."

All the drinking, all the smoking. Skipping school all the time and lying to everyone. I lost another band, my parents are pissed, and my grades are shit.

I need to fix everything, but I don't know how.

"I know what I don't want to do anymore," I tell her as tears start to burn my eyes. "But I don't know what to do instead."

Gertrude lets out a deep breath, like she'd been holding it since I first came to see her nearly five weeks ago.

"Logan," she says, pressing her lips together. "Thank you for trusting me enough to tell me that."

It's not at all what I was expecting her to say. It catches me totally off guard and kind of makes my throat feel tighter than it already was.

I nod.

"I know these last few weeks have been difficult, but you've been doing great work. Grief is tricky. But we can figure it out with a little bit of patience and a lot more of what you so generously just offered to me."

I must look confused, because Gertrude says, "Honesty." Then she grins a little. I smile back.

I talk about Bram for the next forty minutes. I don't talk about the mess he'd gotten himself into or any of my crazy detective work. I don't even mention the sex tape. I just talk about Bram the person. I tell Gertrude about how he used to cross his eyes at me from across the room at parties or if we were in detention together, how he'd always bring a Cherry Coke to our tutoring sessions. I tell her about how great he looked in the tights that were a part of his football uniform and that sometimes he'd wear them around his apartment when I came over, just because he knew I liked them. I tell her about how he named my band.

And she listens. Sometimes she smiles, and other times she writes things down. But mostly she just watches me. She asks me questions, and when I answer them . . . I know it sounds stupid, but it feels like she holds each truth I give to her in the palm of her hand.

"I've been writing songs again," I tell her. "I just hope I don't always need something super dramatic to happen to write. That would suck."

Gertrude looks thoughtful, and I can't tell if she's going to drop a truth bomb or push me to say more.

"Maybe it's not the trauma that sparks your creativity," she says after a moment.

Truth bomb it is, then.

"Maybe," she continues, "it's you speaking your truth. Remember how you told me once that secrets were safer?"

I nod.

"Maybe they're more dangerous than you think."

On the bus ride home after my session is over, I push in my earbuds and queue up a few of the live recordings I have of Unraveling Lovely playing this teen club, The 715, last summer. I'd set up my phone on the side of the stage before every show, so I have hours of us playing, sounding like fucking badasses, ripping up the stage, as if we owned the place.

Dante, Rohan, and I had talked about recording an album after the tour, but post–Battle of the Bands, it never happened. We were the real thing. We had something special, and everyone who came to see us thought so.

I turn the music up louder when the song I'm playing gets to my favorite part. It's a bridge that me and Rohan wrote together, and even as the critic in me is picking every single note apart, I close my eyes and sit back. I love the song that much. It's imperfect, but I want everyone in the whole world to hear it.

My parents kind of ambush me when I walk into the house a half hour later. My mom is holding an official-looking letter in her hand. I can see a seal at the top of the stationery, but that's about it. Even though my dad has his arms crossed, it still looks like he's seconds from ripping my head off.

"Can you explain yourself, young man?" my dad asks before I even take my coat off. He only calls me young man when he's "really disappointed" in me or when he knows I don't have a legitimate excuse for whatever I've fucked up.

"Um," I say. I don't even know what they're mad about. I've been such a shit show lately; it could be anything.

Then it's Mom's turn. "Logan, we know you're better than this," she says. That's when she hands me the letter she's holding.

It's from school. It says that as of last week, I'm officially on academic probation. Luckily, I had a strong first semester, and that's keeping me afloat. But if my grades drop any more between now and finals, I can kiss graduation goodbye.

"Shit," I say.

"Logan, language," my mom says at the same time as my dad says, " 'Shit' is right."

"I can try to ask for extra credit. There's only two classes where I need to bring my grade up," I lie. I try to remember the last time I did homework for *any* of my classes, and then I remember what I decided before I left Gertrude's office—to stop lying. To stop keeping secrets.

"That's actually not really true," I say. "I probably need to ask all my teachers if there's anything I can do to help my grades. And . . . there might not be enough." I look at the letter. I'm even flunking phys ed, though I feel like I have a legit excuse for that one.

My mom looks like she's gonna cry, and God, I fucking hate the look on her face.

"If I totally screwed myself over, I'll go to summer school. I never really wanted to go to college anyway," I tell her. Then she actually does start crying. She turns and presses her face into my dad's chest. I look at him, like *Can I go?* He nods and gives me a face, like *We'll discuss this later.* I'm grateful.

Before the letter, my head had been full of memories of Dante and Rohan, so it's weird when I get to my room, flip my laptop open, and see a message sitting in my inbox from our old band manager, Shay.

She says Rohan has a new band that isn't nearly as good as Unraveling Lovely. She says she wants to surprise him and get us all back together at least for one night. Dante has already told her he's in. Then she proceeds to tell me I owe her, I owe all of them, and she isn't wrong. The last line of the message says, I don't know what was going on with you that made you do what you did, but knowing you, it wasn't just nothing. You don't have to tell me what it was, but we can't make this show happen without you. Something about that line is what makes me want to do it. Considering that Undying Light is moving forward without me, I'm feeling pretty expendable at the moment. Her message makes me feel wanted; necessary. And that's exactly what a cocky dick like me needs to feel.

She signs the message:

> Don't be a dick,
> Shay

And I remember what it was like taking orders from a bossy sophomore while we were on tour. I grin.

I look at the letter from school basically telling me I'm a total fuck-up, which, if I'm being honest, I already knew. Then I look at Shay's note telling me I'm a fucking rock star (I mean, that's basically what she's saying). I know I have to deal with both, but it's easy to know which to respond to first.

27

SHAY

**BAMF // SASHA'S SENSES REVIEW . . .
UNRAVELING LOVELY**

Looks like: falling apart

Smells like: teen spirit (duh)

Sounds like: every band you've fallen in love with and
nothing you've ever heard before

Tastes like: bittersweet symphonies

Feels like: being put back together again

5/5

Logan Lovelace, Feb. 8, 11:59 p.m.

Shay,

It's so crazy that I got your message today. Funny

thing is, I hadn't written much for a while, but lately, something is different. I wrote three songs yesterday. Lol. So would I be down to meet up with Dante and Rohan? Absolutely. I'm more worried they won't want to see me. I know I owe them an apology. I owe you one, too.

L

That's what is waiting for me when I open my laptop a few days after sending Logan the message about the reunion show. I was pretty sure he wasn't going to respond at all.

"Yes, yes, yes!" I yell out loud. I pump my fists into the air. I text Callie to see if she found out what spring dates The 715 has available for the reunion show.

Then I call Deedee to make sure Rohan is still in the dark.

I send a group text to Dante and Logan, asking them if they're free around seven. By noon, I've heard back from both of them, and they can make it. So I send them the details about when and where they should meet me. A few minutes later, they both agree.

I'm ecstatic, and I'm dying to tell someone. I can't tell Rohan because the surprise is for him, and Callie and Deedee already know. I text Jerome, but I know he'll probably just text me back with "Ok" or "Cool"—he won't give me the enthusiasm I need. So I walk to Mom's bedroom and knock on the door.

"Come in," she says. When I open the door, Mom is sitting in the middle of her bed, her laptop open, her cell phone vibrating, and a planner and a few pens all around her.

"Oh, sorry," I say. I'm kinda sad that Mom is working on a Saturday morning when she promised she was going to try to work less, but at least she's home instead of at the office. I guess a drastic change like that doesn't happen overnight. I start closing the door again.

"No, Shay, come in," Mom insists. "I was just—" She flaps her hand, dismissing all the stuff around her. "It's not important. Come here." Mom pats the bed beside her.

And I can't help it. I dive onto the bed, Mom laughs, and I tell her all about Unraveling Lovely and my brilliant surprise for Rohan.

I get to The 715 right before the show starts. Our Numbered Days is performing first. I'd wanted to get here early, but Mom took forever doing my hair. I'm rocking a few thick cornrows in front and an afro in back, a hairstyle I've only ever let Sasha do for me. It makes me feel closer to her, even though it was Mom's fingers knitting together my bushy hair instead of my sister's. I still can't believe I actually asked Mom for her help.

I maneuver through the dense crowd to the table I asked Rohan to reserve for me—it's right up against the left corner of the stage. There's a bigger band playing tonight after Our Numbered Days, so the place is exceptionally full. When I finally push past the last human wall surrounding the place where my table should be, I see Callie and Deedee waving. Then I notice Logan's red hair around the same time as I spot Dante's mop of black.

"You guys made it!" I shout, reaching out and pulling Dante in for a hug.

I look at Logan, and he says, "Look, I know I'm a dick, but the music is about to start so I'll make this quick. I fucked up at Battle of the Bands. I'd just broken up with my boyfriend, and I couldn't deal. I'm not trying to make excuses—there are no excuses. I just want you to know what was going on with me. Anyway, I'm sorry. And . . . I'm sorry about Sasha."

He says this in a rush, and I cock my eyebrow at him, but I get it. I reach out to hug him, like I'd planned to do all along. "I forgive you, I guess," I say, and he squeezes me even tighter. "You're still a dick, though."

"I know," he says.

"Hi, Autumn," I say, hugging her next. And I notice Dante looking at her, like she's a secret he doesn't want to share.

When Our Numbered Days takes the stage, I yell the way I normally would. But a part of my heart stays at the table, where two-thirds of the band I really love is sitting.

I know the exact moment when Rohan spots us in the crowd. He's in the middle of the first song, and he glances our way. He frowns a little, like he can't quite make us out, which he probably can't with the bright lights and the crowd. But as the song ends and the spotlight swivels away from him, he looks in our direction again, and his eyes get two times wider.

Holy crap, he mouths. *Holy crap.*

I tap Dante and Logan on the shoulders to make sure they see Rohan seeing them together for the first time in way too long.

Forty-five minutes later, Rohan climbs offstage and pushes his way through to us.

"What are you guys doing here . . . together?" he shouts so we can hear him over the house music that's playing while the next band gets set up. He grabs Dante's hand and slaps his back in an embrace. He hesitates with Logan until he leans toward Rohan and whispers what I assume is an apology in his ear.

"Shay messaged us," Dante says. "Says you were thinking about giving Unraveling Lovely another chance."

"Although," Logan adds, "Our Numbered Days isn't half bad."

Rohan grins and then turns to me like I'm a lighthouse and he's lost at sea.

"You did this?" he asks, and I nod. "Why?"

I want to tell him that it's an apology for how I've been running away from him and everyone else. And that it's a thank-you for the intervention; for always being there for me, even when I made it hard for him. But it's more than that, too.

"I guess I just wanted my old job back," I say. "Really, really badly."

He laughs. "Thank you," he says. "Seriously, I don't even know what to say." I try to look away, but he won't let me.

"Ro, it's cool. I mean, I want to go to another UL show probably as much as you want to play another one. Plus, you know Sasha would love it." I grip his shoulders, and before I can say anything else, he lifts me up off the floor, and I scream until he puts me down.

"So," he says when my feet are planted on the floor again. "You guys want to come over or what?"

"Duh," Dante says.

As we head out to the parking lot, I'm right beside Logan.

"What kind of songs have you been writing?" I ask.

He pushes the door open with one hand and squints into the

301

dark, like he's thinking. The sun went down hours ago, but the stars still haven't shown up.

"I've written, I shit you not, twelve songs in the last week, after a pretty long dry spell. So, to be honest, it's a little bit of everything and kind of all over the place." He turns around to look for Rohan, and he's right behind us.

"They're probably total trash. But I'd love to pick that dude's brain and see if he thinks they're any good."

In Rohan's dim garage, Logan unrolls the notebook that's been peeking out of his back pocket all night, and he and Rohan huddle together looking through the pages of scribbled writing, like they're sacred scripture. Dante and Autumn flip over a few buckets they find in a corner, and then Dante gets a pair of drumsticks from his car. He beats out quiet rhythms while Autumn looks at her phone and hums along.

Deedee is taking pictures of everything. She has an idea for an ongoing series for BAMF called Remaking the Band. Callie just asked me to brainstorm interview questions to go with Deedee's photos, so we sit down to work on it.

When Logan and Rohan identify a song they both like, they go over to Dante, and Autumn joins us on the sidelines.

"How's he doing?" I ask Autumn, nodding in Dante's direction. She gives me a slight shrug.

"And you?" I say, remembering that Dante had told me that Tavia was Autumn's best friend.

"Okay, I guess. As good as can be expected? I don't know. It was a month on the thirteenth. Seems like it's been longer. And I guess shorter at the same time."

I nod.

"It's been four months for me. Since Sasha, I mean."

Autumn nods. "I was at her memorial. I'm sorry," she says really looking at me, and something passes between us that doesn't really need to be said out loud. It's awful and lovely at the same time. I don't remember her being at Sasha's service, but I don't remember much about that day at all. I touch her shoulder and smile. "Thanks for being there," I say.

When Unraveling Lovely's music fills the room a few minutes later, all the empty space inside me feels a little less hollow.

28

AUTUMN

FEB. 9, 2:26 P.M.

Everything is different without you here. Especially me.
But I'm starting to think that maybe that's okay.

*Tavia may not be on Hangouts right now. She'll see your
messages later.*

From: HeCalledItAutumn@gmail.com
To: TaviaViolet@gmail.com
Sent: Feb. 10, 6:11 p.m.
Subject: <none>

I'm starting to remember what I was like before, or,
I guess, who I am now without you here. That I love
classical music and sketching people's faces when they

don't know I'm watching. That I'd prefer to stay home
and watch a movie instead of going out to a party.
And books. I'd forgotten all about books.

We go to the library today because Dante needs to study, and
I want to check out a book. I couldn't turn him down when he
said the word "study," and besides, it's been almost two months
since I've read anything other than your photo captions and the
lyrics to UL songs. I'm leafing through one of the newer nov-
els, its plastic-wrapped jacket crinkling under my fingers, when I
hear someone whisper my name.

"Hey, Autumn."

When I turn around, Perry's there, his dark blond hair
mussed and messy, like someone had just pulled a hat from his
head against his will. His cheeks are dotted with stubble. He's
wearing his glasses, which he almost never wears, but I can still
see his quiet, translucent eyes behind the lenses, shining like a
shallow forest pond. His lacrosse stick is poking out of his backpack, and he's holding a fat fantasy novel. It's the first time I've
really looked at him since the day on the beach. He looks like a
different person here, in those glasses, holding that book. I could
finally see the version of him that you loved.

I push the book I'm holding back onto the shelf and run my
finger along the spine of the one beside it so I don't have to look
back at those eyes. So I won't have to endure the nakedness of
his expression again.

"Hey, Perry. How've you been?" I ask, even though I've been
avoiding his sadness, like it's a sickness, especially since that fight

with Dante. Especially since I screamed at him on the beach. And it's strange making small talk considering that the last time I saw him, I was yelling in his face, telling him he's the reason why you're gone.

"Not too good, but okay, I guess." He slouches his backpack from his shoulder and drops it on the floor between us. He leans his head against the shelf right beside my hand, and he's quiet for a second or two before he says my name again. I keep staring straight ahead, reading the spines of the books in front of me like they're pages instead.

"Autumn. Can you look at me?" His voice sounds dark and desperate, so I do.

He lets out a long sigh, and his bangs flutter in a way that makes him seem like a little kid. He looks up at where a mural of the night sky is painted across the domed ceiling. I haven't been here in so long that I'd forgotten about it.

"Tavi would always point out the Big Dipper in here," Perry says before he aims those eyes of his back at me. He smiles and shakes his head. "Or Orion's Belt. When we were dating, she would pull me into that last aisle, and we'd lie on the carpet looking up until her giggling got us kicked out."

He takes a step so that he's even closer to me. When he swallows, I can see his Adam's apple bob, and he lowers his voice a bit more before he speaks again.

"What you said, on the beach . . . ," he starts, but he trails off almost right away. The rest of his sentence, his question, hangs in the air between us, and neither one of us wants to finish it.

I turn my head back toward the shelves and read a few of the spines in front of me before looking down at my shoes. I'm in the *W* part of the fiction section, and almost all of Alice Walker's titles remind me of you:

Anything We Love Can Be Saved.

The Color Purple.

Hard Times Require Furious Dancing.

The Way Forward Is with a Broken Heart. . . .

"I shouldn't have said that," I whisper. Perry flares his nostrils, so I know he heard me. "I shouldn't have said any of it."

"But was it true?" he asks, like my answer can change something. "Was she really on her way to see me?"

I don't know if it will help him more if I lie or tell the truth. I look away from him because I know my face will give it all away.

"Autumn," he says, his voice too soft to belong to a lacrosse bro, to the boy who fought Dante. But soft enough to be the voice of the boy who you loved.

"Yes," I say. "It's true. She still loved you."

Perry sticks his hands into his hair, and then he takes off his glasses. I keep talking.

"She wanted me to come to the party with her to find you. To tell you that she made a mistake—that she wanted you to be her boyfriend again. And when you weren't there . . . You know how Tavia was. She still had to tell you that night. So she started driving to your house."

I don't want to talk about it. I don't even want to think about it. But Perry is staring at me with his watery, water-colored eyes, and the words just pour out of me under that ceiling full of stars.

"The day before, she wouldn't stop talking about how you were going to be at the party. About how we had to go. I told her I didn't want to, so she went without me."

The tears fill my eyes so quickly, I barely feel the sting of them. I know Dante's a few aisles away at a table, and I ache for him, but I decide to be brave.

"I told you it was your fault, but really, it wasn't. I think I'm only starting to realize now that blaming you or myself or Dante— or even Tavia—is only making everything harder."

Perry's chin is trembling, his happy-go-lucky attitude about everything nowhere to be found. I'm hoping he doesn't cry because I don't know how to comfort him, even when he's in his wrinkled T-shirt. Even though he's holding that nerdy book. I suddenly, desperately, need to say out loud that none of us could have saved you.

Perry puts down his novel. He touches my shoulders with his big hands, both of them at the same time. And he says it for me.

"You're right," he says. "It wasn't anybody's fault."

When I look up at him, he's smiling a little.

"I know that she was your best friend. And at first, I wanted to be there for you because I know what it's like to lose someone and to feel like nobody gets it."

He squints almost imperceptibly, a ghost from his past touching the edges of his face. But the look is gone before I can even be sure that I saw anything.

"But you wouldn't talk to me. And then you wouldn't stop screaming at me. And, I mean, if you need to yell, you can yell— everyone deals with this crap differently."

He swallows, like it's painful, and I know what those lumps feel like, when you're fighting tears and forcing them back down your throat. It does kind of hurt.

"But all I ever wanted to tell you was that I get it. I think about her all the time."

He looks up at the ceiling again and then takes his hands off my arms. Then he picks up his book and throws his backpack over one of his shoulders. He swipes a hand across his eyes and levels me with a look I can't describe.

"All I ever wanted to say was that I love and miss her too."

"I'm so sorry, Perry. She would have been pissed at me for yelling at you like that."

He smiles a little more because he knows I'm right.

When we leave the library, Dante takes me back to my own house for once. I have a pile of books, and I'm eager to read them, so I shower, even though it's still early. I crawl into my bed with three of the five books I checked out, and I start reading.

Right before dinnertime, Willow shows up. No one knew she was coming home, so my mom is freaking out, worried that she hasn't cooked enough *samgaetang* (even though there's an entire chicken in the pot), and my dad rushes home from work. But my sister comes straight to my room.

She places my stack of books on the floor and climbs into bed with me. She hugs me hard and long, and when she asks how I'm doing, I lose it. Minutes before, I was fine, but something about the sweet smell of her skin and the gentle sound of her voice breaks me. I bawl against her university sweatshirt until my tears have stained the light gray in patches that almost look black. And when I calm down a little, she asks me if I've found anything at all that helps, and I tell her about all the messages and emails I've sent to you.

"A, you can't do that forever" is what she says right away. She picks up my laptop and finds the browser tab with my email. She looks through the sent folder, and I let her. Next, she searches my chats and looks at all the messages there. Then she frowns in my direction, and she starts crying too.

"Why didn't you tell me things were this bad? I knew you were hurting, but I could have come home more often. I could have called to check in every day."

I clear my throat and walk over to the stereo. I put on the Unraveling Lovely EP, look back at her, and shrug.

Willow chews the inside of her cheek and stares out my window. I look too. Two little dark-haired girls are playing in the cul-de-sac, and they could have been you and me when we were little.

"You know what you have to do, right?" Willow says. She'd logged me out while I was putting on the music. When I go back to my bed, my sister hands me the laptop. She knows I know your email address and password. And I know she wants me to delete your email account without her saying anything else.

"I can't," I tell her, my throat squeezing, like I'm allergic to the thought of getting rid of anything related to you. "I need it."

Neither of us says anything for a few minutes, and the music fills the room. I watch the little girls through the window and pull my sleeves over my hands.

Willow's thinking. I can tell because she's quiet and still, two things that she normally isn't. She takes my laptop back, opens a new tab, and creates a new email account: AWillowInAutumn@ gmail.com.

I smile a little at the name. When she looks at me, her eyes are soft and warm and still a little wet. "The next time you want to talk to Tavia, want to try writing to me instead?"

I swallow hard and nod slowly. I promise to try. Then I finally tell Willow I want to go on the trip with her this summer. She asks my mom for her credit card, and we book our tickets to London and Paris, Brussels and Amsterdam.

So, I may not be sending any more emails to you. Earlier today might have been the last time I type your email address, but I won't let it be the last time I write your name.

Willow falls asleep in my bed after dinner, but I'm not tired yet. I rummage around in the basement until I found some sidewalk chalk; then I walk outside, to the spot where the little girls were playing earlier. I write "A+T Forever" on the asphalt and look for Orion's Belt in the dark sky, as if you're right beside me. I realize then that I haven't listened to the voice mail you left me in a while, and something about that makes me feel sad and proud.

I want to call Dante. I want to send you a message. But I just look at the stars.

29

LOGAN

BRAM IS BORED so he makes a video channel.
892 views | 10 months ago

Undying Light has been climbing the Battle of the Bands leaderboard since they found Lo, so I'm wondering if the girl just had a backlog of a zillion songs. I open my laptop and listen to their latest one. It's good. It's a little *too* good. But practicing with Unraveling Lovely is making me a lot more gracious about the other UL's success than I would be otherwise.

I go to Bram's channel with Undying Light's song still playing in the background in a different tab. I scroll through all of his uploaded videos until I get to the first one he ever posted. He looks a little different in the tiny freeze-frame square; younger than in the more recent videos and all the photos I've been obsessing over since Christmas—more fresh-faced and cute, and his hair is longer; curly and flopping in his face. I pause the song, then press play on Bram's video.

"*Heeeeeeeeyyyy,*" Bram says. He's really close to the camera, so the whole screen is his face, and then he backs up a little and grins.

"*So here's the deal. I'm Bram. And I'm always so damn bored. So I thought I'd make a video channel.* Why would anyone want to watch you? *you might be asking yourself. Or I guess I'm asking myself that. And I don't really know the answer. But I like doing stupid stuff, and people love stupid stuff, so I thought I'd marry my love of attention with your love of giving me attention. Or something . . . I guess. Anyway, this is video numero uno. The next one will be much more exciting. I SWEAR. 'Kay. Cool. Bye.*"

The video is super boring. But it's his face and his voice, so I could watch it for hours. I don't, though. I only watch it one more time because there's something important I have to do today.

I lace up my shoes, and my eyes are instantly wet because it hits me that I'm going to Bram's grave. Gertrude and I planned this little field trip during my last session, and even though I'm not supposed to go alone, I don't really want to go with Yara or Nico. I don't want to ask my parents. And I don't want to put it off any longer.

The sky is overcast when I step outside, and by the time I get to the cemetery, it's foggy as hell. I feel like I'm in a goddamned horror movie with a really uncreative director, but I'm grateful for the clouds. If it was sunny, that would feel all wrong.

I didn't come to the cemetery the day they buried Bram. The

funeral was hard enough, and I knew watching his body disappear would seriously fuck me up. So I skipped it. I snuck out of the church and away from my parents. I called Aden and got drunk in his dorm room while I was still wearing my suit. I lied when he asked why I was all dressed up.

But I'm here now, and it's creepy as all hell. The fog isn't helping. I'm going through row after row, looking for the right plot. I have a folded piece of paper in my hand instead of flowers.

When I find it, I almost want to laugh. It's a big block of a stone, smooth and a darker gray than I expected—almost like modeling clay instead of limestone, or whatever pale rock is usually used for this kind of thing.

But here's the kicker: it looks like the tombstone from the Vonnegut book. The cartoon one with the quote across the front of it. The quote's size is smaller, of course, but the font looks the same and everything. It's so weird to see it in real life after seeing it in Bram's room. I shouldn't be surprised that Ms. Lassiter knew her son that well, but some part of me is. Parents usually don't know shit.

I stare at it for a few more minutes, reading Bram's favorite quote, his name, the day he was born. The day he died. I didn't think I would cry, but I feel that annoying tightness in my chest anyway. He's gone, and here's the proof. There's no denying it now.

I clear my throat, even though no one's around and I'm not about to talk. I walk a little closer to the grave and reach out my hand. I run my fingers along the top of the stone, and it's smoother than I expected it to be.

I unfold the paper I've been gripping like mad and try to smooth it out against my leg.

I wrote a song. I can't bear to be lame and start talking to the stone, like it's Bram, and I'm sure as hell not singing or even reading what's on the sheet in front of me. Instead, I stoop down so that I'm eye to eye with the part of the quote that says EVERYTHING WAS BEAUTIFUL. There's a pile of old bouquets at the foot of the stone; some completely brown, some just starting to lose their color. I don't want to disturb them too much, but I move the oldest ones to the side until I can see the ground. I find a few small stones and use them to pin the paper down. I don't want my words to blow away.

I think about the poem Yara left on Bram's video a month or so ago. How pissed I was about it. But now I get why she did it. There's something about being able to say things you never had a chance to that feels so damn good.

I touch the stone one more time before I stand up. I pop the collar of my peacoat because the wind is picking up again. Maybe it'll rain, and the ink on the paper will bleed into the ground. It might snow, and my words will be buried, just like the person I wrote it for. But I guess it doesn't matter now. I said what I needed to say. I gave it to the person who needed to have it.

It's all I can do, and even though it will never be enough, it fucking has to be.

UNBEARABLE

If you'd asked me years ago,
"What does love look like?"
I wouldn't have known to say
pink lips that spew lies,

green-golden eyes,
and a smile that melts my insides.

If you'd asked me years ago,
"What does love sound like?"
I couldn't have described
the tremor and hum,
the almost electric thrum
of your voice making my whole body numb.

If you'd asked me years ago,
"What does love feel like?"
I never would have guessed
at our hearts beating,
our chests heaving,
and the unbearable ache of you leaving.

Our hearts beating,
our chests heaving,
and the unbearable ache of you leaving.

If someone asked now,
"What does love look like?"
I'd tell them it was
the lies in your eyes.

If someone asked now,
"What does love sound like?"
I'd tell them it was
your thrum that made me numb.

If someone asked now,
"What does love feel like?"
I'd tell them I don't know.
But my heart's beating.
My chest's heaving.
It's unbearable—you're really leaving.

My heart's beating.
My chest's heaving.
It's unbearable—you're really leaving.

My heart's beating.
My chest's heaving.
I'm not breathing.
And you're gone.

Three Months Later

SHAY

Unraveling Lovely is scheduled to take the stage in just a few minutes, but Logan still hasn't shown up. Dante is pacing, banging his drumsticks against his thighs, and Autumn is looking at her phone, her eyes following only him whenever she looks up.

Rohan is alternating between tapping his thigh, retuning his already-tuned guitar, and trying not to look nervous, but I notice a pile of crumpled wax paper in the chair beside him. In addition to tapping his leg when he's anxious, Rohan eats taffy the way other musicians chain-smoke cigarettes, so I know he must be worried about Logan being MIA.

"This is just like Battle of the Bands," Rohan says to Dante, and it makes me want to scream at someone.

"Where the hell is he?" I say loudly, to no one in particular, hoping he doesn't screw Rohan over. Or Dante. Or all the people who are already here. It's May, and they've been practicing for this show since February, refining their sound—rediscovering their chemistry. Logan has been like a different person since he showed up at Rohan's show and made nice with everyone, so if he screws us over tonight, I don't think any of us will ever forgive him *again.*

I poke my head around the edge of the doorway to see the caffeine-fueled gathering of kids. I think it's even more crowded now than it was ten minutes ago, and definitely more crowded than it was ten minutes before that. I don't know what I've gotten us into, and I have no idea what I'll do if Logan really doesn't come.

"Can you call him?" I ask Rohan, even though I know he's freaking out. I hope doing this will distract him from being so stressed. "I've already sent him a text, and messages in every app I have on my phone, but he isn't answering."

"I guess," Rohan says, stepping away from me. "He better show up."

He turns and heads down the hall that leads to the backyard, where there's a pretty deck encircled by twinkly lights, a bunch of tables, and a separate bar. It's so weird how half of this venue is used for underground bands and the other half is regularly booked for weddings.

My phone buzzes, and I lift it hoping it's some form of contact from Logan, but it's just Jerome. I answer because I've already tried to contact Logan in every way I can think of, and there's nothing else for me to do now except wait for him to get here.

"Hey, J, are you here? Because Logan still isn't. Can I call you back?"

"I need you," he says. "Come to the stage. I think the right speaker might be broken."

"J, what are you talking about? How can the speaker be broken? They had a show here last night and—"

"Seriously," he says.

I hang up and open the door again, but this time, I look at the dark stage instead of the audience. Jerome is on the opposite side of the stage from me, fiddling with one of the plugs behind a huge speaker.

"For fuck's sake," I say. I storm across the stage, grateful for the darkness, when a spotlight comes on out of nowhere and shines directly on me. I freeze, wondering if all the electronics in the place are going haywire.

The audience screams, and they roar even louder when a second spotlight hits Jerome, who stands up and turns toward me.

He's wearing his grandfather's red suspenders, but all the other clothes are his—and he's in a pair of black jeans, a white T-shirt that says IN LOVING MEMORY OF, and he's handwritten "GRANDDAD CHARLIE." Lots of people tonight are wearing this shirt—we wanted this show to be for anyone who needed it. My shirt and Rohan's have Sasha's name. Dante's and Autumn's have Tavia's.

Jerome's holding a stack of giant poster boards, and just then, the speaker beside him, the same one he claimed was broken, starts playing "Silent Night."

"What the actual . . . ?" I say, looking around.

"Hey," he says. "Just look at me."

I do. And he proceeds to reenact Keira Knightley and Andrew Lincoln's last scene from *Love Actually* in its entirety.

When he gets to the third cue card, everyone in the audience has gotten the reference, and girls are cooing "Aww," and I'm trying to keep it together. When he gets to the "To Me, You Are Perfect" card, I literally start crying, but the next one isn't the line about his wasted heart loving me forever. The last card says WILL YOU GO TO PROM WITH ME?

Goose bumps march like a tiny army straight up my spine, and I shiver a little, even though I'm not cold, because *holy crap.*

I run across the stage to him. We haven't kissed in months, but when we collide, I kiss him hard and long, in front of a hundred screaming strangers.

Rohan walks in with Logan seconds after Jerome and I push our way through to backstage again. Logan's reddish hair is wind tossed and wild, like he'd just run a mile to get here. He unzips his leather jacket and flutters his thick eyelashes. His diva behavior is annoying, but I'm so happy he actually showed up that I don't let it bug me. His T-shirt says IN LOVING MEMORY OF "BRAM."

"Did I miss the promposal?" he asks, and everyone tells him he did. "Dammit," he mutters.

His dark eyes are lined with kohl, so they pop like crazy looking glassy and bright. They seem to say several things at once: That he missed his band mates. He missed the music. He missed it all.

"Well, what are we waiting for?" Logan asks.

"You, idiot," Dante says. And we all laugh.

Logan grabs Dante by the shoulder and slaps Rohan on the back. "Let's do this, then, bitches!"

I'm supposed to announce the band, but I'm all flustered from Jerome's surprise, and I'm not exactly having a panic attack, but I'm totally unfocused. Plus, I kinda just want to make out with Jerome. I've missed his lips. I flail wildly, saying help to Rohan with my eyes and arms, and he jogs over, guitar in hand.

I point to Jerome. "I'm still a little . . . shaken up, but you guys need to be introduced." I'm actually shaking, so Rohan believes me.

The crowd starts chanting: "LOVE-LY! LOVE-LY! LOVE-LY!" and I flail more.

Then Autumn, who I never would have expected to volunteer for anything involving a stage, and who must have been watching and listening the way wallflowers sometimes do, pipes up from her quiet corner of the room. She says, "Um, I can do it." Her voice almost matches the small sound leaves make as they fall from trees.

She pockets her phone and hesitates by the door that leads to the stage. She looks nervous, but kinda determined, too. Dante starts toward her, and I have no idea if he's going to try to stop her or if he's planning to egg her on, but before he even reaches her, she pushes the door open and steps out onto the stage. The crowd goes crazy, probably just because there's more movement at the front of the venue. I peek through the door, and Autumn turns back and grins over my head at Dante. She seems to be taking a few deep breaths before stepping out of the shadows.

I try to contain the giddiness I feel about the show, about Jerome, about all the possibilities jumbled up together in this single moment. I jump up and down in place, and I kiss Rohan's cheek, wishing him luck, and then I press my lips against my Sasha tattoo before making sure Dante has drumsticks and Logan has water and Rohan has extra guitar strings.

When Autumn first steps into the spotlight, she freezes. Dante shout-whispers, "Autumn, the mike." She bends down slowly and picks it up. A squeal of feedback peals through the whole club. Autumn cringes and says "sorry" so far from the microphone that no one but us hears her. When she steps back up to fit the mike into its stand, though, she rallies.

"Who's ready to UNRAVEL?" she says into the mike, and when I look over at Dante, it's like he can't believe it. His eyes are wide, but he's smiling like crazy in Autumn's direction.

Everybody screams.

"Who's ready to get LOVELY?" she says next, and the crowd cheers even louder. I step back from the door and tell Rohan I'll be back as soon as I can pull myself together.

"I won't miss this," I say, guessing what he's thinking. "I swear."

As I push my way out of the building, pulling Jerome behind me, I can hear Autumn's soft, amplified voice again.

"You asked for it, you got it. Logan, Dante, and Rohan are back! Here's Unraveling Lovely!"

I step out onto the deck and I miss my sister. The lights twinkle in the dark and I miss my sister. I can only hear a hint of UL's first song—Rohan's first strum of the guitar ringing out strong and loud, Logan laughing into the mike, Dante hitting the drum tentatively, once, twice, three times—as I look up at the darkening sky. I'm so happy, but I still miss my sister.

I take a deep breath with my eyes closed before I turn to Jerome. "That was a pretty epic promposal."

"You liked it?" he asks.

"Yes," I tell him as my eyes well. "but I miss my sister." He

ACKNOWLEDGMENTS

I'll be honest. I wasn't sure this would ever happen. I hoped. I prayed. I wished in every way a person can wish. And it really, finally happened! You're holding it in your hands: a real book. A whole book written by *me*. But in no way did I do this alone. In no world could I have ever done this alone.

I have to start where I started: with my spectacular parents. A man who dares to dream big and a woman who has never shied away from hard work. Daddy, thank you for making the sacrifices that gave me the permission to do whatever I wanted. Momma, thank you for telling me for as long as I can remember that I could be anything. You both made me feel special instead of weird, hopeful instead of afraid, and loved more than anything else. You are the best parts of me personified. I hope that I have made you proud, because you are the best humans I know. My love for you is ceaseless.

To Cass—for every evening when you make me dinner or cups of tea or keep me well-watered with beer or wine (or all of the above); for the twelve-plus years of love and support and kindness; for helping me keep it together when I feel like I'm not good enough, or like everything's falling apart; and most of all, for all the days and nights and weekends that you've said to me,

"Bae, why aren't you writing?"—thank you. I've loved you since I was nineteen. I'll love you forever.

To all my showstopping friends: Kell Wilson, Jess Elliott, Alyssa Anzur, Stephanie Kelly, Jessie Edwards, May Choy, Ania Klem, Kiera Haley, Brielle Benton, and Alex Sehulster, who read bits and pieces, and dozens of drafts of this Frankenstein's monster of a book as it came together little by little—I would be nothing without you.

A special shout-out to the Melissas: Yoon and Brice. Melli-Belli, you've probably read this novel more times than my editor has. Thank you for inspiring Autumn, and always rooting for her and Dante. Thank you for being one of the best friends a girl could ask for, for over a decade. I love you, awesome nerd, and you're, like, really pretty.

Brice, I know how hard it was for you to read this novel because of your lost loves, Nerissa and Alex. I want to say a special thank-you to you for reading it anyway, and for giving me all your amazing feedback despite the pain it brought up for you. You are beautiful and selfless, girl. You are so brave. I didn't know Nerissa or Alex, but I hope you know I thought of them, and you, as I wrote. They are still important. They will always be important because, though their lives were short, their love is lasting. Nerissa Jean Hackman and Keith Alexander Lynch: I hope you know just how much you are missed.

Beth! Beth, Beth, Beth! Beth Phelan, you are the best, most compassionate shining star in the biz. The agent of my dreams—for real. You see me, you hear my characters' voices, and you believe, body and soul, in the importance of the stories I want to tell. This book wouldn't have found its home without you. Thank you will never be enough.

To my amazing editors (this little book of mine was lucky enough to have two): Rebecca Weston, thank you so much for reading and loving this novel enough to buy it, and for sticking with it even as it was becoming harder and harder for you to work as you once had. Your influence is still felt. And to Kate Sullivan, who fostered and then adopted me: working with you has been everything I dreamed it would be and more. Together we have taken a block of marble and carved our very own *David*. I look forward to many more lunches spent talking about tattoos and story ideas, and hours spent figuring out what the hell my characters should be doing. You are everything.

To my sensitivity readers: Robby Brown, Meredith Ireland, and Nic Stone—thank you for lending your minds and hearts to this project. It is better in every way because of you.

And thank you to the entire team at Random House Children's Books, my old stomping grounds. Beverly Horowitz, Mary McCue, Tamar Schwartz, Colleen Fellingham, Angela Carlino, Alison Impey, and Tracy Heydweiller: I know it takes a village. Thank you a million times over for being a part of mine.